STYLE

AND

FAITH

STYLE
AND
FAITH

GEOFFREY
HILL

COUNTERPOINT
A MEMBER OF THE PERSEUS BOOKS GROUP
NEW YORK

First edition
Book design and composition by Jeff Williams
Printed in the United States of America on acid-free paper that meets
the American National Standards Institute Z39–48 Standard

COUNTERPOINT
387 Park Avenue South
New York, N.Y. 10016–8810

Counterpoint is a member of the Perseus Books Group.

Library of Congress Cataloging-in-Publication Data

Hill, Geoffrey.
  Style and faith / Geoffrey Hill.
    p. cm.
Includes bibliographical references and index.
  ISBN 1-58243-107-8
  1. English literature—Early modern, 1500-1700—History and criti-
cism. 2. Christianity and literature—England—History—16th cen-
tury. 3. Christianity and literature—England—History—16th cen-
tury. 4. Christian literature, English—History and criticism. 5.
English language—Early modern, 1500-1700—Style. 6. Authorship—
Religious aspects—Christianity. I. Title.
  PR428.C48H55 2003
  820.9'3823—dc21

                              2003002001

03 04 05 / 10 9 8 7 6 5 4 3 2 1

P. K. W.
olim Eliensis

CONTENTS

Knowledge cannot save us, but we cannot be saved without
Knowledge; Faith is not on this side Knowledge,
but beyond it; we must necessarily come to *Knowledge* first,
though we must not stay at it, when we are come thither.

—JOHN DONNE

If it were not for Sin,
we should converse together
as *Angels* do.

—BENJAMIN WHICHCOTE

PREFACE

In his exegesis of Psalm 11—and his approach here is applied equally to the other psalms—John Calvin asks whether the translation from the Hebrew is correct in point of detail. Of verse 5, 'Jehovah approves the righteous man', Calvin notes: 'The Hebrew word *bachan*, which we have rendered *to approve*, often signifies *to examine* or *try*. But in this passage I explain it as simply meaning, that God so inquires into the cause of every man as to distinguish the righteous from the wicked. ... God distinguishes between the righteous and the unrighteous, and in such a way as shows that he is not an idle spectator.'

I am prepared to argue, and indeed this book is an attempt at such an argument, that it is a characteristic of the best English writing of the early sixteenth to late seventeenth centuries that authors were prepared and able to imitate the original authorship, the *auctoritas,* of God, at least to the extent that forbade them to be idle spectators of their own writing.

As a generalization such implications of authority are also true of the best writing of later periods, though I would contend that here such excellence is more isolated and more beleaguered. In saying this I have no desire to add my voice to the chorus of contemporary cultural lament, a centrifugal movement in which immense generalizations are produced out of solipsistic rancour.

It strikes me that the sentences from Calvin with which I began could stand as an epigraph to John Donne's several presentations of an essential theme throughout his devotional writing: that of God's grammar. It is a question whether we now understand, let alone receive, this grammar as Donne intended us to grasp it:

> The Holy Ghost is an eloquent Author, a vehement, and an abundant Author, but yet not luxuriant; he is far from a penurious, but as far from a superfluous style too.

With Donne, style *is* faith: a measure of delivery that confesses his own inordinacy while remaining in all things ordinate. To state this is to affirm one's recognition of his particular authority in having achieved the equation; one recognizes also such authority in Milton and Herbert. They are not, generally, otherwise to be equated.

In most instances style and faith remain obdurately apart. In some cases, despite the presence of well-intentioned labour, style betrays a fundamental idleness which it is impossible to reconcile with the workings of good faith.

GEOFFREY HILL
Brookline, Massachusetts

STYLE

AND

FAITH

Common Weal, Common Woe

It is touching, as well as contingent, that the publication of the Second Edition of the *Oxford English Dictionary (OED)* should have taken place in the centenary year of Gerard Manley Hopkins's death.* Though Hopkins was not formally associated with the great enterprise—as he was with Joseph Wright's *English Dialect Dictionary*—his lifetime (1844–1889) coincided, as James Milroy has pointed out, 'with the heyday of English philology'. He was in his fourteenth year when the proposal to inaugurate a New Dictionary of the English Language was carried at a meeting of the Philological Society; when the first section (A–ANT) appeared from the Clarendon Press in February 1884, *The Wreck of the Deutschland* had been in existence eight years. When the final sheets of the *Dictionary* went to press in January 1928, 'almost exactly seventy years from the date' of the Philological Society's resolution, *Poems of Gerard Manley Hopkins* had been before the public for a decade. Its small first printing, sponsored by Robert Bridges, friend both of Hopkins and of the *Dictionary* and

---

***The Oxford English Dictionary*, Second Edition, prepared by J. A. Simpson and E. S. C. Weiner. 20 volumes. 21,728 pages. Oxford: The Clarendon Press, 1989.

memorialist of James Murray's chief associate, Henry Bradley, sold its last copies in the year of the *OED*'s completion.

Although, as these collocations indicate, Hopkins cannot have drawn in any significant way on the *Dictionary* itself, few would dispute his indebtedness to its forerunners and their sometimes inaccurate etymologies; particularly to Richard Chenevix Trench, by whom, as the *Dictionary of National Biography* recorded in 1899, 'the Oxford English dictionary, at present proceeding under Dr Murray's editorship, was originally suggested and its characteristics indicated'. Two of Trench's books, *On the Study of Words* (1851) and *English Past and Present* (1855), gained a wide readership, and each went into numerous editions during Hopkins's lifetime. *Disremember* Trench noted as 'still common in Ireland', and Hopkins may have discovered it there: 'Spelt from Sibyl's Leaves', in which the word appears, is a Dublin sonnet of 1884–1886. He was not the first author to adopt *disremember*. It occurs in Mrs Gaskell's *Mary Barton* (1848), and Ouida anticipated Hopkins by a few years. The original *Dictionary* cited Gaskell, Ouida and three other examples spanning the years 1836–1880. Although the *Supplement* of 1933 found two further citations, one from 1815, the other from 1928, it overlooked or ignored Hopkins, whose *Poems* had gone into a second edition in 1930. The 1972 *Supplement* added three more quotations, this time including '*c* 1885 G. M. Hopkins *Poems* (1918) 52'. The new Second Edition incorporates the findings of both *Supplements* into the original record.

Such details are worth attention because they exemplify the *Dictionary*'s strengths and limitations. On the one hand they bear witness to an initial vigilance of such generous scope that it can take up an out-of-the-way word, furnished with five instances of its usage, and to a pertinacity of revision that does not grudge time and labour spent in adding a further five citations. On the other hand they make a public exhibition of the contributors', or editors', inability, over half a century, to recognize the one usage which significantly changes the pitch of the word ('qúite / Disremembering, dísmémbering áll now'). The Second Edition heads its entry '*v.* Chiefly *dial.* [f. DIS 6 + REMEMBER *v.* To fail to remember; to forget. (*Trans.* and *absol.*)'. If this may be thought sufficient for the nine other citations, it patently fails to register the metamorphic power of Hopkins's context. 'Disremembering', in 'Spelt from Sibyl's Leaves', is not, as the *Dictionary* presumes, 'failing to remember', 'forgetting'; it is 'dismembering the memory'.

It may be thought that, in arguing the case in these terms, one has confused an English Dictionary on Historical Principles with a mere Dictionary of Quotations and is raising an outcry over some missing gem. This is not so. K. M. Elisabeth Murray remarks (in *Caught in the Web of Words: James A. H. Murray and the 'Oxford English Dictionary'* [1977], to which I am in debt for a number of facts and quotations) that her grandfather 'accepted . . . as axiomatic' the Philological Society's opinion that 'the literary merit or demerit of any particular writer, like the comparative elegance or inelegance of any given word, is a subject upon which the Lexicographer is bound to be almost indifferent', and with this working principle one is in broad agreement. If I say, therefore, that I consider the *OED*'s treatment of Hopkins's language inadequate, I am raising a practical, not a sentimental, objection. My concern is with what the editors originally termed 'The Signification *(Sematology)*' and now call 'The Signification, or *senses*'. For *self-being* the Second Edition adds Hopkins (retreat-notes of August 1880) to the original citations from Golding (1587), Fotherby (*ante* 1619) and Bishop Hall (*a* 1656), and the same meditation also serves to illustrate *selve / selving* (unknown to the original editors and overlooked or rejected by the 1933 *Supplement*). The signification of the word *pitch*, in the same set of notes, remains undefined, nor is the sematology of 'Pitched past pitch of grief' (in the sonnet 'No worst, there is none') adduced at any point in the entries on *pitch* and *pitched*.

Murray had conceded, in his original Preface (later retitled 'General Explanations'), that to 'discover and exhibit' the order in which a word has acquired 'a long and sometimes intricate series of significations . . . are among the most difficult duties' of a dictionary such as this. One would be sympathetic to the suggestion that Hopkins, in his uses of *pitch / pitched*, has pitched its significations beyond the range of the *OED*'s reductive method if it were not for the fact that, in his notes 'On Personality, Grace and Free Will', he has himself offered a model reduction: 'So also *pitch* is ultimately simple positiveness, that by which being differs from and is more than nothing and not-being'. In recent years there have been scholarly glosses on 'the peculiar meaning Hopkins gives to the word' (for example, in Peter Milward's *A Commentary on . . . 'The Wreck of the Deutschland'* [1968]), which the compilers of the O–SCZ *Supplement* (1982) appear not to have considered. Those responsible for the H–N *Supplement* (1976) drew on twentieth-century attempts at definition in their entries for *inscape* and *instress*. The latter word is described there, and in the new edition, as 'the force or energy which sustains an inscape'. Norman H. MacKenzie writes in *A Reader's Guide to Gerard Manley Hopkins* (1981) that, 'though this scarcely covers all his examples, it seems impossible to find a simple definition which will'. I do not think that 'simple definition' is necessarily what one needs or what the founders of the enterprise had principally in mind when they spoke of the need to make 'a Dictionary worthy of the English language'. As William Empson remarked fifty years ago, 'short dictionaries should be improved, because they are intended for people who actually need help'; the *OED* is not for those who 'actually need help' in that sense. Empson's 'general proposal' was that 'the interactions of the senses of a word should be included'; he also referred to words which 'straddle' the logical distinctions. In Hopkins's *pitch* several otherwise distinct senses can be felt as 'going together', as Empson would say.

The *Dictionary*'s first editors sometimes dealt firmly with blurred or uncertain significations in cases which involved chronological descent or collocation of various authors. Thus, 'From *c* 1550 to *c* 1675 *silly* was very extensively used in senses 1–3, and in a number of examples it is difficult to decide which shade of meaning was intended by the writer'; or, 'Ingenious II. Used by confusion for INGENUOUS or L. *ingenuus*'; and 'Ingenuous 6. In 17th c. frequently misused for *ingenious*: see INGENIOUS 1–3. *Obs*'. They edit less authoritatively those cases, equally characteristic of the seventeenth century, in which distinct, even opposed, senses of a word alternate in the work of a single author, changing that 'long and sometimes intricate series of significations' into a stylistic field where the compounding of language with political or religious commitment may be either a matter of deliberate display or a case of unwitting revelation. In the entry on *dexterity* ('2. Mental adroitness or skill . . . cleverness, address, ready tact') the reader is apprised that Sense 2 occurs 'sometimes in a bad sense: cleverness in taking an advantage, sharpness'. The citation from Clarendon's *History of the Rebellion* ('The dexterity that is universally practised in those parts') is ambivalently placed and, in its brief citation, elusive in tone. Read in context (towards the end of Book Eight) the phrase still holds a good deal in reserve. Clarendon is alluding to the manners and morals of Antrim's Irish and Montrose's Scottish highlanders, from whose ranks it was planned to raise an army 'that was not to depend upon any supplies of money, or arms, or victual, but what they could easily provide for themselves, by the dexterity that is universally practised in those parts'. How far, if at all, does Clarendon's sense of his word conform to the editorial definition? This is not a case to be explained by 'sometimes . . .'. Whatever is happening to the 'good' and 'bad' connotations is happening within the space of eighteen words, where what is 'good' is determined by the necessities of the 'good' cause and what is 'bad' by the unexplored hinterland of 'what they could easily provide for themselves'.

No one reading the *OED* entry would be able to deduce that *dexterity* was one of the rhetorical janus-words of seventeenth-century politics or that Clarendon was a master in his style of deployment. One may compare his characterization of the constitutionalist Royalist Falkland, whom he admired, with his treatment of the republican Sir Henry Vane the Younger, whom he hated. Of the former Clarendon writes, 'he had a memory retentive of all that he had ever reade, and an understandinge and judgement to apply it, seasonably and appositely, with the most dexterity and addresse'; and of the latter, 'Ther neede no more be sayd of his ability, then that he was chosen to cozen and deceave a whole nation, which excelled in craft and dissemblinge, which he did with notable pregnancy and dexterity . . .'. When I say that Clarendon was a master of his style I mean that *dexterity* is a word embedded by the usage of the time in what Clarendon terms 'the common practice of men', the 'temper and spirit' of the age, the 'posture of affairs', and that his partiality and animus are notably successful when they are contriving their own exceptions in the midst of this common medium.

One misses, in the *OED*'s treatment of this word, the kind of succinct annotation which accompanies the definition of 'common weal, commonweal 2. The whole body of the people, the body politic; a state, community. = COMMONWEALTH 2'. The editorial note reads, 'This use was adversely criticized by Elyot: see quot. 1531'. And indeed the quotation from *The Boke named the Gouernour* proves to be one of those exemplary citations in which the quality of a mind at work in its domain, a compounding of discursive plainness and hauteur, at once comely and ungainly, is conveyed in a few characteristic clauses:

'Hit semeth that men haue ben longe abused in calling *Rempublicam* a commune weale. . . . There may appere lyke diuersitie to be in Englisshe between a publike weale and a commune weale, as shulde be in latin, betwene *Res publica, & Res plebeia*'. In the original text the phrases here strung together by the editorial ellipses are divided by five sentences. The trimming is self-evidently at one with the editorial principles and practices reviewed by the April 1928 issue of the *Periodical,* the house publication of the Clarendon Press, in its salute to 'The Completion of the Oxford English Dictionary 1884–1928':

> Some quotations [on the 'slips' submitted by contributors] have been excerpted with such brevity as to be obscure and need filling up from the original source. More often they are too long to print as they stand—a sagacious worker is careful to copy out ample context, where the meaning might otherwise be uncertain—and need cutting down; the quotable portion is indicated to the printer by underlining in coloured ink or pencil.

The *OED*'s contributors and editors appear to have responded well to those pre-Elizabethan Tudors, Catholic humanists and Protestant reformers, whose stylistic strengths sprang mainly from the need to make radical distinctions and to prescribe the limits of signification, as in the case of Elyot ('The significacion of a publike weale . . .'). The *Dictionary* is therefore indispensable for autodidacts drawn to the study of the noble, dreadful and at times farcical history of English civil and religious conflict.

Murray, in a series of photographs (reproduced in *Caught in the Web of Words*) taken in the Oxford Scriptorium, immersed in, or looking up from, his labours, white-bearded, wearing his velvet cater-cap, resembles a memorial portrait of some immolated biblical scholar of the Reformation. The resemblance was not wholly accidental (*Caught in the Web of Words*, Index, page 382: 'martyrdom, sense of . . .'; page 383: '—opinions on: academic robes . . .'). The imperative to 'discover and exhibit' a 'long and sometimes intricate series of significations' appears morally correlative to, if not derivative from, theological disputations at the time of the Reformation, when the fate of souls could be determined by a point of etymology or grammar. It is no disparagement to suggest that the labours of successive editors and associate editors between 1879 and 1928 seem more akin to the 'diligence' of Tyndale or of Ascham's *Scholemaster* than to the visionary philology of Trench's spiritual mentors Coleridge ('For if words are not THINGS, they are LIVING POWERS . . .') and Emerson ('Parts of speech are metaphors, because the whole of nature is a metaphor of the human mind'). Murray's editorial stamina, his 'iron determination and capacity for unremitting work', may be preferred to Coleridge's spasmodic, though intense, labours. One cannot, however, dismiss Coleridge's words. The man who wrote that, in Shakespeare's poems, 'the creative power, and the intellectual energy wrestle as in a war embrace' and who thought of images in poetry as 'diverging and contracting with the . . . activity of the assimilative and of the modifying faculties' was making sense in a way that bears upon the nature and function of such a work as the *OED*. In the original argument between Murray and the Delegates of the Clarendon Press there was a mistaken premise, or false equation, and the implications of this continue to confuse debate. The contention quickly became a self-parody in which 'famous quotations' were set in judgment over 'crack-jaw medical and surgical words' and language taken from the newspapers. At this level of absurdity one has no hesitation in declaring for Murray; his acerbic reference to the Delegates' apparent inability to 'acknowledge contemporary facts and read the signs of the times' was fully justified. But on both sides of the argument one is aware of a polite blank gaze turned upon those elements in language which Coleridge and Trench constantly endeavoured to bring to the attention of a national readership.

In his 'General Explanations' to the *OED*, Murray wrote that 'to every man the domain of "common words" widens out in the direction of his own reading, research, business, provincial or foreign residence, and contracts in the direction with which he has no practical connexion: no one man's English is *all* English'. Murray edited four texts for the Early English Text Society before his acceptance of responsibility for the *Dictionary* foreclosed upon every other 'practical connexion', a restriction which he bitterly regretted. One cannot doubt Murray's selflessness 'in the interest of English Literature'. At the same time, as his granddaughter's biography reveals, his trust in the rectitude of his own literary judgment was magisterial: 'He held all his life to the opinion that novel reading was a waste of time'. Under constant pressure from the Delegates to save space and money by cutting 'superfluous quotations', he conceded grudgingly, recording in the 'General Explanations' that

> the need to keep the Dictionary within practicable limits has . . . rendered it necessary to give only a minimum of quotations selected from the material available, and to make those given as brief as possible. It is to be observed that in their abridged form they simply illustrate the word, phrase, or construction, for which they are given, and do not necessarily express the sentiments of their authors.

One notes the characteristic scrupulousness; one notes further that 'express the sentiments of their authors' consorts oddly with such phrases as 'a long and sometimes intricate series of significations'. One is inclined to question how closely, in instances of crucial deci-

sion, the kind of judgment implied by 'express the sentiments'. . .
can apply itself to 'intricate . . . significations'.

One feels a similar unease in reading Robert Bridges's memoir of
Henry Bradley, the *Dictionary*'s second editor, whose philological
knowledge has been fairly described as 'of an unusually wide and accurate nature'. Bridges sought Bradley's opinion, during the compilation of the anthology *The Spirit of Man* (1916), regarding quotations
from Shelley. 'Bradley knew Shelley, but not so well as I did, and he
was surprised by the accumulated force of the chosen passages, and
by the true insight that underlay the rich poetry'. I accept that we are
here seeing Bradley through Bridges's eyes, but, judging by opinions
quoted elsewhere in the memoir, I do not think that Bradley's literary sentiments are misrepresented. As in the case of Murray, one
senses a sharp discrepancy between the remarkable accuracy of
Bradley's philological knowledge and the postprandial murmurings of
literary 'taste': 'the sentiments of their authors', 'true insight', 'rich poetry'; 'the author can *write*, which few Germans can . . .'. Was Bridges
more at ease with such condescending tattle than with Hopkins's poetry, of which he had been the loyal, though at times obtuse,
guardian? His memoir of Bradley first appeared in 1926, eight years
after his edition of Hopkins's *Poems*. For almost twenty years, c.
1871–1889, he had been the recipient of letters, from Stonyhurst,
Liverpool, Dublin and elsewhere, containing some of the toughest
yet most tactful literary criticism of the nineteenth century. That
Bridges should cherish Hopkins's work while remaining impervious
to its discoveries is strange yet not uncommon. In this he seems entirely representative of that long and unbroken succession in English
letters which, while always ready to embrace 'sentiments', is itself
without feeling; which is oblivious, most of all when in its presence,
to the creative 'tact' that Coleridge describes in his July 1802 letter to
William Sotheby. When *The Times,* in support of Murray's editorial

policy, stated that for the illustration of verbal nuance, 'any respectable and recognized publication . . . may very likely be more apt for the lexicographer's purpose than a literary masterpiece' it was untroubled by its own nuance. 'Literary masterpiece' here looks complacently down—to adapt T. H. Green's phrase—on that which it belittles by the imposition of such a compliment. It seems to me no real answer to say, 'Well, the principle is perfectly sound' since, in the work undertaken by Murray and his colleagues, the principle is inseparable from the nuance, as the wording of the *Times* piece simultaneously argues and betrays.

Hopkins, who so revered common speech, was the one writer of the 'heyday of English philology' fully to comprehend that principle is inseparable from nuance. The main burden of his poetic argument, both in theory and in practice, was to guard the essential against the inessential, the redundant, the merely decorative. There was a price to be paid, as Eric Griffiths has demonstrated, in effects of 'willed contrivance', in 'those declarations [which] often ring with a worried exaggeration because [Hopkins] feels himself so misapprehended by his readers'. 'Feeling', in this kind of context, is not readily separable from what Hopkins's fellow Scotist Charles Sanders Peirce called 'the Brute Actuality of things and facts'. What Griffiths calls, with a slight but significant shift, 'a simultaneous character of independent life and of willed contrivance' and 'this double character of independent life and willed contrivance in the words' is to be judged against other manifestations of 'doubleness' and simultaneity. One might fairly ask: What was Murray, if not simultaneously a dedicated 'man of science', as he describes himself, 'interested in that branch of Anthropology which deals with the history of human speech', and a reader who professed indifference to a significant part of that literature on which his science relied? 'I am not a literary man. . . . I am not specially interested in Arthur & his knights, nor in the development of the modern newspaper'. As with those other terms of brokerage and taste—'famous quotations', 'literary masterpiece', 'true insight that underlay the rich poetry'—it makes no difference whether the words are uttered in homage or contempt. In either case it is, as Wordsworth said, the language of 'men who speak of what they do not understand'; it is the 'sciolism', as Coleridge named it, the 'pretentious superficiality of knowledge' *(OED)* of the literary amateur, indivisible, in Murray's case, from philological knowledge and lexicographical ability of the highest order. It is a fact at once perplexing and illuminating that, while the making of the *Dictionary* disclosed a vast semantic field in which the brute actuality of English misapprehension could be charted as never before, some of the most telling evidence failed to lodge itself in these pages. One does not find, in the entries for *undiscerned, undiscerning*, any recognition of Hobbes's tribute to Sidney Godolphin, 'unfortunately slain in the beginning of the late Civill warre, in the Publique quarrell, by an undiscerned, and an undiscerning hand'. *Leviathan* is cited in the 'List of Books Quoted in the Oxford English Dictionary'. Murray in 1879 had asked his team of voluntary readers to 'give us, not only all the *extraordinary* words or constructions in their books, but also as many *good, apt, pithy* quotations for ordinary words as their time and patience permit'. In which category would *undiscerned, undiscerning* find their niche? I would say that in Hobbes's use of them they are ordinary words raised to an extraordinary pitch of signification. How is it possible that a reader of *Leviathan*, specifically briefed to pick out both extraordinary and ordinary usage, could fail to register the reciprocating force of these words? Or how is it possible for an editor, with the *Leviathan* citation before him, to believe that it is less apt, less pithy, than the two seventeenth-century examples he finally sends forward for printing?

In attempting an answer one is bound to meditate on the application of the word 'reduce' to a variety of editorial activities. The

Periodical (15 February 1928) acknowledged 'the volunteer sub-editors
. . . by whom the millions of slips were reduced to a form in which
the various staffs could readily handle them without loss of time'; in
the 'Historical Introduction' to the 1933 edition this became 'handling and reducing to alphabetic order . . . three and a half millions
of slips'. Murray, in his 'General Explanations', wrote that 'practical
utility has some bounds, and a Dictionary has definite limits: the lexicographer must, like the naturalist, "draw the line somewhere", in
each diverging direction'. In his dealings with the Delegates he was
constantly resisting demands that the scope of the *Dictionary* should
be drastically reduced. The entry for the word *reduce* (in the July 1904
fascicule, edited by W. A. Craigie and his assistants) is an exemplary
'reducing' (as in: 'reduce. 14*a–c*') of its own 'series of significations',
running to just under seven columns of print. It may justly be added,
however, that among the many consequences and effects of such 'reduction' one is as likely to encounter those which 'break down' and
'lessen' as those which 'refer (a thing) to its origin' or 'bring to a certain order or arrangement'. Murray and his colleagues strike one as
being finely attuned to English usages which are themselves reductive, collocative, analytical (as in the notes on Elyot's 'publike weal' vs
'commune weale', or on *sensuous*, 'Apparently invented by Milton, to
avoid certain associations of the existing word *sensual*'). When they
are presented with 'the assimilative and . . . the modifying faculties' at
work in language, when they encounter reciprocity or simultaneity,
the outcome is sometimes less happy.

The entry for *private* is inadequate to the protean energy of that
word in seventeenth-century English. At the level of practical utility,
Milton's 'hee unobserv'd / Home to his Mothers house privat returnd'
is markedly more 'apt' and 'pithy' an illustration of the quasi-adver-
bial use than is the quotation from Pepys which the editors preferred.
At the same time one notes that the play between 'unobserv'd' and

'privat' so modifies the pitch of the latter word that, while fulfilling the terms of the *OED*'s simple definition ('privately, secretly'), it holds something of its signification in reserve. This 'reserve' has to do in part with Christ's nature, as envisaged by Milton, in part with his cir-cumstances (having conquered the temptation to make himself world-famous and immensely relevant) and in part with the capacity of the imagination to be at once constrained and inviolable. As usual, the *Dictionary* copes well with the reductive uses of *private:* for ex-ample, its occurrences in liturgical rubrics and legal clauses dealing with rights of property. It notes *(private 5c)* 'Private judgement' and (under *privy* III.8) 'privy verdict, a verdict given to the judge out of court'. It does not record, under 'private' or under 'verdict', Bunyan's 'who every one gave in his private Verdict against [Faithful] among themselves, and afterwards unanimously concluded to bring him in guilty before the Judge'. Is Bunyan's 'private Verdict' omitted because the citations for 'privy verdict' and 'private judgement' are deemed to have precluded any action by the modifying faculties? It would be hard to find a use of 'private' with more pith than this; 'private ver-dict' is not a synonym for 'private judgement' or for 'privy verdict'. Bunyan depicts collusion between private malice and public sanction and suggests that legal procedures and terminology may be entirely subsumed by a monstrous unlawfulness of self-will.

One is discovered, at this point, returning upon the proposition that the lexicographer's responsibility is to the genius of the language (*genius,* '3c. Prevailing character or spirit, general drift, characteristic method or procedure') rather than to the 'literary masterpiece' or to any associated notion of individual 'genius' (the sematology of that term in the eighteenth and nineteenth centuries is cogently reduced in the introductory note to Sense 5). After the introduction of such caveats, however, one remains open to persuasion that the genius of the language is peculiarly determined by, and is correlatively a determinant of, 'the special endowments which fit a man for his peculiar work' (Sense 4). When Hobbes writes of 'the knavery of such persons, as make use of . . . superstitious feare; to passe disguised in the night, to places they would not be known to haunt', he allows his own language to be visited by a shade of Caroline fancy. The irony at the expense of the 'timorous, and supperstitious' who are so deceived is modified by a recognition, embodied in the syntax and cadence, that he is himself much taken with the modifying notion 'haunt' and with his own ability to give it the last word. This touch of stylistic self-delight does not precisely match Hobbes's views on 'exact definitions first snuffed, and purged from ambiguity' which, like the pronouncements of the Philological Society, are generally 'taken as axiomatic'. In such instances language appears sharply conscious both of its own workings and of the 'general drift' of assumption, the 'prevailing character' of human nature in the mass, against which the words of special endowment, such as *haunt,* appear as if illuminated from within. It is arguable that Hobbes regarded even a model discourse composed of 'Perspicuous Words' as being potentially chargeable with 'juggling and confederate knavery' and that it is the equivocal nature of his regard that gives the style its particular edge.

In an undergraduate essay of 1867, Hopkins maintained that 'the run of thought in the age braces up and carries out what lies its own way and discourages and minimises what is constitutionally against its set: different times like a shifted light give prominence by turns to different things'. Throughout the seventy years from inception to 'completion', the *OED* drew upon an inheritance of two such opposing energies. Coleridge, constitutionally against the 'set' of the age, whose style, in prose argument, is characterized by phrases descriptive of resisting the current, became, through the influence of the *Lay Sermons, Aids to Reflection* and the book *On the Constitution of the Church and State,* the source of a powerful 'run of thought' during the remainder of the nineteenth century. Philosophically speaking, the *OED* developed, at several removes, from Coleridgean ideas of organic unity; practically speaking, its methods of compilation were bound to expose the limitations of second-hand philosophical doctrines and the myths of nationhood. The Philological Society's call for a dictionary worthy of the English language was committed to a form of words apparently succinct but dissolving into infinite suggestiveness. As a directive it compares poorly with Tyndale's injunction 'that the scripture oughte to be in the english tonge'. Any mythic power that Tyndale's words might transmit to nationalists of later generations would be a romanticizing of his plain practicalities. In the making of the *OED*, the protracted arduous procedures were an elaborate scientific descant on a simple theme: from Trench's flourish of 1855, 'The love of our native language, what is it in fact, but the love of our native land expressing itself in one particular direction?' to Bridges's 1926 valediction to Henry Bradley, who had 'devoted forty years of his life to the Oxford Dictionary. He recognized the national importance of that work. He understood thoroughly the actual conditions of our time, and the power of the disruptive forces that threaten to break with our literary tradition'. Such statements return us once more upon Murray's separation of the signification of words from the 'sentiments' of authors. If one distrusts Bridges's general sentiment about 'disruptive forces' in the 1920s it is because one has reason to distrust the particular signification that 'our' and 'literary' and 'tradition' had acquired in his keeping. If sentiments could be treated as volatile essences one would be rid of these perplexities; one would be free to concur with Bridges 'whole-heartedly', as they say. Coleridge claimed, in the first chapter of *Church and State*, that 'it is the privilege of the few to possess an idea: of the generality of men, it might be more truly affirmed, that they are possessed by it'. John Colmer, in his edition of *Church and State*, glosses this as 'an interesting recognition of the largely unconscious ideas that "possess" ordinary men and that partly account for consensus, social cohesion, and the continuous life of institutions'. Empirical observation suggests that in the making of the *OED*, the possessors were at once, and indistinguishably, the possessed. One might observe that the *OED* began as an 'idea' and ended as an 'institution', a 'consensus'. One might add that it began as an 'idea' and became, through scientific application, a 'conception' ('bringing any given object or impression into the same class with any number of other objects, or impressions, by means of some character or characters common to them all'). Such application, whether in etymological science or in the mere toil of writing English, constrains, and may even destroy, the 'privilege' of the 'idea'. It is a blessing, both for the genius of the language, and for the 'peculiar work' of the writer, that this is so. Melville, in 'The March into Virginia', one of his *Battle-Pieces* of 1866, evokes the young Union soldiers, in their untried blitheness, who will 'die experienced ere three days are spent— / Perish, enlightened by the vollied glare'. We 'see' the silhouettes of the soldiers as they are simultaneously illuminated and extinguished in the blaze of musketry; we 'feel' the shock of their recognition as they are 'instructed' in the 'Brute Actuality of things and facts', their blithe ignorance erased in an 'illuminated' instant, together with their lives. The verb *to enlighten* has both physical and metaphysical significations; Melville achieves a shocking coincidence in sematology. The *OED* recognizes, under Sense 2 ('Now chiefly *poet.* or *rhetorical*'), some words by Longfellow: 'Thou moon . . . all night long enlighten my sweet lady-love!' Such 'sentiments'—they were published in 1843—may be thought of as furnishing in a small way the blithe inexperience that stumbled into the enlightenment of the vollied glare. Melville redeems the lexicographer's tag 'now chiefly *poet.* or *rhetorical*' in the instant that he renders it void.

James Murray argued, in his 1910 'Lecture on Dictionaries', that 'Every fact faithfully recorded, and every inference correctly drawn from the facts, becomes a permanent accession to human knowledge ... part of eternal truth, which will never cease to be true'. Here, as elsewhere in the history of the making of the *OED*, one becomes aware of the discrepancy between a lexicographer's 'inference correctly drawn from the facts' and the kind of correct inference which is drawn—for example—in Melville's poem. 'Perish, enlightened by the vollied glare' is an accession to human knowledge of the distinction between fancy and imagination as 'enlighten my sweet lady-love' or 'Cannon behind them / Volley'd and thunder'd', or even 'part of eternal truth, which will never cease to be true' are not. When a lexicographer commits himself to the idea of a sublime communion between his science and 'eternal truth' is he able, scientifically, to draw the correct inference from his own platitudes? One remembers Johnson's sardonic allusion, in the Preface to the *English Dictionary*, to 'the elixir that promises to prolong life to a thousand years'.

Considered pragmatically, Murray's desperate optimism was a splendid quality. Without it he could not have withstood the manifold burdens: unremitting drudgery, financial insecurity, constant attrition in his dealings with the Delegates of the Clarendon Press. One may question whether the hyperbole of the 'Lecture on Dictionaries' is itself an effect of attrition, of necessary compromise. His biographer has noted that 'the recognition of the Dictionary as a national asset was sealed when James Murray suggested that the whole work should be dedicated to Queen Victoria'. Miss Murray is never less than judicious in her use of words: 'was sealed' is both pact and fate, or pact *as* fate; an 'asset' is 'a single item appearing on the debit side'. It is not what Coleridge had in mind in his reference to 'national benefits'.

That the great work of Murray, his associates and his successors is a matter of immeasurable national indebtedness should be a proposal not subject to debate. That the very nobility of its achievement is inseparable from the stubbornness of its flaws is possibly a more contentious suggestion. As I have attempted to indicate, there are particular intensities of signification—indicated by Coleridge's 'activity of the assimilative and of the modifying faculties' and by Empson's 'interactions'—which none the less seem inessential to 'consensus, social cohesion, and the continuous life of institutions'. The *OED* is an institution with its own 'continuous life', and the computer is now operating in the interests of cohesion: *'Data capture by ICC, Fort Washington, PA'* (see imprint page). If there had been an original bias or imperception (the suggestion is, I have conceded, contentious) I would not now expect it to be reconsidered. Where the quality of an entry can be improved by the simple fact of being brought up to date, the new edition is excellent. *Populism, populist,* had been so overtaken by political circumstance that the 1933 entries were virtually unusable. They are now much improved. The entries under 'private, *a.*' have been extended (see, for example, additions to 'private enterprise'), and significations unknown in 1933 are now recorded. In place of *7a–b* we have *7a–l,* of which *7k* is 'private language: a language which can be understood by the speaker only'. The first citation is from Anscombe's 1953 translation of Wittgenstein; I choose to make of this an instance of exemplary irony. The sixteenth- and seventeenth-century entries for 'private, *a.*' have been slightly retouched. There is a new—and I would have said unnecessary—citation (for 1673) under *2a*. What I have called 'the protean energy of that word in seventeenth-century English' is still off the record. It might well appear to the consensus as 'a language which can be understood by the speaker only'. Hopkins's coinage *unchancelling* of 1875–1876 is ignored ('Thy unchancelling poising palms were weighing the worth', *Deutschland,* stanza 21). There is difficulty about the meaning, as Peter Milward says, though he and others have committed their conjectures to print. I think one might have a quarrel with the *Dictionary* people over this. Is it (as by their silence they imply) a nonce-word, a sliver of private language, 'understood by the speaker only', or is it, by virtue of its particular belonging, a word of real, though 'difficult', signification? *Tofu,* picked up by the 1933 *Supplement,* with citations going back to 1880, receives further samplings (1981, *Guardian:* 'In the United States . . . tofu has become an "in" food'). Is the name of an easily analyzable substance that has appeared on a million menus more real than a word, peculiarly resistant to analysis, which has lodged itself in a few thousands of minds?

Most of what one wants to know, including much that it hurts to know, about the English language is held within these twenty volumes. To brood over them and in them is to be finally persuaded that sematology is a theological dimension: the use of language is inseparable from that 'terrible aboriginal calamity' in which, according to Newman, the human race is implicated. Murray, in 1884, missed that use of 'aboriginal'; it would have added a distinctly separate signification to the recorded examples. In 1989 it remains unacknowledged.

In what sense or senses is the computer acquainted with original sin?

Of Diligence and Jeopardy

Tyndale's translation of the New Testament was first printed in 1525–1526. A revised version appeared in 1534, and it is upon this later text that David Daniell's new edition is based.* N. Hardy Wallis, in the publication undertaken for the Royal Society of Literature in 1938, also preferred Tyndale's revised text. *Tyndale's New Testament*, as now published by Yale University Press, is a 'modern-spelling edition'. The decision to modernize is to be regretted, and one regrets also that the opportunity was not taken to reissue and put into wider circulation the Wallis edition.

The modernizers appear to have a strong common-sense case for proceeding as they do. Those who plead for the retention of old spelling are perhaps sentimentalists, dilettanti of 'form and pressure', self-deluded in their passion since the pristine orthography may in fact be the flourishes of a secretary or an amanuensis rather than the marks of the maker; other details may represent nothing more than the conventions and aberrations of a particular printing house.

Tyndale's New Testament, translated from the Greek by William Tyndale in 1534. A modern-spelling edition, with an introduction by David Daniell. 429 pages. New Haven and London: Yale University Press, 1989.

Variants, eccentric even by the standards of the time, in a 1535 New Testament were once received as pious imitations of rustic speech, in the spirit of Tyndale's Erasmian reply to 'a certeyne deuine': that 'ere many yeares, hee would cause a boy that driueth the plough to know more of the Scripture than hee did'. They are now attributed either to the uncertainties of Flemish compositors or, as A. W. Pollard argues, to the phonetic enthusiasm of a 'bookish' English press-corrector working for the Antwerp printers.

It must also be conceded that whereas Francis Fry's 1862 reprint of Tyndale's first New Testament, like his reprint in the following year of the same translator's 'Prologe' to 'The Prophete Jonas', is a true fac-simile, reproducing not only the black-letter typeface but also the spellings, contractions and virgules of the original, several of the most valuable modern old-spelling editions of Tyndale (for example, J. I. Mombert's 1884 reprint of the Lenox Library Pentateuch and the Wallis New Testament of 1938) are 'verbatim' rather than 'facsimile' texts. As he himself makes clear, Mombert's edition 'does not give the *letter* in facsimile'. He emphasizes that he had in mind 'the ready use of the volume by a large number of readers' and that the 'first inten-tion of reproducing the Original . . . in the same type . . . had to be abandoned as incompatible with the ends to be served' by his edition. Wallis's 'alterations', such as the substitution of roman for black-letter and the removal of contractions, were undertaken 'in order to clarify the text' for the benefit of that 'large body of readers and Bible stu-dents' envisaged by Isaac Foot when he proposed the edition.

There is a superficial similarity between such ideal motives and those of the new Yale 'modern-spelling' edition 'dedicated to showing the accessibility of Tyndale's New Testament even after 450 years'. In matters of speech and writing, however, we cannot regard motive as something which lies outside the contextual frame; it is through 'the processe, ordre and meaninge' of the 'texte' that motive declares or betrays itself. There is in fact an incompatibility between the Mombert and Yale editions which could be characterized as the difference between an old humility, not unworthy of Tyndale, and a newer spirit of accommodation. Mombert, in his Preface, alerts his reader to 'the imperfection which marks all human effort, especially where it aims to avoid it', and which, despite the 'great pains . . . taken to secure accuracy', may have left inaccuracies undetected in his edition. The pains of the Yale edition are different: 'It is uncomfortable . . . when a late Middle-English word, long ago defunct, suddenly jars the reader and needs glossing'.

For Mombert, the jarring (labour, diligence, anxiety, the anticipation of self-reproach) is inherent in that vocational 'effort' to which he is dedicated. The Yale editor's dedication to the task of revealing the 'accessibility' of his client seems paramount and self-descriptive: 'There is . . . a powerful case for a modern-spelling Tyndale. In the clangour of the market-place of modern popular translations, Tyndale's ravishing solo should be heard across the world'. Yale University Press, in common with its rivals in academic publishing, has, doubtless, a fair understanding of the 'clangour of the market-place', and one would be a little surprised if any reader, apart from a few valetudinary conservatives, were to feel in any degree 'uncomfortable' with, or 'jarred' by, the striking inappositeness of such promotional lyricism. A sense of jarring, of discomfort, as things naturally inherent in the common processes of endurance and endeavour, belongs to a different, outmoded, order of understanding; the understanding in which Tyndale added his colophon 'To the Reder' at the end of his first New Testament ('Count it as a thynge not havynge his full shape / but as it were borne afore hys tyme / even as a thi[n]g begunne rather then fynnesshed') or in which Luther composed—and Tyndale translated and amplified—the 'Prologe to the Epistle of Paule to the Romayns' ('Lyke as a sicke man cannot suffre that a man shulde desyre of him to runne to lepe and to doo other dedes of an whole man').

Increasingly during the last fifty years commentators on Augustine have been willing to concede that 'the doctrine of original sin has become for modern men and women unintelligible and unbelievable' and that, in consequence, 'there is ... to the modern mind, a certain unreality' in such discussions. Original sin may be described not only in terms of concupiscence and wilfulness, our nature 'gredie to do euell', as Tyndale declares in his marginal gloss on Romans 5:25, but also as that imperfection which stamps all activity of the graceless flesh, a category from which much achievement of a high order, much scrupulous and indeed noble endeavour, cannot be excluded, if the work is done 'without faith', 'with oute the sprite of God'. This sense of natural inborn helplessness, 'when a man wills to act rightly and cannot', is a significant thread, yet no more than a thread, in the Pauline Epistles and in Augustine, and has been cogently summarized, albeit as a 'pseudo-concept', in Ricoeur's 'le mal est une sorte d'involontaire au sein même du volontaire, non plus en face de lui, mais en lui, et c'est cela le serf-arbitre'. I have called it no more than a thread. In the Epistles the prevailing pattern is one of 'grace and apostleshyppe' (Romans 1:5), and both Luther and Tyndale affirm this faith. My capacity to make any judgment on these matters is confined to the field of semantics, and one must therefore face the prospect that what Luther, in his *Lectures on Romans*, calls the 'terrible curving in on itself' of the life of mere nature is apparent even within the small compass of these words. I am not indifferent to Ricoeur's warning: 'We never have the right to speculate on either the evil that we inaugurate, or on the evil that we find, without reference to the history of salvation' (Peter McCormick's translation), nor am I oblivious to the danger and responsibility which may be incurred when, for whatever reason, one is unable to give real assent to the terms of Ricoeur's caveat. In such a circumstance it is possible, or even probable, that criticism, committed to examine 'the involuntariness at the very heart of the voluntary', is revealed as a symptom of that which it claims to diagnose.

It should not be too promptly concluded, however, that criticism, in such straits, becomes a mere travesty of itself. Criticism lives with travesty as its natural condition, that condition of 'ioperdy', 'ieopardye' or 'ieopardie', as Tyndale or his printers variously spell it, by which mankind is variously threatened and distressed. Jeopardy, we could say by way of summary from Tyndale, compounds 'all the synne which we doo by chaunce of frailte', 'ouermoch busyenge and vnquyetynge thy self a[n]d drounynge thy self in worldly busynesse vnchristenlye', 'the dampnacion of the lawe and captiuite of ceremonies', the 'Idolatrie of . . . imaginacion', a condition from which only those that 'dyed in the faith' are assuredly exempt. Even so, it is far from evident that Tyndale's, and others', belief in such mortal jeopardy marked either their lives or their writings with ineluctable gloom. Erasmus's *Enchiridion* (1503), which impressed Tyndale and which he is known to have translated (though the anonymous English version first published in 1533 may not be his), argued that 'some affections [passions] be so nygh neyghbours to vertue / that it is ieopardous leest we sholde be deceyued, the diuersitye is so daungerous and doutfull', but the tenor of the argument at this point is one of cheerful instruction: 'These affections are to be corrected and amended / and may be turned very well to that vertue whiche they most nygh resemble'. Tyndale, in *The Obedience of a Christen Man*, is tougher than this. Despite Tyndale's early interest in the *Enchiridion*, the Florentine Neoplatonism which informs Erasmus's book seems remote from the work of the English reformer. Yet even Tyndale's charge that Christ's closest followers 'after so lo[n]ge hearinge of Christes doctrine were yet ready to fyght for Christ cleane age[n]st Christes teachi[n]ge' is free from any tincture of fatalism. Such betrayal, such restoration, is seen as in all senses exemplary: 'yf christes disciples were so lo[n]ge carnal what wo[n]der is it / yf we be not all perfecte yᵉ fyrst daye'.

I take issue with the manner in which the argument is stressed on page xxiv of the introduction: 'at pro-Establishment moments . . . as in Titus 3, where Tyndale has "Warn them that they submit themselves to rule and power, to obey the officers . . ." the Authorized Version has (and the capitals appear in 1611 and many following editions) "Put them in mind to be subject to Principalities and Powers, to obey magistrates . . . "'. If the editor wishes to associate 'the ring of Establishment authority' with the shift from 'rule and power' to 'Principalities and Powers' it is disingenuous to suggest, as he clearly does, that the 1611 translators shoulder the blame for 'distancing' Tyndale. The change was effected by those who revised the Geneva New Testament between 1557 and 1560. 'Warne them that they submit them selues to Rule and Power to obey, that they be ready vnto all good workes' (1557) became, in the Geneva Bible of 1560, 'Pvt them in remembrance that they be subiect to the Principalities [&] Powers, [&] that they be obedient, [&] readie to euerie good worke . . .'. The *OED* shows an identical shift, between 1557 and 1560, in Ephesians 6:12 (1560 'For we wrestle not against flesh and blood, but against principalities [1557 'Rulers'] against powers . . .') and in Colossians 1:16 (1560 'whether they be Thrones, or Dominions, or Principalities, or Powers [1534 Tindale to 1557 Geneva, 'maieste or lordshippe, ether rule or power']').

To dispute the direction, or bias, of a polemical argument is a rather different matter from challenging the occasional point of fact. One is moving from matters of scholarly detail to tenebrous questions of power and purpose. By 'polemical' I refer to the Yale editor's militant claim that 'in their new allegiance to "relevance", publishers and the public have been allowed to forget the man who laid the foundation of the Bible in English' and to his tone of 'aggressive controversy' when considering translators' 'committees', whether of 1611 or of 1970 ('Tyndale was not a committee'). Indifference and forgetfulness are lamentable characteristics of our time, but this introduction does not really resist such trends. Despite a brief token listing of books for further reading, it has, in the presentation of its case ('Tyndale's Bible translations have been the best-kept secrets in English Bible history', etc.), its own manner of forgetting. Such a coyness as 'best-kept secrets' slights the memory of those earlier scholars who dedicated themselves to the just recognition of Tyndale's achievement: Francis Fry, James Isidor Mombert, A. W. Pollard, Henry Guppy, R.W. Chambers and Isaac Foot, among numerous others. *The Work of William Tindale* by S. L. Greenslade (1938), cited in the Yale edition's 'Further Reading', not only 'has a short selection of his works', it also contains an essay, 'Tindale and the English Language' by Gavin Bone, which anticipates by fifty years the present editor's praise of Tyndale as a writer who can sound strikingly 'modern', whose short sentences hit home, whose simplicity is an adjunct of conscious craftsmanship. If 'the significance of Tyndale as a highly conscious craftsman' remains unestablished, as the new introduction insists, one can only respond that, in the domain of the review-fed intelligentsia, the power of established fact is scarcely distinguishable from the potency of transient reputation. Norman Davis (*William Tyndale's English of Controversy*, 1971) states, by no means rashly, that 'the excellence of Tyndale's translations has been recognized almost from the time they appeared, and has often been analysed and justly praised', but in the world of amnesia and commodity this kind of established fact is no longer thought sufficient. 'Tyndale's ravishing solo' must now be 'heard across the world' as if he were some dissident poet in line for the Nobel Prize.

Mombert, in the 1884 Preface to his edition of Tyndale's Pentateuch, alludes to the recent unveiling, by the Earl of Shaftesbury, of the monument on the Thames Embankment to 'the Apostle of Liberty, who, at the cost of his life, gave to the people of English tongue much of the English Bible'. This simple equation of Tyndale's apostleship with the emancipatory ethos of, say, William Wilberforce or Abraham Lincoln goes happily enough with the century's run of thought but is theologically anachronistic, as is the present editor's 'Tyndale spoke for all humanity'. It is true that in *The Obedience of a Christen Man* he attacked the 'bloudy' doctrine of Rome 'in as moch as we be taught euen of very babes / to kyll a turke / to slee a Jewe / to burne an heritike' and that, in the 'Prologe' to his translation of Exodus, he showed how God, 'when all is past remedye a[n]d brought into desperacion', 'then fulfilleth his promises, and that by an abiecte and a castawaye, a despised and a refused person . . . '. Even so, it now takes as much innocent ingenuity to suppose that such eloquence anticipates the 'Family of Man' culture as it formerly took to believe that Tyndale shared the spirit of Shaftesburyan philanthropy. For all its insistence on the 'goodly lawes of loue', Tyndale's doctrine is one of election through faith: in the New Testament colophon 'To the Reder' he writes of 'the edyfyi[n]ge of Christis body (which is the co[n]gregacion of them that beleve)', and this is a far cry from notions of secular 'egalitarian' openness and availability.

It may be objected that I am wilfully reading this nonsense about the 'egalitarian' 'caring' society into the present editor's remarks and that, in context, what he claims is no more and no less than that Tyndale created an English style which was eloquent, cogent and free from the 1611 Bible's 'Latin-inspired' cadences framed by and for the 'mandarin classes'.

The *OED*'s first record of 'mandarin class' is 1947—John Hayward's British Council pamphlet *Prose Literature since 1939*: 'If literature is to extend its civilising mission among the literate masses; if it is not to become the arcane cult of a mandarin class; it must impose its values, and insist on their supreme importance . . .'. The Yale editor writes, 'The Authorised Version panel, Latin-inspired, spoke for the mandarin classes in the unforgettable "Sufficient unto the day is the evil thereof". But Tyndale spoke for all humanity in his, even more memorable, "For the day present hath ever enough of his own trouble"'. So to present Tyndale partly recalls Dean Milman, Gosse, Logan Pearsall Smith and others, on Donne's preaching style, his 'incomparable eloquence' before this or that 'great concourse' of Jacobean 'noblemen and gentlemen': it also partly recalls a thinner style of semi-official high-mindedness ('The opinions expressed . . . are . . . not necessarily those of the British Council'). Hayward had critical integrity and did the best he could with his otiose brief; it could fairly be said, however, that his 'civilizing mission among the literate masses' is almost certainly more 'mandarin' than the opinions entertained by Laurence Chaderton or those members of the 1611 committee who thought like him.

The Yale editor would probably argue, and with some justice, that he does not see himself as an ingenuous disciple of the half-hearted British Council style of 'civilising' mission and that the introduction makes clear his dislike of applying any kind of diffusive wash to the clear intent of Tyndale's work. 'Cleaue vnto the texte and playne storye' and 'The litterall sense is spirituall' are injunctions, claims, of a somewhat different kind from the assumption that 'literature' must 'impose its values', and the Yale Introduction is sharp enough with those whose main justification for the 1611 Bible is its status as 'Sublime English Literature', 'a particular glory of English

letters', 'the acme of achievable literary perfection'. But it is also re-
grettably the case that if one cleaves to the text and plain story of the
introduction one finds it a sad jumble of stylistic solecisms and illog-
ical conclusions. You cannot, with equity, sneer at 'Sublime English
Literature' or pass judgment on 'committees of people with no ears'
if your own 'hearing' permits the use of such phrases as 'best-kept secrets in English Bible History', 'Tyndale's ravishing solo', 'the vivid,
powerful, desert-wind intensity of much of Hebrew prophecy', 'enor-
mous and popular tome' (*cf* 'smothered under tomes of what
amounted to free association'), 'epoch-making', 'the bad press that
Tyndale has had', 'give us Tyndale any day', 'yet Tyndale can do
equally well what Sir Walter Scott, in another context, called "the Big
Bow-Wow Strain", as the Pauline Epistles and Hebrews show'. I anticipate the common-sense retort: that all these instances are entirely
adequate to their expository purpose and that for such a purpose the
stylistic finesse of Henry James is not required. It is shocking, none
the less, that this gesture of mediation between Tyndale's 'solitary
music' and 'today's reader' so markedly lacks every quality and characteristic sustained by the original work; the 'wonderful ear', the
'trenchant reasoning'.

When the various concessions to common sense have been made
(for example, the amount of editorial discretion in the old 'verbatim'
editions which even purists are willing to accept; the current availability of exact photographic reproductions of black-letter texts), it is here
that one's case against this modern-spelling edition of Tyndale finally
rests. A tractable 'English' project ('accessible Tyndale') has insinuated
itself into Tyndale's intractable purpose (to make the New and Old
Testaments accessible, in English, to 'the laye people'). This is not so
much transmission as a kind of contamination. It is commonly supposed that mediation calls for mediocrity, as though for a guarantee of
sincerity and good faith. The Yale editor writes in the apparent belief

that there is little to distinguish 'today's reader' from Tyndale's 'laye people' whom it was 'impossible to stablysh . . . in any truth, excepte yᵉ scripture were playnly layde before their eyes in their mother tonge'. He appears to work on the assumption that ignorance at the end of the twentieth century is not to be distinguished from ignorance in the first quarter of the sixteenth. Our ignorance, however, results from methods of communication and education which have destroyed memory and dissipated attention. Tyndale, who constantly laments and rebukes common ignorance, none the less follows Luther in his emphasis on memory and attention. His 'Prologe in to . . . Deuteronomye' calls it 'a boke worthye to be rede in daye and nyghte and neuer to be oute of handes'; in the translation-adaptation of the 'Prologe to . . . Romayns' he writes, of Paul's Epistle, 'I thynke it mete, that euery Christen man not only knowe it by rote and with oute the boke, but also exercise him selfe therin euermore continually, as with the dayly brede of the soule'. Gavin Bone noted how, in such writing, sense and rhythm, and 'the old punctuation of bars drawn across at the end of the rhythmical clause', go together (today's reader of the Yale edition may compare and contrast page 62 of the text with the photographed page from the 1534 volume used as frontispiece). Luther and Tyndale encouraged rumination ('the moare it is chewed the plesander it is'); modern re-interpretation of their design is at once excitable and inert: 'Tyndale understood how to get variety of secondary stresses to make an even flow that pulls the reader along'. To be 'pull[ed] along' is to be passive, helpless; St Augustine, with whose thought Tyndale, like Luther, was well acquainted, depicted (in *Enchiridion*, VIII, 26) mankind's involvement in the consequences of original sin 'quo traheretur per errores doloresque diuersos ad illud extremum . . . sine fine supplicium' (Ernest Evans translates, 'dragged through divers errors and sorrows . . .'; Albert C. Outler gives 'led, through divers errors and sufferings . . .').

If I am here implying that the Yale editor seems not fully to comprehend the semantic implications of his theology, my suggestion is not without a trace of fellow-feeling. An invitation—to make Tyndale accessible to today's reader, or to write a review article—is accepted, and the trap is sprung. One is from that moment committed to suffer the 'involuntary' at the heart of the 'voluntary' undertaking. The Yale introduction claims that Tyndale's work is 'uncovered' by the modernized spelling: an extraordinary choice of word if one thinks of Leviticus 18 in the 1611 version, though the astonishment is muted for the reader of that chapter in Tyndale's Pentateuch, which has 'discouer' in almost every instance. One wishes that the involuntary comminatory power of the curious usage had been attended to even as the sentence volunteered its speciousness and absurdity to the editorial gaze: 'With modernised spelling, and no other changes at all, that translation is here uncovered to show it as the modern book it once was'. This claim, I am bound to say, is an impertinence. To make Tyndale's revised New Testament of 1534 'accessible' to 'today's reader' is not to discover it as the modern book it once was. The modern book it *once* was remains in the sufficiency and jeopardy of 'its difficult early-sixteenth-century spelling': 'The ne- / we Testament / dyly / gently corrected and / compared with the / Greke by Willyam / Tindale: and fynes- / shed in the yere of ou / re Lorde God / A.M.D. [&] xxxiiij. / in the moneth of / Nouember.'

The present editor, I have already observed, objects to those who cherish the Bible, particularly the 1611 version, in an exclusively secular fashion as 'the acme of achievable literary perfection'. Such protest is not new. Gavin Bone flustered the cogency of his admirable essay of 1938 with such exclamations as 'There is no vestige of literariness in [Tyndale's] writings' and 'think of a Bible written by Pater'. Norman Davis retorted, in his 1971 lecture, that 'writing for purely literary effect perhaps there is not, or not much; but effect in the sense of getting results was what Tyndale wanted'. Such conclusions appear, in principle, faithful to Tyndale's own priorities ('though we read the scripture [&] bable of it never so moch, yet if we know not . . . wherfore it was geven, . . . it profiteth vs nothinge at all'), but the arguments on which they depend are in fact simplistic and inequitable. The underlying assumption, betrayed by such phrases as 'no vestige of literariness' and 'purely literary effect', is that those who cannot give real assent to Tyndale's intentions and 'results' ('It is not ynough therfore to read and talke of it only, but we must also desyre god daye and night instantly to open oure eyes . . .') are perforce mere parodists and self-parodists, 'ydle disputers, and braulers aboute vayne wordes'. It seems to me, however, that those who coin, or adopt, dismissive phrases which pivot on the words 'literature', 'literary', 'literariness', are themselves in thrall to the very negligencies and sentimentalities which they condemn. 'Pater' is brought into the quarrel because, though they are justly angered by the confusing of grace with refinement, election with elitism, their terms of judgment are still dictated by the stereotypes which their arguments reject.

This kind of self-impacting, the oxymoron of prejudicate opinion, is not uncommon even among those students and editors of Tyndale who might be expected to have taken his precepts to heart. In 'W. T. Vnto the Reader' (1534) Tyndale declares that 'in manye places, where the text semeth at the fyrst choppe harde to be vnderstonde, yet the circumstances before and after, and often readinge together, maketh it playne ynough etc'. Tyndale has his own style of equity, though he dispenses it somewhat differently from the Elizabethan Jesuits Campion and Southwell, for whom the word 'equitie' itself is a keynote in their polemic eloquence of 'reason', 'good method' and 'plain dealing'. Tyndale's sense of equity is characterized by the gait of his clauses from 'at the fyrst choppe harde' to 'playne ynough etc' and by the stress on the final words, in which the

impression of a diligent constancy and the impression of some urgent
extempore business are shrewdly maintained. Tyndale's grammar, the
'litterall', conceives of the 'spirituall' as though within a heart-sense
of the verb 'apply': 'to put a thing into practical contact with another'
(his 'that we maye applye the medicyne of the scripture, every ma[n]
to his awne sores' antedates by some eleven years the *OED*'s earliest
citation for Sense 3 *trans*). I would say that he required intense application from his 'brethren and felowes of one fayth': 'diligence' is
one of the characteristic words by which we know him. And his so-
licitude for 'the weake stomackes' defies translation into the market-
research idioms of his latest advocates and successors, the 'team' responsible for the Revised English Bible (REB) (1989), who feel 'that
since the Bible is the ultimate guide to the Christian faith, then it
must respond to the changing demands of the times we live in'.*
There is no end to the 'demands' which the 'times' will make. The
'Age', in this, is like any other moral or emotional blackmailer. Why
must it be left to a distressed and errant lay person to instruct trained
theologians, or those who act and speak for them, in such elementary
truths? For Tyndale, as for Luther, the 'demands' issued, at one and
the same time, from the 'bloudy' hierarchy of Rome and from the
tyranny of original sin. The old partisan savagery may have sunk
from sight, together with much else of historical remembrance, in
the latest ecumenical 'think tank', but I find it hard to accept that the
immanence of 'corrupt nature' is now supposed an archaic concept
or that such words as Tyndale's 'even as a man wold obtayne yᵉ fau-
oure of wordely tirantes' can be treated as merely the utterance of
some irrelevant ancient prejudice. The Yale editor appears to dislike

---

*The Revised English Bible with the Apocrypha. A revised edition of the New
English Bible of 1970, with a preface by Donald Coggan, Chairman of the Joint
Committee on the Revision. Oxford and Cambridge: Oxford University Press and
Cambridge University Press, 1989.

the merchants of 'relevance' as much as I do. But it must be added that, although he is with me in spirit, in the 'process, order and meaning of the text' he is with them. What has the Luther-Tyndale 'Prologe to . . . Romayns' to do with the kind of 'powerful case' assumed by him and by the puffers of the Revised English Bible, except to judge it across a void? The law and the faith proclaimed by Luther and Tyndale are not user-friendly; they are 'terreble . . . a[n]d to be tre[m]bled at', as Tyndale wrote of Deuteronomy 28 and 29. The paragraph on predestination in 'Prologe to . . . Romayns' is likewise 'terrible'. There are those who find the words, in the 1549 Communion Service, about unworthily receiving the sacrament ('for then wee become gyltie of the body and bloud of Christ our sauior, we eate and drinke our owne damnacion') equally terrible and to be trembled at. This I understand. I do not 'understand' this comment of Lord Coggan's, published in an REB press release: 'When my wife and I celebrated our 40th wedding anniversary I bought her a piece of jewellery and I did *not* wrap it in newspaper. So it is with the Bible—the greatest treasure of all must likewise be presented worthily'. 'Presented worthily' must mean something apart from 'leatherex boards, with attractive gilt blocking', though it calls for charity (not, I think, love) to allow the point. The First Prayer Book's 'yf wee receyue the same unworthely' is recognizably of the same spiritual and temporal world as Tyndale's 'yf they . . . runne at ryotte beyonde his lawes and ordinaunces'. It is a world so beyond comprehension that the ambition to render it 'accessible', 'available to today's reader', is in every sense vain. The doctrine, the faith, of Luther and Tyndale are an alien tongue; it was an element of Barth's greatness, in *Der Römerbrief*, to recognize this foreignness: 'The Kingdom of God is a foreign country . . .'. He also wrote that 'The Gospel . . . does not negotiate or plead . . .'. Those responsible for programming what the REB's press materials call 'A "New Look" for the Good Book' are committed to negotiation and pleading before all else: 'If the Bible's language becomes too difficult, then the Churches run the risk of losing touch with their congregations'.

I anticipate the protest that in so emphasizing the promotional material I overlook the achievement which is thus promoted; that I am confusing the accidental with the essential and substantial, the contingent with the necessary. My answer would apply Tyndale's remark about grammar to these other 'circumstances before and after'. The language of the REB scholars, in setting out their premises and principles, is hardly to be distinguished from the idioms of the hired publicist: 'The revision has been concerned to avoid archaisms, technical terms, and pretentious language as far as possible'. This is specious syntax. An archaism can be historically determined and described by lexicography; a technical term can be defined; 'pretentious language', as used here, is a small balloon of prejudice and ignorant self-approval. The statement may indeed betray 'the involuntariness at the very heart of the voluntary', but it is no accident. It is intimately and palpably of the same substance as 'the times we live in'.

The times we live in justly demand and approve proficiency, meticulousness, in laboratory work. Provided one asks no more than this the scholarship of 'the REB team' can be duly acknowledged. 'The translators and revisers have taken into consideration not only the evidence presented in recent editions of the Greek text, but also the work of exegetical and literary scholarship, which is continuing all the time' (REB: NT, iii). I do not question the scope and precision of their data-processing. I would further acknowledge that where 'process' is itself the theme of the biblical narrative, as, for example, in Jeremiah 32, the account of the prophet's purchase of a piece of land, the new translators can supply an idiom wholly in keeping with the requirements of the age: 'Fields will be bought and sold, deeds signed, sealed, and witnessed, in Benjamin . . .' (verse 44, REB; New

English Bible reads 'shall'). Contrasted with this, the sixteenth-century Bibles pay their words out, slowly, on the nail: 'yee londe shalbe bought for money, [&] euyde[n]ces made ther vpon [&] sealed before witnesses in the countre of Ben Jamin'. One is reminded of Bone's observation that 'each sentence of the old prose is a monument. . . . It is not a facet of truth, to be merged with another quick facet as that falls uppermost'. I am not sure about 'monument', but it is true that the ordonnance of the 'old prose' seems able to work in complete harmony with the injunction, in Leviticus, to 'kepe myne ordinaunces' (19:19; Tyndale's English). The new style ('deeds signed, sealed, and witnessed') is that of the quick turnover; it has its own brusque cogency; it is untouched by that sense of the travail of knowledge, the knowledge of travail, which can whet the eloquence of the 'old prose' but which can also sound repetitious and burdensome. It has been the 'guiding principle' of the REB team 'to seek a fluent and idiomatic way of expressing biblical writing in contemporary English'. Jeremiah 32:44, in the new style, is undeniably fluent. But Jeremiah, in the narrative, had nowhere to go; in Gordon Rupp's words, 'He was a prisoner in Jerusalem which was completely encircled by the armies of Babylon and his field was in enemy-occupied territory'; its purchase 'was a great gesture of faith, that those formidable enemies would melt away . . .'. The ordinant Tudor prose ('Me[n] shal bye fields for siluer, and make writings, and seale them, and take witnesses in the land of Beniamin . . .') endorses the 'great gesture' and seals the 'faith' with the witness of its conjunctions. Conversely, the faith of the REB appears to be that its 'fluent and idiomatic . . . English' will cause its own formidable enemies ('archaisms', 'pretentious language', 'complex or technical terms') to melt away; its 'field at Anathoth' is the patronage of the Book-of-the-Month Club.

One's objection to the Revised English Bible and to the Yale modern-spelling New Testament is not that they are modern. Joyce,

in exile, thought about Dublin properties and the properties of
English as Jeremiah thought about his field and as Tyndale thought
about 'the processe, ordre and meaninge of the texte'. The quarrel
turns, as it usually does, on matters of perception and imperception.
It probably did not occur to 'the REB team' that the Delegates and
the Syndics of the two University Presses would entrust the work of
its lifetime to press agents whose natural locutions include 'it is read
out loud in church' and 'the predominant aim behind the revision
being to produce a work that could be read out loud', who cannot
perceive the awful risibility of describing the Bible as 'a living tool'.
But as Bible scholars they ought to have foreseen this; the obligation
to do so is inherent in those teachings about grammar, 'diligence' and
the 'flesh' which have come down to them from Tyndale ('the circumstances before and after') and ultimately from Augustine ('quo
traheretur per errores doloresque diuersos', etc.).

The moral attitudes of the REB 'team', or of those who address
the world on its behalf, resemble those of the 'group' responsible for
the Second Edition of the *Oxford English Dictionary* (1989).
'Conscientious Bible translators' are 'sensitive' to occurrences of 'sex-
ism in the Bible', says one REB press release. The *OED* group recently emasculated (Sense 2*b esp*) James Murray's century-old
'General Explanations'. Where he wrote, 'For to every man the domain of "common words" widens out in the direction of his own
reading, research, business . . .', it silently emends, 'For the domain of
"common words" widens out in the direction of one's own reading,
research, business . . .'. I am not the first to point out that it takes a
lot of nerve (Sense 10*b colloq*) to interfere in this way with the prefatory matter of a work devoted to 'historical principles'.

The purpose of that apparent digression is to lay the ground of
my contention. The English Bible and the English Dictionary, the
two great recorders of our memory, conscience, travail and diligence,

have been given over to those whose 'law' is derived less from Tyndale than from Wemmick ('The office is one thing, and private life is another'). In the mechanics of their office they are meticulous collators and scrutineers. In 'private life' their taste in reading appears to conform to the unexacting standards of the professional middle class. But since Wemmick's Law is a fallacy, 'private' taste recoils upon public function: 'The Joint Committee was concerned that *The Revised English Bible* should be written in a fluent style, and advice was sought from prominent literary figures such as the late Philip Larkin, the poet, and the novelist Mary Stewart' (press release). This self-sanctioning of one's own limited capacities and predilections is not the 'due humility' for which Lord Coggan vouches in his preface; it is a serene imperception.

Those who read my objection as an unjust elitist contempt for what Lord Coggan terms 'intelligibility', or for the needs of worshippers drawn from 'a wide range of ages and backgrounds', might ask themselves how it was that in 1910, Everyman's Library could bring out its edition of *The First and Second Prayer Books of Edward VI* with a scholarly introduction by the Bishop of Gloucester and with the original Tudor spelling unchanged. J. M. Dent, the founder of the series, and Ernest Rhys, its first editor, were not insensitive to the needs of 'the weak stomachs' among their wide readership, but, like some other men of letters at that time, they showed respect for the intelligence of 'ordinary' people by occasionally making demands upon it. To set the old Everyman text and introduction against the introduction and text of the Yale New Testament, or to read Lord Coggan's preface to the REB after the Bishop of Gloucester, is to begin to understand the irreparable damage inflicted, during the past ninety years or so, on the common life of the nation. 'Intelligibility', 'accessibility', do not make sense, do not cohere, without 'diligence', as Tyndale defines it.

Does he 'define' it, though? 'Diligently', it must immediately be said, is a jeopardous adverb in his writings. It stands on the title page of *The Obedience of a Christen Man* (1528) and of the 1534 New Testament, as if he were impressing his own literal and spiritual imprimatur for the elect. It is the word that he gives to Herod's practices in Matthew 2:7, 8 and 16 ('dyligently enquyred of them'; 'Goo and searche dyligently'; 'which he had diligently searched oute of the wyse men'). In the 'Prologe' to 'Jonas' it is associated with 'ypocrites'. Within the space of a few pages in the 'Prologe in to ... Numeri [Numbers]' it is used to condemn the Pharisees' excessive concern with details of the ritual laws and to commend the reading of 'gods word ... with a good herte'. Preeminently, 'diligence', 'diligent', 'diligently' remain words of covenant, constancy and constant application: 'Yf thou shalt herken diligently vnto the voyce of the Lorde thy God ...' (Deuteronomy 28:1): 'to preache the Gospell with all diligence' (Tyndale's 'Prologe' to 2 Timothy). Tyndale, in the same passage, observes that 'Paul exhorteth Timothe to goo forwarde as he had begonne ... as it nede was, seinge many were fallen awaye ...'. The phrase 'as it nede was' admits jeopardy: so does a clause in the anonymous English version of the *Enchiridion* of Erasmus: 'bycause they can not chose but of necessite be occupyed, and besyed ...'; but the two contexts, though in one sense complementary, are also contrary to one another. Each is cognizant of what Tyndale elsewhere calls 'the worlde of weake people' (Pentateuch 1530: 'a prologe shewinge the vse of the scripture'). Tyndale's words on 2 Timothy draw close to Paul's 'No man that warreth, entanglith him silfe with worldely busynes'; the English *Enchiridion* considers the best intentions and endeavours of 'temporall ... princes' to be necessarily entangled with 'the besynesse of the worlde'. One's understanding of 'diligence', 'diligent', 'diligently', would be that they trace the barely distinguishable spiritual boundary between that which is immersed in and that which is detached from the world's business. In so doing they undertake their own proper business within the grammar of the covenant. 'Diligence' is in part defined by that 'jeopardy' which its task is to resist and endure.

It is clear from Lord Coggan's preface to the REB, and from the several sheets of accompanying press release, as it is from the Yale New Testament's reference to 'accessibility' and 'difficult early-sixteenth-century spelling', that significant numbers of contemporary theologians and textual scholars accept, as one of their major duties, the protection of 'today's reader', tomorrow's worshipper, from the jeopardy of cultural embarrassment or the faintest possibility of mental or emotional strain. This is altogether a different issue from the attainment of increased accuracy, a principle with which one is not in dispute and which Tyndale himself established on his 1534 title page: 'dylygently corrected and compared with the Greke'. One objects to the conflation of textual accuracy with current hygienic fads and fancies ('fluent style', 'best possible page appearance', etc.). The press release, on the 'team''s sensitivity to gender-words, claims that it 'has been careful to use inclusive or unspecific words whenever it judged that that sense belonged to the ancient texts . . .'. Revision of this kind is, in itself, not new. The REB, Job 1:19, reads 'which fell on the young people' where the 1611 Bible had 'it fell vpon the yong men'. As the Hebrew word means 'youths and maidens', the change to the 'inclusive' term is entirely justified. But in making this alteration the REB is merely following the example set by the NEB and, before that, by the Revised Standard Version. What is new is the opportunist pitch of the REB's press agents in compounding a well-established scholarly procedure with the 'concerned' jargon of the trade. The 'Joint Committee' and the 'team' may throw up their hands and declare (in all good faith) that they had not thought to become entangled with worldly business. It seems to me, none the less, that they have been confused in their dili-

gence. There are signs that the word 'diligence' itself is an embarrassment to them. Although not obsolete or archaic, it is scarcely 'contemporary . . . idiomatic' (the latest citations, in the new *OED*, for
'diligence' are 1871, and 1875 [*Law*], for 'diligent' 1887, for 'diligently'
1894). One might suppose that an 'attempt . . . to use consistently the
idiom of contemporary English' (REB: NT, iv; *cf* REB: OT, xvii)
would apply itself to a thorough revision of this word which so evokes
sixteenth- and seventeenth-century moral energy and scruple. But I can
find no consistency in the REB's practice. When Tyndale, in
Deuteronomy 28:1, uses 'diligently' (1611: 'diligently'), REB retains it
(see also Deuteronomy 13:14). In Deuteronomy 6:17, where the 1611
Bible reads, 'You shall diligently keepe the Commandements . . .' ('diligently' is not in Tyndale's version), REB gives, 'You must diligently
keep the commandments . . .'; in 2 Peter 1:5, 10, Tyndale's 'And hervnto
geve all diligence' and 'brethren, geve the moare diligence' (1611 'give
diligence') become, in the REB, 'You should make every effort' (NEB,
'you should try your hardest') and 'do your utmost to establish' (NEB,
'exert yourselves to clinch').

When Tyndale, in *The Obedience of a Christen Man*, argued that
'it is better to suffer one tyraunte th[an] mani [&] to sofre wronge of
one the[n] of every ma[n]', he was, as the lesser evil, compounding
with political necessity, to which he gave a kind of credence but
which was none the less contributory to 'yᵉ stro[n]ge fyre of tribulation and purgatorye of oure flesh' (*Pentateuch*, 1530: 'A Prologe
shewinge the vse of the scripture'). In such 'business', the diligence of
grammatical understanding ('the circumstances before and after') was
made both a reflection of and a means of looking upon the contest
between the circumstances of the world and of the spirit. The best
one can say of the REB translators and revisers is that, though they
are masters of the apparatus of scholarship, they lack diligence of the
imagination. One can hardly distinguish, as they go their 'fluent and

idiomatic' way, the word of scholarly discrimination from the euphemism of the letter of reference. The worst that one can say of them is that they have surrendered without a qualm to 'the worlde of weake people' which they have dreadfully confused with that of 'a boy that driueth the plough'. Their work is consequently in thrall to the 'many tyrants' of commerce and society. The crassness and imperviousness of the publishing jargon seem so perilously close to Tyndale's 'bondage of their awne ymaginacions and inuencions', so inimical to Barth's 'The Gospel does not expound or recommend itself. It does not negotiate or plead, threaten, or make promises. It withdraws itself always when it is not listened to for its own sake' (Edwyn C. Hoskyns's translation).

I had intended to say that the Word of God in English could now withdraw from the clamour of its 'promotion' into the 'inaccessibility' of Mombert's edition of Tyndale's Pentateuch or Wallis's edition of the 1534 New Testament or, best of all perhaps, the old Everyman edition of *The First and Second Prayer Books of Edward VI*. But maybe that is too tempting to be right. The alternative conjecture would be that the Word diligently withdraws *into* the modern world's jeopardy, the 'captiuite of ceremonies', to make there its 'affirmation of resurrection'.

Keeping to the Middle Way

Robert Burton projected several attributes of his persona Democritus Junior, eminent among them his collateral vocations as 'Divine' and as 'schollar'. There is not always, with writers, complete reciprocity between what is projected and what is felt and expressed, but in Democritus Junior there is a more complete interrelationship and exchange than one might in reason expect from the author of a post-Ramist anatomy:

> It is most true, *stylus virum arguit,* our stile bewraies us, and as Hunters find their game by the trace, so is a mans *Genius* descried by his workes.

Burton's translation of the tag is not wilful: 'bewraie' fairly represents the several implications of *arguere;* so much for the 'schollar'. The 'Divine' (I parody anatomy) hears the phrase within the contexture of English scriptural renderings (Tyndale to King James): 'Surely thou also art one of them, for thy speech bewrayeth thee'—Matthew 26:73—Peter's accent gives him away, and in truth he denies the truth. It is not scriptural truth that Burton is here defending but a form of verity that may exist chiefly in contexts of declaration that are also occasions of self-revelation, self-exposure. Although 'descried' is an innocuous retracing of 'arguit', even to leave such a trace can be dangerous, if not fatal. Who among the most ordinary of Protestant readers—exercising the retentive memory prescribed by Tyndale—would forget the scriptural paradigm? But because Burton so places it, the further suggestion that a writer's essential character stands forth in his 'stile' is self-evidently nothing to be ashamed of. The emphases are held in apposition, not felt as confrontation. The effect more closely resembles William Empson's 'tug between two interests', except that in this case 'two' is restrictive: if one retains the idea of pairs, there must be several pairings—fecundity and measure, diligence and folly, unity and variety, plenitude and the void. What is traced or followed here is not—or not evidently—a matter of rhetorical formalities. Burton in the guise of Democritus Junior appears to scorn paradoxes, rating them with the 'unrighteous subtleties' of papists, the 'mad pranks' of atheists and anabaptists. He moves, more tactfully than formal rhetoric might allow, and yet with a hunter's instinct, through resonances that are themselves part of the accumulating memory of post-Reformation written and spoken English. And this particular 'genius', at this particular time, is not Burton's property alone. Shakespeare has it in superabundance, but he is richly anticipated by Nashe, and quarries him. Even Hobbes, who would clamp down on this kind of contextual memory as on a lode of well-buried abstruseness, knows perfectly well how to work its seams.

What I am here adumbrating seems more inclined to Erasmian *copia* than to Ramist anatomy; I find Father Ong's instructive *Ramus, Method, and the Decay of Dialogue* (1959) too abrupt in its ascription of Burton's work simply to a Ramist 'fad', together with Nashe's *Anatomie of Absurditie* and Lyly's *Anatomy of Wit*. Though Burton professes that he was unmethodical in his reading, he claims 'method' for the work itself, although Ramus figures only once among the many whom he elects, by quotation and marginal citation, as names to dress his story. 'Divines use *Austins* words *verbatim* still, and our Storie-dressers doe as much, hee that comes last is commonly best': Burton 'does best' because in an important sense he too 'comes last'. He writes in commanding knowledge of ancient and modern predecessors—'the composition and method is ours onely, and shewes a Schollar'—and in the sharp awareness that priorities and circumstances are in process of change ('is ours onely' could be read as 'my sole contribution is the method' or as 'my mastery of synthesis is unique'). A sense of authorial pride and a sense of massive and grateful indebtedness seem to hold together in Burton as they do in Nashe and, with significant differences of emphasis, in Donne. One misses such gratitude in *Leviathan* (except for the noble tribute, first and last, to Sidney Godolphin). Burton, Nashe and Donne are memorialists as well as innovators, but, with Godolphin dead, it remains for Hobbes to conclude, as it remained for John of Patmos to prophesy, that the former things are passed away.

Burton was pre-eminently what he declared himself to be: a scholar. He was, less evidently to readers of a future time but evidently to himself and for the congregation to which he conscientiously ministered, a man in holy orders, a priest of the Ecclesia Anglicana. He suggests, here and there, that he has no taste for 'controversie' and for that reason, though not exclusively for that reason, he may be seen as keeping largely (rather than narrowly) to his rooms in Christ Church. I would suggest that he follows, as closely as Donne, though tracing a somewhat different game, the diligent mediocrity of Jewel's *Apologie,* Whitgift's *Answer to the Admonition* and Hooker's *Ecclesiasticall Politie.* 'The *medium* is best' is Burton, as is 'sobriety and contemplation joyne our soules to God' and, from Proverbs, 'keepe thine heart with all diligence'.

I do not say that one must submit to *Ecclesiasticall Politie*, as though its 'laws' had the status in Christian history of Tertullian's *regula quidem fidei una omnio est, sola immobilis et irreformabilis.* Though Hooker incorporates this same 'rule' into his Third Booke, he does so in order to establish a crucial distinction between the 'rule of faith', which is 'immoueable', and the 'lawe of outwarde order and politie', which may be 'varied by times places persons and other the like circumstances'. Behind his powerful and elusive arguments stand other tacit and explicit forms of appeal, which it is his purpose to reconcile by sweetness of presentation, as if, though demonstrably recalcitrant, they were yet open to reason. What I here call 'sweetness' is not mellifluousness but rather a quality to be understood through Donne's 'oftentimes Judgement signifies not *meer Justice*, but as it is attempred and sweetned with Mercy'. Those elements of dispute, to which Hooker thus tempers his sentence, I would take to include the recusant witness ennobled by William Rastell's 1557 folio of *The Workes of Sir Thomas More* and the Protestant martyrology gathered and perpetuated by John Foxe's *Actes and Monumentes* of 1563. The publication of Rastell's edition during the Marian reaction, with its dedication to the Catholic queen, and the regular appearance during Elizabeth's reign of augmented editions of Foxe's book give sufficient evidence that Hooker, as champion of the *via media,* was not fighting straw men or empty air. The case of Foxe presented complications, as *Actes and Monumentes* celebrated not only the founding martyrs, the presiding saints and confessors, of the reformed English Church but also those from whom the most radical and acrimonious of Calvinist Puritans and separatists drew their inspiration. In matters of style and faith, which are the main burden of the present discussion, the post-Henrician conditions of church and state politics determined that Burton's analysis of religious melancholy had been preceded by 'Roman' and Genevan forms of the practice: forms which

Burton was not fully at liberty to recognize. His work has a number of substantial citations from More's Latin *Utopia* but none, so far as I can tell, from *A Dialoge of Comfort Agaynst Trybulacion*, in which More submits to self-examination on such questions as an individual's ability to endure penal solitary confinement as 'an horrour enhauncid of our own fantasye' and confronts the immediate 'terrour of shamfull & paynfull deth'. J. R. Knott, in his *Discourses of Martyrdom* (1993), footnotes a modern psychoanalytical urge to read Foxe as a mere record of 'compulsive neurotic and pathological behavior' but rightly points out that Foxe himself took some account of the psychology of fear, the occasions of faltering, and agrees with Warren Wooden that the flaws are part of Foxe's portrayal of the full humanity of witness among those whose sufferings he relates in reiterative harrowing detail.

The crux that unites the incompatibilities of More and Foxe is the acceptance of 'persecucion for the fayth' as inevitable, even necessary. Although such persecution was to continue in England throughout the seventeenth century, Burton's professed attitude to such things is that they are among a myriad horrors born of human superstition and fantasy: 'No greater hate, more continuate, bitter faction, warres, persecution in all ages, then for matters of religion'; 'It is incredible to relate, did not our dayly experience evince it, what factions . . . have beene of late for matters of Religion in France, and what hurlie burlies all over *Europe*, for these many yeares'. The phrase 'did not our dayly experience evince it' exemplifies the manner in which Burton's style itself evinces precisely why, and how, it is as it is. It must set itself to record, like a day-book, the minutiae of monstrous confusion; it must perforce run and reel with the dreadful European 'hurlie burlies', and yet reduce all to the idea of a quotidian Christian life as it might be: a sanative commitment to honest charity ('even all those vertuous habits . . . which no man can well performe, but he that is a Christian, and a true regenerate man'). The inherent danger with such an unremittingly busy style is that it will become, or will be understood as having become, mere cynical worldly prattle. I have a sense that Burton would take the French *politiques* as a model if he were not constrained to present them as 'loose Atheisticall spirits . . . too predominant in all kingdomes'.

I do not say that Burton wrote either directly or indirectly in the full comprehension of Hooker's achievement that we, with the benefit of hindsight, believe we possess. As various scholars have observed, *Ecclesiasticall Politie* caused no great stir when the first four books appeared in 1593, and its reputation remained (perhaps deliberately) shrouded during the early decades of the next century. Nevertheless Helen Gardner has claimed (and I accept) that Donne 'absorbed Hooker's conception of the *via media* so deeply that it [became] the basis of his own thinking'. I suggest only that to know Hooker on the need to free 'our mindes . . . from all distempered affections' and to read Donne on 'inordinate melancholies, and irreligious dejections of spirit' (and on the resorting to 'fooles' and 'comedies' as vain antidotes) is to comprehend Burton on the 'immoderate' nature of carnal and religious melancholy, and the inanities with which men seek to divert it. As Hooker says, 'We are naturally induced to seeke communion and fellowship with others' and 'all men desire to leade in this world an happie life. That life is led most happily, wherein all virtue is exercised without impedime[n]t or let'. Burton anatomizes melancholy in its hydra-headed forms; he dissects its monstrous capacity to hinder communion and fellowship.

When Burton writes that 'our stile bewraies us' or that 'the method is ours onely' the pronoun hovers in its senses between the proud singular ('a mans *Genius* descried by his workes') and the penitential collective of *The Book of Common Prayer* ('our manifolde sinnes and wickednes'). The English 'common prayer' itself derives from ancient Latin usage, the *Publica est nobis et Communis Oratio* of the Church Fathers to whom both Rome and Lambeth appealed in their contentions. It is to be noted that Hooker's English retains the Latin order ('the loue of publique deuotion . . . the very forme and reuerend solemnite of common prayer dulie ordered . . .'), but, while that is strictly the case, to read the Anglicans is to be aware of a particular strength of resonance in their use of the word 'common' itself. It is resonant because it is ambiguous, and Hooker, Donne and Burton (and Nashe also) play it across the full range of its ambiguities. I receive the impression, from Jewel's *Apologia Ecclesiae Anglicanae* (first English translation 1562), that 'common' signifies an English reformed 'Catholike' order of charity ('to thintent that the people, as Paule doth admonish vs, by ye co[m]mon praier may receaue a co[m]mon profit' and that such forms of common observance are to be distinguished from 'ye multitude of idle cerimones' which now signify the public worship of Rome. I do not claim that one could safely generalize from such particulars; I say only that the suggestion appears to hold for a particular context and may do so in others. Hooker names 'common advise' as that body of right counsel which validates and rectifies 'whatsoeuer is herein publiquely done' and blames sectaries who judgew 'any blinde and secret corner' to be 'a fit house of common prayer'. 'Common advise' seems to me to take up Jewel's 'all the good fathers & catholike byshops, not only in the old testament, but also in the new' and excludes as usual, therefore, all that is covered by Hooker's 'the vulgar sort amongst you' or Burton's 'the gullish commonalty'.

Some evidence to support my suggestion may be found in that common stand-by, Elyot's *Boke named the Governour*: his contention that there 'may appere lyke diuersitie to be in englisshe betwene a publike weale and a commune weale, as shulde be in latin, betwene *Res publica, & Res plebeia*'. There is no doubt here as to Elyot's pitch, and he strikes me as being isolated in the certitude of his definition. In contrast, the Anglican apologists are masters of tonal indeterminacy and ring changes on 'the common good'. My reference is in part retrospective: to a semantic opportunity (or possibly opportunism) that had accompanied the small grammatical shift from the Church in England to the Church of England; and to the apparently slight differences of grammatical opinion which, between 1555 and 1558, had sent members of the reforming party (or schismatic faction) to their excruciating deaths. To this I would add a sense of the continuance, into the late years of the century, of that formal reasonableness established in the preface to the 1549 *Booke of the Common Prayer*, 'to appease all suche diuersitie (if any arise), and for the resolucion of all doubtes . . . for the quietyng and appeasyng of the same'.

The doubts to be resolved, however, do not encompass matters of papistical conscience but matters of reformed practice. The people may require assistance in coming to terms with the new language of authority. The authority itself is now to stand unquestioned. Hooker is magisterially persuasive in ranging across the senses of the word 'common', but none of his uses would make good case-law. He moves us to the affective equivalent of a reasoned conviction, or a proof, that we have been given a secure intermediary, even intercessory, term between the alien, and alienating, power of the Bishop of Rome and the alienated private interpretations of Puritan enthusiasts. When common supplications are made to God out of the midst of common sufferings, we forget the 'gullish commonalty', and the sufferings themselves are reduced (in comely theory) from extortionate private musings to the comfortable words of common confession and absolution. Burton again:

> I [the melancholic] am a contemptible and forlorne wretch, forsaken of God, and left to the mercilesse fury of evill spirits. I can-

not hope, pray, repent, &c. How often shall I [Burton] say it, thou maist performe all these duties, Christian offices, & be restored in good time.

In citing such arguments and examples, however, I am also anticipating the major differences of emphasis that make *The Anatomy of Melancholy* a radically different work from *Ecclesiasticall Politie.* Burton quotes massively and with marked equity from the pieties of pagan as well as Christian authors; Hooker too gives judicious attention to the axioms and precepts, the *loci communes,* of Plato, Aristotle and Cicero. From neither Hooker nor Burton does one gather any sense of disdain for that common inheritance of experience and wisdom, and in this they are true heirs of Calvin's magnanimity. But Hooker puts the 'pouertie' of modern 'Ramystry' firmly in its place: 'Of marueilous quicke dispatch it is, and doth shewe them that haue it as much almost in three dayes, as if it dwell threescore yeares with them'. One can see how a question of rhetoric might well be construed as a matter of spiritual fidelity and how 'stile' might indeed 'bewraie' the author.

Burton could pass, or even stand, for Hooker's 'diligent obseruer . . . of circumstances, the loose regarde whereof is the nurce of vulgar folly', but where Hooker places law and reason at the centre of comprehension and Christian offices at the heart of polity, Burton, like Nashe, is a parodist of 'loose regarde' and a hunter of vulgar folly: 'It is a wonder to read of that infinite superstition . . . as he that walkes by Moonshine in a wood, they groped in the darke . . . which the Divell perceaving, ledde them farther out [that is, out of the right way, further into the dark]'. This passage, which I am constrained to give piecemeal, is worth pondering as a whole. One recognizes how Burton stands halfway between two other great comedians: Shakespeare, of *A Midsummer Night's Dream,* and Hobbes, of

'Apparitions or Visions' and 'The Kingdome of Darknesse'. 'It is a wonder to read of . . .': philosophically and morally the words adjure us to keep our hearts with all diligence; tactically, they catch the excitement of the romances and voyages, of the theatrical opportunism that Sidney deplores and Nashe appropriates. Burton, like Nashe and unlike Hooker, exposes his own method of diligent observation to the dangerous forces of circumstance; in doing so he is at least in part an adventurer, an ambivalent faculty which again he shares with Nashe.

But they are all Romans 13 and 'Litany and Suffrages' men, really. They are also, by diverse ways of inheritance and in differing forms, spiritual heirs of the moderate reformers in the first half of the sixteenth century: as strongly against enclosure, engrossing and brokage as they are opposed to levelling and 'mu[n]grel *Democratia*'. Burton's 'For that which is common, and every mans, is no mans' is the same commonplace as Nashe's 'That which is disperst, of all is despised'. Burton's 'Sheepe demolish Townes, devoure men, &c' repeats More's protest in *Utopia*. Nashe's 'vnder-hand cloaking of bad actions with Common-wealth pretences' (1592) closely recalls charges of double-dealing during Somerset's Protectorate (1547–1549) and as closely anticipates Donne, in his Christmas Day sermon of 1621: 'pretences of *publique good*, with which men of power and authority apparell their oppressions of the poore'. To proceed by analogy: it is as if the authorial voice in Nashe's *Christs Teares over Iervsalem*, in Burton's declaration of his 'Utopia', and in Donne's Christmas sermon, inherits the public responsibility of those 'censorys' or 'conseruaterys of the commyn wele', as Erasmian humanists in the 1530s had envisaged such positions of justice (though with little if any discernible influence on actual Henrician legislation). To analogize further, it is as if the effort 'to translate wisdom into political action' which baffled humanists like Elyot and Starkey translates itself, in the prose of Nashe and Burton, into the praxis of an individual style. The energy has to go somewhere; since it cannot realize itself as a legislative act, it turns back into the authority and eccentricity of style itself. When Burton writes of the universality of human folly that 'to insist in every particular were one of Hercules labours, there's so many ridiculous instances, as motes in the Sun', his sentence is simultaneously a ridiculing dismissive hyperbole and a ridiculous 'mote' in a huge, dogged, half-comic endeavour to perform what the author is, by this very token, saying cannot be done. Nashe, and Burton also, are like the 'artificers' described in 'Democritus to the Reader': 'that as *Salust* long since gave out of the like, *Sedem animae in extremis digitis habent,* their Soule, or *intellectus agens,* was placed in their fingers ends': the pen moves with erudite instinct—*stylus virum arguit*—and their 'curious Workes' are their books, evidence of genius and industry in a land where 'only industry is wanting'. W. R. Mueller observes that Burton's concern is 'not only . . . the melancholy person but also . . . the melancholy kingdom, particularly England. He sees a definite relationship between the two, and is seeking national, as well as individual, salvation'. We have, in any case, Burton's own words on the matter; but Mueller is right to stress its significance.

Donne, who would have questioned Mueller as to the exact meaning of 'salvation', stands more than a little apart on the status of *intellectus agens,* closer to Hooker yet not wholly with him. He redefines the *Commune bonum,* to which Nashe refers, as the *Bonum simplex* of Augustine and submits the curious works of his profane making to the divinely reasonable order of *Ecclesiasticall Politie:*

> When I behold with mine eyes some small and scarce discerneable graine or seede whereof nature maketh promise that a tree shall come; and when afterwardes of that tree any skilfull artificer vndertaketh to frame some exquisite and curious worke, I looke

for the euent, I moue no question about performance either of
the one or of the other.

The first part of Hooker's sentence is the methodical opposite of
Burton's 'To insist in every particular . . .'; its conclusion stands as
though in opposition to Burton's endorsement of *Sedem animae in
extremis digitis habent.* Hooker's crucial phrase is 'I moue no question
about performance'; Burton's method is to move such questions repeatedly *in extremis digitis;* Nashe's moral and verbal curiosity works
well *in extremis.* Hooker simply (as it appears) relegates 'any skilfull
artificer' and 'some exquisite and curious worke' to stand as exemplary details in the pattern of a greater whole, a final unity. And yet,
of course, Hooker and Burton reprove the same kinds of vain curiosity. Donne, in his funeral sermon for Sir William Cokayne,
December 12, 1626, described the mid–1620s as 'our narrow and contracted times, in which every man determines himselfe in himselfe,
and scarce looks farther'. He would be in two minds, I think, about
Burton's Herculean labours, understanding them to a great extent as
Burton himself comprehended his own intelligence and industry but
also judging them as complicitous with '*spiritus vertiginis,* the spirit of
deviation, and vaine repetition', failings for which Donne drew upon
himself as a perverse example to his own congregation: 'I pray giddily,
and circularly, and returne againe and againe to that I have said before, and perceive not that I do so'. But here, finally, they would concur: on the unremitting vigilance needed if the diagnosis is not to become one more addition to the list of symptoms of that which Donne
calls 'spirituall wantonnesse'; a state which he, like Burton, would
wish to see precisely distinguished from 'a spirituall drunkennesse in
the Saints of God themselves'.

Burton, like Nashe, read in and quoted from Erasmus, and both
authors have a grasp of 'abundance' and of its dissipated twin, redun-

dancy. Erasmus observes particularly of the English that they are not 'frugal' and, in dedicating the first version of *De Copia Verborum* to John Colet, praises the 'great fruitfulness' of Colet's educational reforms (*Collected Works*, 24). Nashe, who cites the *Copia* and *Moriae Encomium,* celebrates 'increase', 'liberalitie', 'bounty', even the 'sumptuous', though he does so in a book dedicated to the red herring and titled *Lenten Stuffe*. There is a strong counter-turn running among Nashe's abundant figures; it stresses 'profligated labour' and 'bounty' made 'bankerupt'. He contrives to show the 'generous high-mindedness', for which Erasmus praised Colet, travestied by the social climber and academic careerist Gabriel Harvey: 'how affluent and copious thy name is in all places, though *Erasmus* in his *Copia verborum* neuer mentions it'.

Erasmus, in amiable disputation with Colet, associates fecundity with multiplicity in scriptural interpretation, while his respondent argues that 'it is the function of that very fertility to bear not several things but some one thing, and that very thing the truest'. Speaking emblematically, I see Colet presiding in spirit over Donne's sermons and Erasmus as abetting the style of Nashe and Burton. Donne, naturally attracted by what Colet calls 'exuberant fertility and abundance', dedicates his sacred art to their reduction. Nashe and Burton, by inclination and vocation 'adamantine persequutor[s] of superstition' (as Burton said of Lucian), in practice derive a method from the literal meaning of *'persequor'*: they give superstition and 'ferall vices' of all kinds the run of the field so as to 'find their game by the trace'. The *OED* is in no doubt that Burton's 'ferall' is from the Latin *feralis* and means 'deadly', 'fatal'; I do not question the correctness of that derivation. It also cites a work that Burton consulted, Thomas Wright's *The Passions of the Minde* (1601), for 'ferall' from the Latin *fer-a.* a wild beast: 'Some . . . arrive at a certayne ferall or savage brutishnesse'. Though Burton, despite some local appearances to the contrary, would not prescribe or encourage the fancy to run wild, I cannot think that his imagination was shut against the suggestiveness of this particular semantic overtone.

For Erasmus, multiplicity is intellectual and spiritual bounty, and I believe that Nashe and Burton think so too. If they had thought otherwise, we would not have their books (or not the books that we have); but knowing bounty as they do, they also know the voraciousness and sterility of ignorance, ambition and ingratitude—Nashe's 'whole catalogue of wast authours', his 'greedy seagull ignorance . . . apt to deuoure any thing', Burton's 'gallantry and misery of the world', 'wise men degraded, fooles preferred'. Democritus Junior, like the other pleaders of the 'common good', has scarcely a good word for clamant and crowding Demos: his 'boiles of the common-wealth', Donne's 'expert beggars' (as distinct from 'them who are truely poore'), Nashe's 'rubbish menialty', Hobbes's 'the more ignorant sort, (that is to say, the most part, or generality of the people)', Clarendon's 'dirty people of no name'. What he has, in common with others who are here discussed, is an attitude of challenge towards questions of social origin. He is less direct than either Hobbes ('I am one of the common people') or Bunyan ('my father's house being of that rank that is meanest, and most despised of all the families in the Land'). Burton, a scion of the minor gentry, uses philosophical personae and syllogistic sophistry to balance a point of mockery where all pretension to wisdom is reduced to a common baseness, a 'commonalty' in which, by an ambiguous grammatical sequence, he appears willing to include himself. He is neither like Hobbes, the pleb matching himself with the best that Great Tew has to offer, nor like Bunyan, exaggerating the baseness of his origin in order to prove all the more emphatically his election to a domain of 'Grace and Life' denied to those of 'high-born state according to the flesh'. Burton finds himself where he has put himself, betwixt-and-between, as a slightly truculent Bergamask to the serious pace of his *via media*.

Wyndham Lewis, who is like Nashe's belated twin, strangely misconstrued 'the brilliant rattle of that Elizabethan's high-spirited ingenuity, stupefying monotony . . . empty energy'. I would say that Nashe, like Burton, understands that sphere of action, which the Gospels and Epistles call 'this world', to be *'Mundus furiosus'*, the domain of stupefying monotony and purposeless energy. The 'high-spirited ingenuity', which Lewis allows, is the verbal strength and adventurousness which Nashe brings to the investigation of torpor and satiety. Burton's word for this domain is *ataxia* (the English form 'ataxy' got into print in 1615, six years before the first appearance of Burton's book). The 'empty energy' that motivates 'this world' is, in the macrocosm, the force of Democritus' atoms colliding in the void; within the microcosm, it is 'so many heades, so many whirlegigs' and, as Nashe most directly and empirically knew, the endless wear and tear of—and on—inventiveness itself, subject to the ever-increasing demands of the public press.

If 'Democritus to the Reader' has any advantage over Nashe's *Piers Penilesse,* it is because Burton's persona, which he may well have taken from Erasmus's *Moriae Encomium,* so perfectly matches microcosm to macrocosm, the minutely tactical to the grandly conceptual, a once-for-all stroke of luck and genius. Nashe's own self-fulfilling, comprehensive discovery is the red herring, the 'king of fishes' to all of good faith and stinking fish for papists and other infidels. I sense more sharply in Nashe's 'light friskin of . . . witte' than in Burton's 'extemporean stile' (as he is pleased to name it) a strain of what Pound calls the 'intelligence at bay'. 'Caveat' is a term that Nashe regenerates from the jargon of the day: 'May wee not then haue recourse to that caueat of Christ in the Gospell, *Cauete ab hipocritis'*; 'I cannot forbid anie to thinke villainously, *Sed caueat emptor.* Let the interpreter beware; for none euer hard me make Allegories of an idle text'. The suggestion that 'emptor' means 'interpreter' springs from the same animus that

interprets 'carnifex' as 'scholler' or even as 'meat-eater' (a red herring
taken with due acknowledgement from the jest of a certain Dr
Watson). Democritus Junior in his turn forewarns 'melancholy men
. . . warily to peruse that Tract . . . & *caveant Lectores ne cerebrum iis
excutiat*', while his next-to-last words are 'CAVETE FAELICES'.

   If Burton's motto is 'expertus loquor' or 'experto crede roberto' or
even 'sed de his satis', Nashe's must be *sed caueat emptor*'. He has been
terribly misread by his purchasers, desirous of a further purchase on
him, even by those such as Wyndham Lewis (and the present author,
mea maxima culpa) who greatly admire him. That we do so miscon-
strue him is partly his own devising. He deals with the reader, as the
witty Dr Watson dealt with his 'fleshly minded' acquaintance, by 're-
torting very merily his owne licentious figures vpon him'. In their
sense of what 'licentious figures' do, and where and what they lead
to—Hell—Burton and Nashe have marked similarities. Compare
them on the final straits of wit: 'We [devils] that to our terror and
griefe do know their [Poets', Philosophers'] dotage by our sufferings,
reioyce to thinke how these sillie flyes plaie with the fire that must
burne them'; 'Their [pagan philosophers'] wittie workes are admired
here on earth, whilst their Soules are tormented in Hell fire'. Each
sees the damned as suffering in a redaction of this world's cruelties. A
phrase of Burton in particular—'naked to the worlds mercy'—springs
from that common synthetic philosophical marl (Pauline,
Augustinian, Senecan, Erasmian, etc.) upon which 'Democritus
Junior' grows his wit. Hobbes writes 'Of Man' and 'Of the Kingdome
of Darknesse', as if in felicitous memory of such 'reliques' that, at the
same time, he wishes to consign, together with those 'senselesse and
ambiguous words' which he works so felicitously, to the oblivion of
their own darkness ('wandering amongst innumerable absurdities').

   There is a particular phrase in *Leviathan* which links it to an earlier mode of moral observation (as represented, let us say, by

Cornwallis's *Discourses upon Seneca the Tragedian* of 1601). In Cornwallis, it is a maxim: 'Patience is founded in the true discourse of the minde'; in Hobbes, an anatomy summarized: 'In summe, the Discourse of the Mind, when it is governed by designe, is nothing but *Seeking,* or the faculty of Invention, which the Latines call *Sagacitas,* and *Solertia;* a hunting out of the causes, of some effect present or past; or of the effects, of some present or past cause'. The nature of the true discourse of the mind seems to me to be the central issue of *The Anatomy of Melancholy* and to be much more than a marginal concern in Nashe. For Nashe, the true discourse of the mind is to be found in the faculty of invention, 'hellish' as this may be. With Burton, it is finally made clear that he does not wish to rest in invention, nor are we finally scorned and baffled purchasers of his activity as we are of Nashe's. Paradoxically, that which establishes the ultimate difference between writers drawing on such common Christian humanist stock is movement. 'It is most true, *stylus virum arguit*', and the factor which distinguishes Burton from Nashe, Burton and Nashe from Hooker, and Hobbes from all of them, is pace. They pace themselves differently. Democritus Junior's anatomy of his own style—'*effudi quicquid dictavit Genius meus*'—reappears as Hobbes's laconic scorn, dismissive of logorrhoea: 'For if he would not have his words so be understood, he should not have let them runne'.

In one of his Lincoln's Inn sermons, Donne writes that 'God speaks to us *in oratione stricta,* in a limited, in a diligent form: Let us [not] speak to him *in oratione soluta*'. Judged by this criterion, as much as by the later priorities of Hobbes, Burton is likely to appear 'loose'. There are repetitions which can scarcely be read as accidents; for example, the account of Democritus surrounded by dissected animal carcasses which appears twice within thirty pages; others, such as the adage 'For he that cares not for his owne is master of another mans life' repeated a dozen pages on, read like trifling oversights. Far from trifling is the manner in which, throughout 'Democritus to the Reader', Burton runs a marginal inventory of a particular word which has clearly snagged his mind in the course of his scholarly reading: *stultus* and its cognates; in this section he supplies some forty to fifty entries for the word. There are precedents for the deployment of words as moral focuses: R. S. Sylvester shows how More, in the Latin text of his *Richard III,* adopts Tacitean words—*pavor, adulatio, accusatores, delatores*—to suggest the likeness of 'close & couert dealing' in Roman and contemporary tyranny. For Burton, even so, *stultus / stultitia* has an exceptionally powerful attraction, and the style which it influences and affects is English, not Latin.

Burton could perhaps be said to have invented, to suit his own sense of decorum (which is strong), an English form of *stultiloquium* (= a foolish babbling) and of the Plautine *stultiloquentia,* several years before 'stultiloquy' appeared in English usage (and, even then, in a pejorative sense: Jeremy Taylor's 'What they call facetiousnesse and pleasant wit, is indeed to all wise persons a meer Stultiloquy, or talking like a foole', 1653). I would hazard the further suggestion that Hooker's sense of 'loose regarde' and Donne's *'in oratione soluta'* here encounter Burton's different order, or range. If 'encounter' sounds too deliberate, let us say that they are brushed aside, in passing, by such locutions as 'We must make the best construction of it', 'Mixt diseases must have mixt remedies', 'Great care and choice, much discretion is required in this kinde'. The last of these quotations is noteworthy: it can be taken—by analogy—to indicate how Burton's 'extemporanean stile' does not run counter to 'discretion' and is indeed, as he says, 'partly affected'. Hobbes's feigning, in the dedication of *Leviathan,* that he is ready to be taken for an opinionated old goose (but a Capitoline goose, no less) is reminiscent of Burton's tactical affectation, though with a forensic edge that Burton does not claim.

If Hooker's assiduous citing of 'reason', in senses that are both definitive and highly allusive, derives from Aquinas; if Donne's public oratory formalizes private traits which may strike us as close to Pauline yearning for exemption from the flesh *(cupio dissolvi)*, Burton's method openly declares its debt to Hippocrates and Galen and to modern physicians, while its theology of healing remains Augustinian. *Be not solitary, be not idle,* the urgent affirmative grammatically placed as a negative, which, so far as I can gather, is Burton's compact enrichment of things said by Hippocrates and by the Portuguese physician Fonseca (d. 1622), concludes the vast argument at 3.4.2.6. The close proximity, as a doubly moral-medicinal colophon, of Hippocrates and Augustine indicates an evenness of regard towards Greek sanity (Hippocrates' pupil Galen is cited even more than his master) and Christian teaching on sin and grace:

> This likewise should we now have done, had not our will beene corrupted, and as we are enjoyned to love God with all our heart, and all our soule: for to that end were we borne, to love this object, as *Melancthon* discourseth, and to enjoy it.

The feral openness of our time may detect a pun in the sharing of an element between Burton's title and the Graecized name of the Lutheran humanist Philipp Schwarzerdt, but I think that on this point at least Burton would reiterate *Sed de his satis.* Where we pluck out 'found poems', Burton, in the Augustinian mode which he shared with Nashe and Donne, would find restlessness, or a treadmill of wit, 'endlesse argument of speech' which, as Nashe concluded, must be broken off 'abruptlie'. The injunction *Be not solitary, be not idle* is not meant to urge self-dissipation amid infinite variety of business, in any 'praecipitate, ambitious age'. Hippocrates' advice has somehow to be reconciled with the Psalmist's 'Be styll then, and knowe that I am

God'. In undertaking to anatomize eloquence such as this, one is exhibiting fragments of a synthesis which, though composed of minute particulars, transcends all Ramist itemizing. Consider in this light one sentence from the final section, 'Cure of Despaire':

> If any man, saith *Lemnius*, will attempt such a thing [exorcism], without all those jugling circumstances, Astrologicall Elections, of time, place, prodigious habits, fustian, big, sesquipedall words, spells, crosses, characters, which Exorcists ordinarily use, let him follow the example of *Peter* and *John*, that without any ambitious swelling tearmes, cured a lame man, *Acts 3*. *In the name of Christ Jesus rise and walke.*

The manner in which the huge, 'loose', referential edifice of *The Anatomy of Melancholy*, the 'confused company of notes . . . writ with as small deliberation, as I doe ordinarily speake', can yet be so tellingly pointed and cadenced by one sentence—the simple authority of 'In the name of Christ Jesus rise and walke'—is wonderful almost beyond words. As Burton was not the prolix 'smatterer' carefully presented in the 1621 postlude, I have little doubt that he fully appreciated the quality of what he had achieved and considered his labours well spent.

It is as if, in his capacity for such fine tuning, Burton realizes the equivalent in words of that 'accurate musicke' which he records as being used against 'agitation of spirits', 'vaine feare and crased phantasie'. 'Accurate musicke' is, and is not, like Donne's 'equall musick' in the peroration to his Whitehall sermon of February 29, 1627–1628: 'where there shall be no . . . darknesse nor dazling, but one equall light, no noyse nor silence, but one equall musick, no fears nor hopes, but one equall possession . . .' The order of Donne's words is analogous to that of Hooker's Christian reason: 'by . . .

steppes and degrees it ryseth vnto perfection of knowledge', where perfection is the confirmation of ultimate equity of redemption in the elect: yet Donne's text, out of which the sublime knowledge arises, is Acts 7:60, the prayer of the dying protomartyr Stephen that the criminal ignorance of his slayers be not imputed to them. Donne's words elsewhere in the sermon are virtually identical with Hooker's; he proposes that 'the name of *Stephen* hath enough in it to serve not only the vehementest affection, but the highest ambition'. Hooker had urged Cartwright, Travers, Whitaker and their fellow Puritans to ask themselves 'whether it be force of reason or vehemencie of affection, which hath bread, and still doth feede these opinions in you'. 'Vehemencie of affection' / 'vehementest affection': in Anglican apologia of this period the line drawn between the inordinate and the ordinate can be as fine as this. Circumstance commands it, but individual genius turns circumstance into an approximate free will. 'Accurate musicke' is a figure that plucks on a variety of strings, and Burton's 'We must make the best construction of it' (by which he means 'if a man put desperat hands upon himselfe, by occasion of madnesse or melancholy . . . as *ex vi morbi*') could have marked him as injudicious, even libertine, in the eyes of Hooker, who would regard him as arguing loosely from 'things doubtfull'. However, this is a principle which Hooker partly concedes, if only to shift his polemical grip on Cartwright, in the 'Preface' to *Ecclesiasticall Politie.* Donne, who left *Biathanatos* unpublished, writes of 'a rule that ordinates and regulates our faith': 'inordinate' is his characteristic pejorative ('inordinate melancholies', 'inordinate sadnesse', 'inordinate love', 'inordinateness of affections', 'inordinate lamentation', 'inordinate sorrow growes into sinfull melancholy'); yet he himself inclines to the inordinate.

There is a body of exegesis which—influenced by Freud—sees Donne so strongly possessed not only by the 'death wish' but also by a lifetime's struggle against it that this consideration should powerfully, even finally, determine our sense of the overall direction and significance of his work. He confesses the temptation on at least one occasion and I cannot disprove the claim that he suffered from a lifelong suicidal tendency, but even those who urge this hypothesis would agree that 'Cupio dissolvi, I desire to be dissolved and to be with Christ', is Pauline theology, notwithstanding the vehement affection which Donne may reasonably be supposed to bring to it.

What I have principally in mind is not so much a broad question of morbid psychology as a minute particular of inaccurate music. I instance the last two words of one of Donne's greatest poems, the 'Hymne to Christ, at the Authors last going into Germany' (1619):

> Seale then this bill of my Divorce to All,
> On whom those fainter beames of love did fall;
> Marry those loves, which in youth scattered bee
> On Fame, Wit, Hopes (false mistresses) to thee.
> Churches are best for Prayer, that have least light:
> To see God only, I goe out of sight:
> And to scape stormy dayes, I chuse
> An Everlasting night.

It is perhaps unnecessary to our sense of this stanza that the fifth line should be recognized as a commonplace found in More's *Utopia*. It is, however, necessary, here as elsewhere in Donne and his contemporaries, to accept that each of those authors could take for granted his readers' intimacy with the Scriptures, either in the Vulgate or in one of several English translations.

From whatever point of witness a seventeenth-century reader might approach Donne's words, 'everlasting night' would surely strike eye and ear as a shocking spiritual oxymoron or wild aural pun: it retorts upon 'The Anniversarie', the celebration of love's 'first, last, everlasting day', but inordinately so. We seem too close in spirit to that 'most fearefull and most irrevocable Malediction' in the fifteenth expostulation of *Devotions* (1624). There is little point in appealing to the mystics. If the night is 'everlasting', it cannot be either the dark night of the soul or the cloud of unknowing.

But of course Donne glosses his own darkness—in the funeral sermon for Sir William Cokayne:

> The Gentils, and their Poets, describe the sad state of Death so, *Nox una obeunda,* That it is one everlasting Night; To them, a Night; but to a Christian, it is *Dies Mortis,* and *Dies Resurrectionis,* The day of Death, and The day of Resurrection; We die in the light, in the sight of Gods presence, and we rise in the light, in the sight of his very Essence.

Not the Scriptures, then, or the mystics, but possibly Catullus *(Nox est perpetua una dormienda)* and Propertius *(Nox tibi longa venit nec reditura dies).* E. M. Simpson writes that Donne 'turns from the Old Testament to Catullus for his associative magic'. 'Associative magic' would perhaps suffice if the poets in question were Thomas Campion and Campion's Catullus or Propertius, but it does not take the measure of Donne's allusiveness, either in the sermon or in the 'Hymne to Christ'. In the sermon, the measure is *in oratione stricta,* in the poem *in oratione soluta.* Compared to the last stanza of 'A Nocturnall upon S. Lucies Day', in which Donne, albeit with pronounced difficulty, offers up the sensuality of *Songs and Sonets* as the sensuousness of rectified affection, 'A Hymne to Christ' ends with an enigma. I would find it hard to accept that an echo of the Latin elegists is a sufficient counter-weight to the alienated New Testament phrase; and though I still regard the 'Hymne' as the greater of these two great poems, it seems none the less that a price was paid and continues to be paid for its particular kind of power. The complicity of elegiac sophistry with spiritual equivocation has a touch of the 'ferall' about it, *ex vi morbi*, as it might be. My reference to 'inaccurate' music must be set directly against Burton's 'Others commend accurate musicke, so *Saul* was helped by *Davids* harpe', as it is my contention that Donne here eludes Burton's progress *ad sanam mentem* and returns his own music to perturbation. Even so I have to concede that rational objection scarcely touches the ultimate power of poetry such as this, and that the quality of the finest seventeenth-century metaphysical writing transforms Bacon's derogation of the scholastics—'fierce with darke keeping'—to claim tribute even from the grudging inventiveness of Bacon's animosity and to reclaim such 'keeping' to the light of spiritual eloquence, as to Hooker's 'The power of the ministerie of God translateth out of darknes into glorie'. Part of that darkness for Donne would be the Neoplatonic mysticism of Pico della Mirandola, which he admired and which, in Edgar Wind's telling phrase, he 'rescu[ed] from degradation'.

I have observed that in the contextures of this writing the inordinate and the ordinate are at times finely separated. The standard rhetorical figures merely trace the outline of such characteristics and, even then, in a relatively crude style. There is, however, a particular complicity of actives and passives invoked by these writers which may take its bearings from Calvin's interpretation of Augustine on free will and the bondage of the will. I have particularly in mind 'Man receaued in deede to be able if he would, but he hadde not to will yt he might be able'. The figures most closely aligned with this doctrinal-grammatical dilemma are perhaps *paronomasia* and *traductio* (I do not find it easy, in particular cases, to distinguish one usage from the other). Nashe, in *Christs Teares over Iervsalem,* engages with *traductio* so intensely as to mimic reprobate treachery. In so far as the nature of women is here being traduced, Nashe is himself subject to reprobation; he carries the infection in his own style: and I am convinced that he knows this:

> Euer since *Euah* was tempted, and the Serpent preuailed with her, weomen haue tooke vpon them both the person of the tempted and the tempter. They tempt to be tempted, and not one of them, except she be tempted, but thinkes herselfe contemptible. Vnto the greatnesse of theyr great Grand-mother *Euah*, they seeke to aspire, in being tempted and tempting.

The pattern 'being tempted and tempting'—passive and active—is repeated in Donne's sermons and *Devotions* ('I am a reciprocall plague; passively and actively contagious'; 'our selves are in the plot, and wee are not onely *passive,* but *active* too, to our owne destruction'). With Burton, as I understand him, the passive is made up of the vast common heap of 'melancholy [taken] in what sense you will, properly or improperly, in disposition or habit, for pleasure or for paine, dotage, discontent, feare, sorrow, madnesse, for part, or all, truly, or metaphorically, 'tis all one'. That ''tis all one' elides a Shakespearian sense of clowning insouciance and fool's comeuppance with a seemingly endless *sorites* of mental and spiritual suffering ('the whole must needs followe by . . . induction'), so minutely recorded that all sufferings appear reduced to a voluminous monotone. With Burton—again, as I understand him—the active declares itself in plain, even severe, statements of faith and practice that stand out from the tragi-comic welter like inspirations of 'God's grammar':

> Thy soule is Eclipsed for a time, I yeeld, as the Sunne is shadowed by a clowd, no doubt but those gratious beames of Gods mercy will shine upon thee againe, as they have formerly done, those

embers of Faith, Hope and Repentance, now buried in ashes, will
flame out afresh, and be fully revived. Want of faith, no feeling of
grace for the present, are not fit directions, we must live by faith,
not by feeling, 'tis the beginning of grace to wish for grace: we
must expect and tarry.

'We must live by faith, not by feeling': this at the heart of several hundred thousand words dedicated to an 'anatomy' of diseased feeling. *In
the name of Christ Jesus rise and walke.*

In an undated sermon (1622?) delivered at St Paul's, Donne at-
tends to an unnamed scholar's act of *paronomasia;* 'depart[ing] from
the ordinary reading [of the Booke of Psalmes], which is *Sepher
Tehillim,* The booke of Praise, and to reade it, *Sepher Telim,* which is
Acervorum, The book of Heapes, where all assistances to our salvation
are heaped and treasured up'. It is fitting, I think, to end here; for it
was not beyond the wit of the author of *The Anatomy of Melancholy*
to conceive his own work as a book of heaps out of a heap of books:
a mere *sorites* to set his name to, even while Bacon was showing forth
to a new age the 'harmonie of a science supporting each part the
other'. Yet in that heap the makings of a finer anatomy, a grander or-
ganum, a richer treasure, a nobler volume of praise.

A Pharisee to Pharisees

Henry Vaughan provided texts for several of his poems, as a priest would for a sermon. 'The Night' has John 3.*

> There was a man of the Pharisees, named Nicodemus, a ruler of the Jews: The same came to Jesus by night, and said unto him, Rabbi, we know that thou art a teacher come from God: for no man can do these miracles that thou doest, except God be with him. Jesus answered and said unto him, Verily, verily, I say unto thee, Except a man be born again, he cannot see the kingdom of God [John 3:1–3].

At what point did Nicodemus see the light? Did he see it because he had come, or did he come because he had seen it? Jesus gently chides him for his questions: 'Art thou a master of Israel, and knowest not these things?' [10].

The narrative makes Nicodemus seem a mixture of inoffensive ignorance, genuine perplexity, and chop-logic: 'How can a man be born when he is old? can he enter the second time into his mother's

---

*The full text of 'The Night' can be found in the Notes section for this chapter.

womb, and be born?' [4]. But Vaughan calls him 'wise' Nicodemus. In making the decision to seek Christ, he was, according to the Scripture, 'doing truth' or 'coming to the light'. Nicodemus was a Pharisee, a leading member of the ruling ecclesiastical party. Coming to Jesus at all was a dangerous thing to do. Therefore he came under cover of darkness. Jesus makes a primary act of conversion, from the literal to the figurative, in seeing this darkling venture as the stumbling of ignorance away from reprobation and towards truth: 'And this is the condemnation, that light is come into the world, and men loved darkness rather than light, because their deeds were evil' [19]. But Nicodemus, although a Pharisee, did not love the darkness rather than the light; in coming to Jesus by night he was declaring his innate love of the light.

We are as yet only being drawn towards the poem; we are to see how the poem stands in the presence of the scriptural episode and its hints of sympathetic pre-cognition, of intuition overcoming rational antipathy (it would have been reasonable for Nicodemus in those circumstances to have felt hostility towards Jesus). Vaughan's feelings towards the scriptural event are intensely sympathetic; he is drawn to it; his rhyme, as we shall discover, will attempt to chime with the theme, as his figures of speech will descant upon the basic measure, night: light.

The narrative of John 3 discovers two men taking each other's measure: 'Nicodemus answered and said unto him, How can these things be? Jesus answered and said unto him, Art thou a master of Israel, and knowest not these things?' [9–10]. Since a poet's concern is with both metre and rhyme we may expect Vaughan to be drawn to demonstrations of measure in its several senses. He must measure up to the task of imagining these natural and supernatural beings as they take the measure of each other and of destiny, of time and eternity, of knowledge and ignorance, faith and doubt; and his own words must be measured against, must chime faithfully with, the received words of Scripture.

Somewhere along the way we have begun to read the poem. Like representatives of Nicodemus, who represented us, we are strongly drawn to it, but drawn also to exercise our chop-logic upon it. In speaking of Vaughan's words chiming faithfully with the received words of Scripture we also beg questions of faith and conformity. His inventive imagination adheres 'to words and rhythms' picked up in his meditative reading, but his brusque departures and rapid conflations are as emphatic as his adherences. The citing of the text and the initial naming of 'wise Nicodemus' provide a focus for manifold soundings and radiations. Throughout the poem, recollections of Exodus 39–40, 1 Kings 6, The Song of Solomon 5:2, Malachi 4:2 and Hebrews 9:14 are as strong as, or stronger than, those of John 3, and there are further darkling allusions which may bring to mind Genesis 18, Boehme, Paracelsus and Vaughan's own prose. I do not think, however, that these allusions necessarily restrict the poem to the communing of initiates. Biblical exegetes from Augustine to Calvin took the view that 'wise Nicodemus' was in some respects rather dim, and Vaughan seems to have 'his own, similar understanding of Nicodemus' limited wisdom'. But the limited wisdom does not preclude 'blest' belief, and the blessing does not exclude human limitations. Once we have turned to the setting, the situation, of John 3, it becomes pervasive, unforgettable, and the relationship of Nicodemus' perplexed desire to the 'sacred leafs', the 'fulness of the Deity', the 'deep, but dazling darkness' of the manifest truth, is unmistakable. I have suggested that Jesus, in taking the physical darkness to be spiritual darkness, performs an initial act of poetic conversion; yet the figure of speech is intended to be literally true. Poetic metaphor is a means of converting the actual into the real. To see the reader of 'The Night' as a lay figure for Nicodemus may be only a late and dusky impertinence. Nicodemus, for all his exemplary academic dimness, was truly 'wise' and truly 'blest'; the reality of Scripture attests to that. The blessing, or the wisdom, involved in any other individual case can be nothing more than conjectural radiations emanating from, or directed upon, that focus. One cannot rule out the possibility, however, that Vaughan, a 'bookish poet', would concur with H. A. Williams's suggestion that 'the academic study of prayer may lead a man to pray'. I would further agree that 'The Night' 'refuses to make any easy divisions between the poet and his corrupt times'. The 'land of darkness and blinde eyes' is Palestine c. A.D. 30, the 'late and dusky' environment may be Wales and England under the Commonwealth, the 'loud, evil days' are, according to Vaughan, his own; but it is to his purpose that we should sense a miry compounding of implication. I concur with those who hesitate to call 'The Night' a visionary poem, since 'vision' is too commonly taken to mean effortless, unimpeded rapture. Vaughan's embroilment in national and personal distress makes him doubly conscious: of impetus and impediment; of a world hastening to catastrophe; of humanity fearfully laggard in its recognition of the apocalyptic signs.

The impetus and the impediment are equally registered in the poem. It 'quickens to a palpable ecstasy', but that ecstasy, in stanza six, is also markedly derivative; and in stanza seven ecstasy itself is narrowed and compacted to an urgent desire:

> Were all my loud, evil days
> Calm and unhaunted as is thy dark Tent,
> Whose peace but by some *Angels* wing or voice
> Is seldom rent

These lines especially in their involvement of annunciation with violence and breaking are, like the visitation they describe, serene yet troubling. 'Rend' and 'rent', in the Scriptures, occur most often in contexts of lamentation, punishment and dread: 'I will surely rend the kingdom from thee' [1 Kings 11:11], 'and [I] will rend the caul of their heart' [Hosea 13:8]. In Matthew 27:51, the veil of the Temple is 'rent', and so are the rocks. Exodus 39:23 describes how the robe of the ephod was bound 'that it should not rend'. Indeed, if there is a direct source for stanzas four and seven it is most likely to be found in the concluding chapters of Exodus, which narrate and describe the building of the 'tabernacle of the tent of the congregation' with its 'mercy seat of . . . gold' and 'vail of the covering', and its covering of cloud. In noting the probable source we note also how Vaughan at once assents to and dissents from that which inspires him. The 'dark Tent', 'calm and unhaunted', is one of his most intense affirmations; the 'mercy-seat of gold', together with 'dead and dusty *Cherub*' and 'carv'd stone', is rejected as a piece of edifying (and possibly Pharisaical) clutter. It is 'living works' that are to be treasured. If it is possible to be faithful both to letter and spirit and yet stand solitary and heterodox in one's conflations or diffusions of letter and spirit, Vaughan's 'The Night' is the autocratic manifestation of that possibility. It makes a mosaic out of Mosaic (and many other) echoes, but the mosaic is a 'living work', like that 'blest Mosaic thorn' celebrated by Christopher Smart. The creative mystery dwells in Vaughan's capacity to vivify a method that might so easily have produced second-rate *appliqué*. 'Others might expound the letter; Vaughan lived the text'.

We would be 'ill-guiding' and ill-guided, however, if we were to suppose that 'living the text' is, for Vaughan, much like that spontaneous overflow of divine immanence which Christ's 'own living works' declare. The poem is acutely aware of immanence, as it is of imminence; there are serene celebrations of indwelling; even so, something remains within and withdrawn when all has been quantified and qualified. The troubling power of the '*Angels* wing or voice' is still unaccountable:

> And the cherubims spread out *their* wings on high, *and* covered with their wings over the mercy seat, with their faces one to another; *even* to the mercy seatward were the faces of the cherubims [Exodus 37:9].

But these serene and noble beings are compounded in the 'dead and dusty *Cherub*' of stanza four. It is true that 'the Lord called unto Moses, and spake unto him out of the tabernacle of the congregation' [Leviticus 1:1], but that recollection does not entirely contain the 'fulness' which I believe Vaughan is summoning to, and from, his own indwelling imagination. Pedantry not only spells constraint; it is also freedom; and 'bookish' Vaughan had anticipated Alexander Cruden in his knowledge that 'tent' signifies 'an apartment or lodging-place made of canvas or other cloth on poles' [Genesis 4:20] as well as 'the covering of the tabernacle' [Exodus 26:11].

> In *Abr'hams* Tent the winged guests
> (O how familiar then was heaven!)
> Eate, drinke, discourse, sit downe, and rest
> Untill the Coole, and shady *Even*.

Though 'Religion' brings angels' wings and voices into a tent it is without any suggestion of the calm being 'rent'. Even so it is possible that in 'The Night' Vaughan is echoing his own poetry as much as he is echoing his own prose. 'Religion' had appeared in the first edition of *Silex Scintillans* (1650); 'The Night' was included in the second, enlarged, edition of 1655. 'Religion' itself has its clear source in Chapter 18 of Genesis:

And the Lord appeared unto [Abraham] in the plains of Mamre:
and he sat in the tent door in the heat of the day; And he lift up
his eyes and looked, and, lo, three men stood by him: and when
he saw *them*, he ran to meet them from the tent door, and bowed
himself toward the ground, And said, My Lord, if now I have
found favour in thy sight, pass not away, I pray thee, from thy
servant [Genesis 18:1–3].

The three men, who are at once angels and the voice of the Lord (it
is Vaughan who sees them as 'winged'), bring blessing and assurance
to Abraham and Sarah but the threat of imminent destruction to
Sodom. Abraham risks the Lord's wrath by speaking up for the 'righteous' who may dwell there. But 'early in the morning' he sees the
smoke rising from the cities of the plain. In 'Religion' Vaughan excludes the wrath and retribution that are a part of the angels' bearing.
In 'The Night' it is as though he elliptically concedes these attributes
in the brusquely disproportionate 'rent' which seems to intrude from
the margins of his recollection.

We may question, however, whether such connotations 'intrude'
or are 'drawn in'. 'One of the largest and most recurrent' of Vaughan's
image-clusters 'has, for common factor, the idea of magnetism', and
he may have been drawn or impelled towards this interest by the hermetical studies of his brother Thomas. The stanza from 'Religion'
makes clear that his ideal of an 'active commerce' between 'the various planes of existence', between angels and men, would be a 'familiar' 'discourse', a quotidian but holy communing, a matter of calm
and untroubled daily practice rather than of clandestine nocturnal
comings and goings. Vaughan, as Royalist and Anglican, was the ad-
herent of twin causes, both defeated. 'By 1650 Vaughan's earthly
Church of England had in fact vanished'. Two of his prose works
published in 1652 and 1654, during the interregnum, bear upon the

study of his poetry, of 'The Night' in particular. 'The logical prose
content [of 'The Night'] is to be found in *The Mount of Olives*'.
Vaughan composed that work, one section of which bears the title
'Man in Darkness', to encourage the practice of solitary devotion
among his readers 'in these times of persecution and triall'. In the
dedicatory epistle to Sir Charles Egerton, Vaughan writes: 'The *Sonne*
of *God* himselfe (when *he* was *here*) had no place to put his head in;
And his *Servants* must not think the *present measure* too hard, seeing
their *Master* himself took up his *nights-lodging* in the cold *Mount* of
Olives'. In the preface to *Flores Solitudinis . . . Collected in his Sicknesse
and Retirement*, 1654, he declares:

> *I write unto thee out of a land of darknesse, out of that unfortunate
> region, where the Inhabitants sit in the shadow of death: where de-
> struction passeth for propagation, and a thick black night for the glo-
> rious day-spring. If this discourage thee, be pleased to remember, that
> there are bright starrs under the most palpable clouds, and light is
> never so beautifull as in the presence of darknes.*

If we regard 'The Night' and its several darknesses in the light of
such evidence we discover how the sympathetic attraction of otherwise disparate images and echoes from Old and New Testaments,
from a variety of non-scriptural sources and from Vaughan's own
writings creates a positive embracing of abnegation, a transferring of
potentiality from the darkness of a stricken soul, a stricken cause and
a stricken church into a visionary intensity. The ecstatic night of The
Song of Solomon, the night of Christ's several cold and solitary vigils
(as recounted in Vaughan's other 'texts' for this poem, Mark 1:35 and
Luke 21:37), possibly that night, also, in which 'an horror of great
darkness' fell upon Abraham and a voice prophesied that his seed
should be a stranger in a land that was not theirs [Genesis 15:12–13],

all these attractive and repellent nocturnal associations are synthesized, transfigured, converted by the dominating metaphor of the darkness which saw the conversion of the Pharisee Nicodemus. 'Conversion' is the key to the metaphysics of *Silex Scintillans* and to the poetics of 'The Night'. Coldness, destitution, deprivation (as in *The Mount of Olives*), darkness, blindness, deadness, silence are made the magnetic points of contact with the Divine Grace. Night is heaven, and heaven takes on some of the qualities of visionary darkness:

> Gods silent, searching flight:
> When my Lords head is fill'd with dew, and all
> His locks are wet with the clear drops of night;
> His still, soft call;
> His knocking time; The souls dumb watch,
> When Spirits their fair kinred catch.

This is Vaughan being 'bookish' again, plagiarizing The Song of Solomon 5:2 and Revelation 3:20 with magnetic originality, as though he were simply catching 'fair kinred' of his thought. There seems no reason to dispute S. L. Bethell's claim that in this stanza the poet 're-creates through sensory material an intuition of eternal reality'. It is significant that Bethell refers to 'sensory material' rather than to 'sensuous experience'. Sensuous experience is what is evoked; the sensory material I take to be language itself.

It would perhaps be generally agreed that a 'poetic' use of language involves a release and control of the magnetic attraction and repulsion which words reciprocally exert. One is impelled, or drawn, to enquire whether that metaphysical rapport felt to exist between certain English rhyme-pairings is the effect of commonplace rumination or the cause of it. Auden, in *New Year Letter*, makes 'womb : tomb' a trick in his 'Devil's' sophistry, implying that the easy availability of the rhyme is complicitous with our trite melancholy and angst. Sir Thomas Browne, meditating in 1658 on funeral urns 'making our last bed like our first; nor much unlike the Urnes of our Nativity', may cause one to suppose that speculative pseudo-logic works independently of the gravitational pull of words; yet he too is 'rhyming' in a sense, only with shapes, not sounds. Sigurd Burckhardt suggests that a pun is 'the creation of a semantic identity between words whose phonetic identity is, for ordinary language, the merest coincidence'. Heard in this way, all rhyming is punning; as, seen in the light of hermetical philosophy, all creation is a form of rhyming, or 'union of elemental extremes', and would be especially so to Vaughan, 'committed as he was to a belief in the validity of the specialized microcosmism of hermeticism'. That which Milton disdains as 'the troublesom and modern bondage of Rimeing' is troublesomely binding as much because it is easy as because it is hard: an imputation endorsed by Aubrey's report of Milton's lofty permission for Dryden to *tagge his Verses*'. The troublesome ease may be inferred too from the work of Thomas Campion, whose *Observations in the Art of English Poesie*, with its reference to 'the childish titillation of riming', anticipates Milton's dismissive tone. His own lyrics from the four books of ayres, in which 'loue' rhymes with either 'moue' or 'proue', or their moods and cognates, in song after song, obligingly demonstrate his contention. Such rhymes are evidently easy for the singing voice; they are also 'tags', that is to say, they show a 'pretty knack', they 'buttonhole' attention, but they are not 'like cleare springs renu'd by flowing', not 'voluble', as is 'Rose-cheekt *Lawra*', Campion's own masterly 'example' of unrhymed verse. At the same time one might be bound to accept, for it would be hard to deny, the way in which a modish metaphysics of love's oxymoronic power accrues from the mellifluous repetitiveness of these rhymes, as Donne appears independently to have noted: his hyperbolic rhyming in 'The Canonization' seems designed to draw attention to the discovery. The impulse of 'loue', at once fixed and flighty, to 'moue' and 'remoue' is an incitement for Campion's singer to 'proue' its falseness or its truth:

> Changing shapes like full-fed *Ioue*
> In the sweet pursuit of loue.

It is fitting that this lordly rhyme should consummate *The Ayres that Were Svng and Played at Brougham Castle . . .* since both change and permanence are in Jove's protean gift.

In Vaughan's poetry a rhyme which occurs with striking frequency is 'light : night', or 'night : light'. Here, too, basic mechanics assume ontological dimensions. S. L. Bethell has remarked on 'the light-darkness opposition in Vaughan', but such a rhyme embodies more than an opposition. It is a twinning: a separation which is simultaneously an atonement ('Wise *Nicodemus* saw such light / As made him know his God by night') and a conjunction which exacerbates the sense of divorce ('And by this worlds ill-guiding light. / Erre more then I can do by night'). In the pairing 'light : night' 'night : light' itself, there is nothing remarkable except its bookish obviousness. Campion is drawn to it several times, notably in the refrain of 'My Sweetest Lesbia'; so is Herbert. Wotton proffers it handsomely ('On his Mistris, the Queen of Bohemia') and Jonson makes it sound both securely traditional ('A Hymne on the Nativitie of My Saviour') and sententiously challenging (in the third 'turne' of 'To the Immortal Memorie . . .'). But in Vaughan the eye and ear are dogged with a particularly dogged tenacity: 'In the first birth of light, / And death of Night' ('To Amoret, Walking in a Starry Evening'); 'I'le leave behind me such a *large, kind light*, / As shall *redeem* thee from *oblivious night*' ('To the River *Isca*'); 'The first (pray marke,) as quick as light / Danc'd through the floud, / But, th'last more heavy then the night / Nail'd to the Center stood' ('Regeneration'); *'(for at night / Who can have commerce with the light?)'* ('Vanity of Spirit'); 'But these all night / Like Candles, shed / Their beams, and light / Us into Bed' ('Joy of my life!'); 'As he that in some Caves thick damp / Lockt from the light, / Fixeth a solitary lamp / To brave the night'; 'Yet I have one *Pearle* by whose light / All things I see, / And in the heart of Earth, and night / Find Heaven, and thee' ('Silence, and stealth of days!'); 'Call in thy *Powers*; run, and reach / Home with the light, / Be there, before the shadows stretch. / And *Span* up night' ('The Resolve'); 'Above are restles *motions*, running *Lights*, / Vast Circling *Azure*, giddy *Clouds*, days, nights'; 'O lose it not! look up, wilt Change those *Lights* / For *Chains* of *Darknes,* and *Eternal Nights?*' ('Rules and Lessons'); 'The Dew thy herbs drink up by night, / The beams they warm them at i'th' light' ('Repentance'); 'Or wil thy all-surprizing light / Break at midnight?'; 'The whole Creation shakes off night, / And for thy shadow looks the light' ('The Dawning'); 'I saw Eternity the other night / Like a great *Ring* of pure and endless light / All calm, as it was bright' ('The World'); 'The first glad tidings of thy early light, / And resurrection from the earth and night' ('Ascension-day'); 'Their magnetisme works all night, / And dreams of Paradise and light'; 'Their little grain expelling night / So shines and sings, as if it knew / The path unto the house of light' ('Cock-Crowing'); 'Dear feast of Palms, of Flowers and Dew! / Whose fruitful dawn sheds hopes and lights, / Thy bright solemnities did shew, / The third glad day through two sad nights' ('Palm-Sunday'); 'Tempests and windes, and winter-nights, / Vex not, that but one sees thee grow, / That *One* made all these lesser lights' ('The Seed growing secretly'); 'Were not thy word (dear Lord!) my light. / How would I run to endless night' ('The Men of War'); 'Who shews me but one grain of sincere light? / False stars and fire-drakes, the deceits of night . . .' ('The Hidden Treasure');

'And onely see through a long night / Thy edges, and thy bordering light!' ('Childe-hood'); 'To thy bright arm, which was my light / And leader through thick death and night!' ('Abels blood'); 'This litle *Goshen*, in the midst of night, / And Satans seat, in all her Coasts hath light' ('Jacobs Pillow, and Pillar'); 'O beamy book! O my mid-day / Exterminating fears and night! / The mount, whose white Ascendents may / Be in conjunction with true light!' ('The Agreement'); 'Should poor souls fear a shade or night, / Who came (sure) from a sea of light?' ('The Water-fall').

It is reasonable to ponder what it is that draws or impels Vaughan towards this rhyme. Is it an instinctual gravitation, or a conscious application to the sensory material of his brother's and other hermetical writers' theories about magnetism and sympathetic attraction? Or is it that Vaughan has so concentrated his mind on the abstract eschatology of 'light-darkness opposition' that he is relatively or even totally indifferent to the monotonous uninventiveness of his word-finding? Such addiction is indeed vulnerable to suggestions that it renders null and void a poet's unique claim to whatever prestige his craft may have: his capacity to invent, to 'compose', to 'find out in the way of original contrivance'; to 'create, produce, or construct by original thought or ingenuity'; to 'devise first, originate', to 'bring into use formally, or by authority'. It could be argued, of course, that the word 'invent' itself contains contradictory implications and that to 'come upon', which suggests chance discovery, is to be distinguished from 'devise' or 'bring into use', which imply forethought and manufacture.

'The Night' itself, it is true, contains powerful contradictory energies, but it must be said that our own readings of the poem are themselves liable to disabling contradictions because, for a variety of contemporary cultural reasons, we 'see not all clear' when we try to calculate the ratios of vision to craft. E. C. Pettet finds the final stanza over-inventive, merely ingenious, 'manufactured', as though 'something of the organic impulse and life of the poem, its intensity and seriousness, has gone'. J. F. S. Post has argued that 'despite the achievement of a timeless vision, no poem of Vaughan's shows better his reluctance to dissolve into rapture'. 'Shows better' and 'reluctance' suggest a fuller understanding both of Vaughan's vision and his perplexities and of his way of 'bringing into use formally, or by authority' the envisioning of perplexity itself:

> There is in God (some say)
> A deep, but dazling darkness; As men here
> Say it is late and dusky, because they
> See not all clear;
> O for that night! where I in him
> Might live invisible and dim.

'Lux est umbra Dei', according to Ficino. Vaughan's contemporary Sir Thomas Browne quoted the phrase in support of his own preference for 'adumbration'. 'Some say' confirms the validity of the poem's perplexed meditation; it does not, in my view, dissipate its 'mystical awareness'. If awareness is to have any value at all as a critical term, it must be allowed to retain that innate sense of being 'on one's guard'. This is surely what the poem's 'full intensity' rejoices in: that Nicodemus came warily but nonetheless came upon the truth and that, as he did so, nature kept vigil and was no less wary than it was entranced ('did watch and peep / And wonder'). Though we too should be wary of reading Vaughan, a 'thorough-going intellectual', as if he were a childlike precursor of Romanticism, our sense of 'awareness' is enhanced when, in stanza six, the God of The Song of Solomon 5:2 and of Revelation 3:20 comes like a mousing owl over the fields by the Usk, with 'silent, searching flight' and 'still, soft call'. To be the 'catch' of Spirits is a fearful rapture.

'The Night' celebrates the absoluteness of 'blest' belief while it asserts a mortal 'consent' to mundane 'darkness' and 'myre'. It is the supposed discrepancy between celebration and assertion that has troubled some readers. But I suspect that Vaughan himself has spotted the catch: he writes of himself as one who is doubly caught. He is both possessed by God and gripped by a sense of his own unworthiness ('*Servus inutilis: peccator maximus*' as he was to remain, in his own mind) and of his own and others' subjection to Cromwellian republican tyranny. If we are persuaded of the validity of Vaughan as poet of the absolute, it is because he has validity as poet of 'contingency', a term which covers 'close connexion or affinity of nature' (1612), an 'event conceived as of possible occurrence in the future' (*a*1626) and mere 'chance', 'fortuitousness' (1623).

> O for that night! where I in him
> Might live invisible and dim.

'Might' is conditional, but so are stanza seven's 'Were all my loud, evil days' and 'Then I . . . / Would keep'. Contingency surrounds, in the form of grammar, syntax and verse-structure, the 'Dionysian' absolute, the 'deep, but dazling darkness'. As Post has observed, 'detached yet "possessed"'; the final stanza 'seems to shuttle between two realms . . . without relinquishing touch with either'.

In the light of this observation one may add that Vaughan's metaphysics, his bookish but spontaneous and sincere paradox of 'deep, but dazling darkness', or his persistent 'light-darkness opposition', working through the rhyme-pattern, poem after poem, transforms contingency itself into a density, an essential 'myre', though without the accidents of language thereby being denied or tamed. Each time the words 'light : night', 'night : light' chime they reassert 'merest coincidence' even while they are affirming a theological or hermetic theorem as clear and absolute in Vaughan's mind as 'the square of the hypotenuse . . .'. One is drawn towards the invention of a term—'metaphysical phonetics'—to try to define what is happening through this reiterative pattern. But this would merely create a further 'theorem', and I am far from convinced that the relationship between vision and language in poetry, or at least in Vaughan's kind of poetry, works according to theorems, particularly hermetic ones.

Frank Kermode has been taken to task for suggesting that Vaughan's 'conversion' 'was rather a poetic than a religious experience'. This claim, though extreme, has the considerable virtue of conceiving language as something other than a mere ancillary of 'vision' or 'experience'. Language is a vital factor of experience, and, as 'sensory material', may be religiously apprehended. Post has written at some length on Vaughan's 'poetics of conversion', meaning principally his transformation of *The Temple* into *Silex Scintillans:* 'No one read Herbert with greater benefit or imagination'. I believe that one could go further and say that Vaughan fashioned regeneration by regenerating fashion. E. C. Pettet has noted how the 'shining ring of eternity' to be found in the great opening lines of 'The World' is 'already intimated' in the pretty secular verses 'To Amoret, Walking in a Starry Evening'. He could have added that the 'light : night' rhyme of 'To Amoret . . .' 'intimates' its own regeneration in the light-darkness eschatology of Vaughan's religious poems, and of 'The Night' in particular.

Father W. J. Ong, deep in the dazzling darkness of his brilliant essay 'Wit and Mystery', tells us that, for Aquinas, 'Christian theology and poetry are indeed not the same thing, but lie at opposite poles of human knowledge. However, the very fact that they are opposite extremes gives them something of a common relation to that which lies between them: they both operate on the periphery of human intellection. A poem dips below the range of the human process of understanding-by-reason as the subject of theology sweeps above it'. The 'awareness' of Vaughan's religious poetry is an awareness of such extremes. That which lies between these extremes, in his beautiful poem 'The Night', is the conversion-conversation of Jesus and Nicodemus in which that which is above understanding-by-reason (theology) and that which dips below the process of understanding-by-reason (the contingent nature of sensory material) are briefly made to chime.

The Eloquence of Sober Truth

It is fortunate for the estate of humane letters, as we have received it from the writers represented in *Early Responses to Hobbes,* that a sense of overall and general truth may be gained as a real effect of such writings, irrespective of whether sincerity or authenticity (as we are inclined to understand them) can be discovered at the source.* The formal admixture of the plain and the florid, of openness and cunning ('wresting', deliberated misreading), of magnanimity and malice, of public application and private referral, of empiricism and ideology, that is to say, the quotidian practical eloquence of controversy evident in these works, finds little or no answering resonance among a specialist or a general readership of our own time. Understandably so. Rightly to evaluate John Bramhall and the first Earl of Clarendon would be to recognize ourselves as barely having moved from under

---

Early Responses to Hobbes, edited by G. A. J. Rogers. Six volumes, boxed (New York and London: Routledge / Thoemmes Press, 1996), 1,699 pages. The volumes discussed in this essay are *A Defence of True Liberty,* by John Bramhall, Bishop of Derry (1655); *Observations, Censures, and Confutations of Notorious Errours in Mr Hobbs his Leviathan,* by William Lucy, Bishop of St David's (1663); and *A Brief View and Survey of the . . . errors . . . in Mr. Hobbes's Leviathan,* by Edward Hyde (Edward, Earl of Clarendon) (1676).

the shadow of their contentions. And such recognition would, for millennial idealists and cynics alike, be asking too much.

Of the authors here represented, it can be said that, although not always knowing where they stood, they knew in general how they stood, from what and from whom they were descended and how they wished to be seen to have stood: in relation not only to authority and precedent but also to posterity. The awareness of providence, agency and delegation, of being required by conscience and circumstance to act as intercessor between flawed past, uncertain present and unsecured future, is suggested most powerfully by the exordium to Clarendon's *History of the Rebellion and Civil Wars in England,* which he began to draft on March 18, 1646: an opening sentence, 'a mighty period of nearly five hundred words', in which details of syntax and word-choice significantly invoke the emphatic cadence of Richard Hooker's exordium to *The Lawes of Ecclesiasticall Politie* (1593). In so committing himself, Edward Hyde (as he then was) eloquently recalled to life a definitive voice of the Elizabethan Church and State, but a voice considerably changed, strained, by the circumstances of the intervening half-century. It was a purposed eloquence which, already under attack when Hooker adopted it and made it his own, had, in less than fifty years, been rendered obsolete. For Clarendon, however, situated as he was, to be, or to sound, obsolete was to be, or to sound, legitimate.

Legitimacy is not sincerity, nor is it the personalist authenticity of Emerson and the Emersonians. The significance of *Early Responses to Hobbes,* for us as much as for seventeenth-century thought and polity, is the preponderance of discourse. The authors argue, often tendentiously, sometimes crudely, very much in their own interest, but they are not, with the possible exception of Robert Filmer, monologuists, nor are they determinists or mechanistic dialecticians; they engage with the (hostile) other as a contending voice among others.

They recognize their own contentiousness, their own partiality, and thereby acknowledge, in a sense, their parity, their common partaking in that condition, that innate incompetence, which Hooker had called 'this our imbecillitie'.

Clarendon's own debt to Hooker evidently comprehends more than the matter of a grandiose but mismanaged exordium. The fluent magnanimity of the *Lawes,* its 'peaceful and lofty sentences' (as A. P. D'Entreves called them), is authentic but not unambiguous. There is a polity to declare and defend, and this is a politic style. It is scarcely conceivable that Hooker believed it possible to disarm by peaceful means the Presbyterian aggression: in a disadvantageous position he sees the advantage to be gained from using words with a marked courtesy towards the quality of reciprocal discourse or, at least, towards a fiction of the desired reciprocity. Such usage represents or affects to represent the writer's 'diligent and distinct consideration', the neglect of which, Hooker implies, is a key failing in his opponents. That Clarendon commences his *History* with an imitation of Hooker's opening paragraph is due mainly, I suggest, to his politic grasp of associational pitch-values. His representation of the issues is frequently neither diligent nor distinct nor considerate, but to arouse the memory—and when it serves, the hollow memory—of peaceful and lofty sentences is eminently worth his time and labour.

There is a semantic doubleness, a double valency, in English public writing of the sixteenth and seventeenth centuries that constitutes its own form of minor tradition, and here also one can see that Clarendon is working in a mode which derives from Hooker. To what extent, beyond the opening tribute, this is always a conscious derivation I would find it harder to decide. To take one characteristic example: in Hooker, 'dexterity' is a word of ambivalent tone, an ambivalence which is even more pronounced when Clarendon adopts it. In one instance in Hooker, it applies to the 'subtiltie of Satan'; in another it affirms the 'works of nature' as they are seen to be 'exact' and 'by divine arte performed'. The 'admirable dexteritie of wit' which Hooker attributes to the original reforming inspiration of Calvin cannot be taken as a term of unqualified respect, though, when Hooker found a theory or practice abhorrent, as he did 'Ramistry', he was not one to mince words. Egil Grislis's observation that '[his] attitude toward Calvin . . . may reflect both respect and censure' is appropriately judicious, and confirms my sense that 'dexterity' was a word typically resorted to, in cases of suspended judgment, by those conscientiously desiring to maintain equity but that it characterized also those whose disabling perplexity of mind gradually works through to the reader and may also have become apparent to the author himself during the process of composition.

Conscious as Hyde must have been, in 1646, that the *History,* as critical of Stuart mismanagement as it was laudatory of Charles I's private virtues, could not be made public in the foreseeable future, its style, in part recollected for an immediate audience of one—his own reflective self—and in part projected for an unfathomable posterity, betrays his divided attention, if not his confusion. The 'mighty' opening period of the *History* is unwieldy; it is also ungrammatical. For 'may loose the recompense dew to their virtue' read 'may [not] loose the recompense dew to their virtue'. Clarendon aimed to write with a persuasive frankness while being not entirely scrupulous in his handling of debatable matters which, as they were in themselves formidable and complex, also on occasion eluded his otherwise formidable style of elegiac-forensic 'vindication'. It is revealing that he too allows a considerable amount of slack in his use of the word 'dexterity'. When he approves the whole constitution of the man, as he does with Lord Falkland, it signifies the ability to apply one's understanding and judgment with celerity, 'seasonably and appositely'. Where he detests his subject, as he does Henry Vane the younger and William Waller, it points to a celerity in self-promotion, a talent to 'cozen and deceave'. The Earl of Strafford, whose 'passions', especially that of 'pride', Clarendon presents as in part responsible for the national catastrophe, 'the late woful calamities in *England*', 'the late execrable Rebellion', but whose inherent strength of character raised him above his accusers, 'made his Defence with all imaginable Dexterity; answering this, and evading that, with all possible skill and eloquence'. The range of implication is perhaps wider in Clarendon than in Hooker; necessity of circumstance, strongly sensed in the *Lawes,* is even more pressingly evident in the *History* and the autobiographical *Life.* In each case, we are simultaneously aware of a particular kind of grammatical structure and a particular theory of moral virtue: dexterity is at once the proper credential of a serious writer and a craft potentially sinister; a cunning spring-trap as likely to catch the magisterial author as it is to deal with the miscreant object of his censure.

Virtually without exception, the various authors represented in *Early Responses to Hobbes* leave little room to doubt that language, in relation to private and public practice, is at the heart of the matter: the matter being principally that of the instauration, destruction and restoration of a true national identity and doctrine. Bishop Bramhall of Derry would be glad enough to stand by the authority of moral axioms—for example, 'deceitfull men do not love to descend to particulars'—but his style is transitional: we see axiom in process of its translation into working exemplar:

A precedent generall deliberation how to do any act, as for instance, how to write, is not sufficient to make a particular act, as my writing this individuall reply[,] to be freely done, without a particular and subsequent deliberation.

In William Lucy's *Observations, Censures and Confutations of . . . Leviathan* (1663), the empirical shifts even further, into satire:

> When he writ his *Leviathan,* there was *motion,* but this *Leviathan,* I hope, is not *motion;* it may, perhaps, in heedlesse Readers, cause *motion* and *commotion,* but certainly it lies still under my paper at this time, and will do all this night.

In Bramhall's *Defence of True Liberty* (1655), the distinction between necessity and freedom is pointed by the availability of the verb forms 'must write' and 'may write' and is affirmed by the judiciousness with which an author chooses between them. The burden of his charge is that Thomas Hobbes constantly 'changeth shapes in . . . one particular' and that such shape-shifting implicates etymology, logic and common honesty. Moreover (according to Bramhall), Hobbes misconstrues as often as he intentionally misleads; his errors stem from simple incompetence as much as from a perverted will; or, rather, the common errors as much as the sophisms are the outward and visible sign of a radical inward desperation. For Bramhall to 'descend to particulars', to 'strike . . . at the root of [the] question', is both to anatomize deceitfulness and self-deception and to establish the ground of right dealing. Lucy, exercised as much by Socinian errors as by Hobbes's waywardness with Scriptural texts, proposes to 'take every word apart, and vindicate it from their several Objections'.

In numerous instances which these authors present, to 'strike . . . at the root' is the same as to clear the 'genuine sense' of a word from Hobbes's specious application of it, or to 'rip up the bottom of [a] business', as in the several pages which Bramhall devotes to eradicating the senses of 'voluntary' and 'spontaneous' planted by his antagonist and to nurturing a genuine sense of them, in keeping with his—Bramhall's—understanding of sense and reason. If I take this to imply that Bramhall and Lucy are more open to Ramist method than was Hooker, my suggestion hangs by a slender thread—that of the term 'anatomy' in English literary usage during the sixteenth and seventeenth centuries—and is also strongly attached to W. J. Ong's observation that Petrus Ramus's *Commentary on the Christian Religion* sets itself 'explicitly the task of illustrating the theological loci'. The early responders, to the Hobbes of the original *De Cive* of 1642 as well as of the later *Leviathan,* are strong advocates and assailants of the loci, but they are primarily turning an emphasis which they may have drawn from a knowledge of Ramus into forms of argument strongly opposed to Ramist tendencies in general, a modification which one also recognizes in Robert Burton's *Anatomy of Melancholy.* This first appeared in 1621 and, together with Philip Sidney's *Arcadia* (1590), commits, but does not abandon, its discourse to that debatable ground where, in the corrupt state of man, private and public interests are determined—but not irretrievably—by the indeterminate.

Bramhall seeks to establish his moral ground against the author of *De Cive* by submitting, at the very outset of the debate, a basic question concerning the scope and limits of self-knowledge in contexts of such contentiousness: whether those 'affections' which 'betray our understandings' may 'produce an implicite adhaerence in the one [person] more than in the other'.

If one could legitimately elide chronological sequence, it would be possible to claim that Bramhall desires to expose 'implicite adhaerence' as the graceless twin of that 'inhaerent' 'vertue' which Hobbes celebrates in his recollections of Sidney Godolphin. Further, it is as if Bramhall enters the tacit caveat that true magnanimity calls for more than a magnificent ingenuity of phrase. As he says elsewhere in *A Defence of True Liberty,* 'this controversy . . . is not about Words, but about Things; not what the words Voluntary or Free do or may sig-

nifie but whether all things be extrinsecally praedetermined to one'.
In so saying, of course, he focuses attention—his and ours—all the
more urgently on questions of language, the nature of meaning. The
unarguable circumstance telling against my chronological elision is
that the private disputation between Bramhall and Hobbes took place
six years before the tribute to Godolphin was made public in 1651; the
source of the dispute, as we have noted, was not *Leviathan* but the *De
Cive* of 1642. A more persuasive response would be that the later
Hobbes is everywhere implicit—and often explicit—in the earlier
writings, and that Bramhall's original objection to his opponent's
'meer Logomachy' in *De Cive* would have been reinforced by a subsequent reading of *Leviathan*. He would not, in 1651, have seen any
cause to retract.

Chronology and its intractabilities notwithstanding, the contention over disparate elements to which I have alluded in the phrase
'true national identity and doctrine' manifestly traces and retraces the
likeness and unlikeness between 'implicite adhaerence' and 'inhaerent' 'vertue'. Although the root cause of Bramhall's objections to *De
Cive* is the apparent inability of Hobbes's argument to grasp the
nature of that 'true morall liberty, which is in question between us',
Hobbes's summoning of the spectre of blind necessity, near the end
of *Leviathan,* in his second reflection on Godolphin's untimely death,
'unfortunately slain in the beginning of the late Civill warre, . . . by
an undiscerned, and an undiscerning hand', challenges all other
examples of contemporary *laus et vituperatio* to approach anywhere
near its tragic resonance, let alone take its measure. Hobbes's nearest
rivals in rhetorical power, in such deploration, are Sidney in the
Arcadia, Walter Ralegh and, in certain instances, Clarendon.

So to elevate into exemplary maxims, epigrammatic conclusive-
ness, as I do here, those turns of phrase which the original contestants
would have considered mere examples of 'tautology' and 'wresting',

the issue of 'meer animosity', 'antipathy', 'melancholy', 'desperate imaginations' (imaginings), on one side or the other, is to risk being taken as assuming a dictatorial privilege of hindsight. The issue remains, even so. If Hobbes's theory of the Passions is 'very far from being *the true Key to open the cipher of other mens thoughts*', as Clarendon avers, and if the caveat is honestly entered (and it may not be), where and how is the 'key' to be obtained? Clarendon chides Hobbes for his 'mirth' at the expense of the 'Schole-men' who, the barrenness of their speculation notwithstanding, at least contributed 'terms of Art . . . which in truth are a cipher to which all men of moderate Learning have the key'. It is apparent, however, that 'cipher' in Clarendon's second sense is not exactly conformable to his earlier use of the term. In the second instance the key is application; in the first it is construal. We are therefore returned to the original point at issue: How are statements to be read? How are they *meant* to be read? It is on this point, or question, that all those who felt themselves called to make 'Animadversions upon' either *De Cive* or the later *Leviathan* appear, on the face of it, to be in agreement. This state of accord, or its simulacrum, derives in no inconsiderable part from Hooker's tactics of politic concord, judicious censure, gestures of magnanimity: a style which he had already established some years prior to the appearance in print of the first four books of *Ecclesiasticall Politie*: 'Conster his [St Paul's] wordes, and ye cannot misconster myne. I speake no otherwise. I ment no otherwise'.

The standard procedure is that of the 'necessary requisite', even though ideas as to what constituted the requisite mean standard differed from author to author. Father Ong stresses the inherent force of the 'commonplace' in the textures of even the most individual style and argument. One would add only that the *idea* of the body of commonplace was itself not only convenient but also powerfully suggestive to writers of this period, as a kind of secular *adiaphora*, indifferent matter, which should figure either as an unfailing reservoir of tried and tested human wisdom and experience or as an immovable bulk of *pseudodoxia*, rumour and common report, supposedly justifying any given author's reasonable contempt for, and distrust of, 'this present age full of tongue and weake of braine', the 'Sophisters and seditious Oratours apply[ing] themselves to the many headed multitude'.

Struck here by Bramhall's choice of words, our automatic response is 'Shakespeare'. But how far, if at all, was *Coriolanus* regard-ed as essential, or advisable, or prudent matter by the 1640s? The phrase 'many-headed multitude' is in Sidney's *Arcadia* and was taken by him and by others from Horace's first *Epistle*. The root question with regard to the use of commonplace at that time relates less to genealogy than to genius, the 'natural ability or capacity' to render significant that which is given; to 'form . . . and model' (Hyde, on William Chillingworth) an individual contribution to the shared dis-course. I infer that among the many reasons for a consensus against Hobbes, as represented by this set of *Early Responses* and by other writings not represented, was a suspicion—or a recognition—that, in his work, style becomes a different kind of individual attestation: an attestation to singular power. Although Hobbes is at pains to assert that laughing to scorn, the 'Sudden Glory' of self-applause when 'observing the imperfections of other men', is itself 'a signe of Pusillanimity', his own negative attributes were pre-eminently, as his foes insisted, pettiness of spirit, cowardliness and timidity (that is, 'pusillanimity'). His genius is that he does not write in accordance with his own prescription. 'The Light of humane minds is Perspicuous Words, but by exact definitions first snuffed, and purged from ambi-guity': yet he is a master of nuance and innuendo, tactics absolutely requiring that our language retains, and is directed so as to retain, a good deal of partly consumed matter, the stuff of contrary feelings and perplexed experience, even a certain amount of bad odour. (See further in Part One, Chapter 2, his play on 'haunt', meaning the malign activity attributed by the credulous to ghosts and apparitions but meaning also the malign activity of 'crafty ambitious persons' who spread 'fearful tales' about a particular location—for instance, a churchyard—so that they themselves may 'haunt' or frequent it for their own nefarious purposes.) And what kind of business does Hobbes conduct with faith and works, meaning and usage, in the following excerpt? He declares 'our Senses, and Experience, [and] our naturall Reason' to be

> the talents which [God] hath put into our hands to negotiate, till the coming again of our blessed Saviour; and therefore not to be folded up in the Napkin of an Implicate Faith, but employed in the purchase of Justice, Peace, and true Religion.

From Tyndale (1526) through to the King James Bible (1611), 'napkin' renders the Greek σουδάριον (Latin *sudarium*), literally 'sweat-cloth', in Luke 19:20, John 11:44 and 20:7 and Acts 19:12. In Luke, it is the piece of cloth in which the bad servant has 'kept' (Tyndale) or 'layd up' (King James) the one talent with which he had been entrusted. In John 20:7, it is the face-covering left in the empty tomb, 'not lying with the linnen clothes, but wrapped together in a place by it selfe' (1611). Hobbes appears to have implicated a secondary sense with the primary sense of his words. In paraphrase, his emphasis is plainly on 'good works', the investing, not the hoarding, of God's gifts. But his secondary sense—the linen 'wrapped together', folded up—happens to be the primary meaning of an essential tenet of Christian belief. The meaning of the resurrection is implicit in the sign of the folded σουδάριον, but an 'implicate faith', a faith that will not come forth into declaration at the very site of the mystery, that remains folded in on itself, set aside, is no faith at all:

the heart of doctrine is here mute witness rather than redemptive and eloquent mystery.

It could be argued that in saying 'Hobbes appears to have implicated . . .', I overstate the case, attributing intention, deliberation, where there may be only misapplication; and that Hobbes is simply hoist with the petard of his contempt for the solecisms of others, 'for if he would not have his words so be understood, he should not have let them runne'. I take it as a crux, a test of interpretative judgment, here. If Hobbes has failed to estimate, allow for, or otherwise register, the weight and power of John 20:7, its capacity to distort with implication the familiar admonition of Luke 19:20, the moral is that, as Donne claims, 'the Holy Ghost in penning the Scriptures delights himself . . . with a propriety . . . of language' and that someone who thinks barbarously and gracelessly will overreach into self-revelation and submission. God is not mocked; nor, finally, is his language. On the contrary, however, I find that sentences such as we have here testify to Hobbes's leaps of imaginative power, and, further, that the clue to the particular quality of his mind is given by another characteristic turn, in Part One, Chapter 4. There, ostensibly, he is simply categorizing particular applications ('speciall uses of Speech') within the 'generall use of Speech'. The fourth of these special uses is exemplified by our ability 'to please and delight our selves, and others, by playing with our words, for pleasure or ornament, innocently'.

Let us consider for a moment 'our selves, and others'. Henry Vaughan wrote, probably in the same lustrum that saw the publication of *Leviathan*:

> But living where the Sun
> Doth all things wake, and where all mix and tyre
> Themselves and others, I consent and run
> To ev'ry myre.
>
> ('THE NIGHT', 1655)

And—earlier—Donne had written, c. 1628:

> Wilt thou forgive that sinne by which I wonne
> Others to sinne? and, made my sinne their doore?
> ('A HYMNE TO GOD THE FATHER')

Behind the *I / other* tenor in both Donne and Vaughan, we may find that of the earliest prayers and collects of the Church of England, 'Catholic but reformed', under Cranmer; as in the prayer for mercifulness from the Edwardian *Primer* of 1553: 'even as thou our heavenly Father art merciful, and promisest that if we be merciful to other, we shall obtain mercy of thee'. Hobbes has a way of playing the stern old formalities into a state of suspended animation, for that is what 'pleasure and ornament' amount to here. I can think of no seventeenth-century usage outside Shakespeare, for instance in Iago's 'honest', that is less innocent than Hobbes's 'innocently', and the comma immediately preceding it is as wicked as it is perfect.

If, as Father Ong maintains, 'the result of the opportunity offered by print was the thousands upon thousands of editions of commonplace books in various guises which flooded the market for some two hundred years after the invention of alphabetic typography', opportunism evidently becomes a factor of style, and style itself, since 'commonplace' is the datum, or base, shifts markedly towards implications of register. By 'register' I intend to suggest—balancing between verb and substantive—a (precise) manner of setting down; an entitlement to set down; a device for admitting or excluding, for example, air, heat, smoke (the first recorded use of this sense is in Ben Jonson's *The Alchemist*, 1610).

The third suggestion, as it will appear the most far-fetched, needs to be tackled at once. 'Heat', as a reading of Clarendon, Milton and others of their contemporaries makes evident, is a term of seventeenth-century ethical polity. Clarendon presents himself as learning to 'subdue . . . that pride, and suppress . . . that heat and passion he was naturally inclined to be transported with'; 'heat', for him, means appetite, 'uncharitableness' and 'ignorance'; he associates it with the political and ecclesiastical agitation of the 1630s: 'heat and animosity' on the one side challenged by 'heat and passion' on the other. With Milton, in *Areopagitica,* the sense of the word is held at the other extreme of the spectrum: 'where that immortall garland is to be run for, not without dust and heat'.

One has to differentiate, even so, between this and the other forms of registration which were becoming more widely established. The mode I have in mind is not the international state-law of 'the incomparable *Grotius*' (as Clarendon addressed him); it is not contracted according to the principles of Comenius's *Great Didactic,* wherein 'the general and particular activities of teaching, learning and knowing can be determined'; it does not proceed by those 'exquisite reasons and theorems almost mathematically demonstrative' which Milton attributed to John Selden's method in *De Jure Naturali.* Clarendon, in fact, contentiously associates the 'Rules of Arithmetic and Geometry' with the 'imaginary Government . . . of which no Nation hath ever yet had the experiment', that phantom issuing from the seditious brain of Hobbes of Malmesbury.

The fundamental pattern of registration in the present set of *Responses* is more conservative; a modulation rather than a modification of already existing forms of ratiocination and eloquence. There is a marked willingness to defend the Scholastic Philosophers against the brutishness—as they read it—of Hobbes's contempt. Both Clarendon and Bishop Lucy, however, refer to 'Etymologie'; Bramhall claims that Hobbes exploits double meanings ('the ambiguous acceptions of the word, free'); Clarendon objects to the 'mist of words' which obscures the 'Fallacies upon which [Hobbes] raises his Structure'.

It is evident, however, that their own arguments are aided—
indeed, abetted—by the contemporary interchangeability of the
terms 'proprietie' and 'property'. Clarendon, for example, refers to
'the Liberty and propriety of the Subject' and, on the following page,
salutes 'the precious terms of Property and Liberty' which must not
be perverted into 'absurd and insignificant words, to be blown away
by the least breath of [Hobbes's] monstrous Soveraign'. 'Property', for
Clarendon, is a 'precious term', as 'Occupancy' is 'a sacred title' to
Lucy. In these three instances, as elsewhere, 'property', 'propriety' and
'occupancy' represent private tenure with secure enjoyment of 'Lands
and Goods' but also, by a slight degree of extension, they indicate
qualities of intellectual and civic deportment which may be claimed
and possessed as self-evident right of title. 'Propriety' is, on this basis,
self-possession (a quality of character) stemming from an assurance of
inalienable right to property, together with the free acceptance of all
duties and obligations pertaining thereto:

> the Copies and Transcripts of antient Landmarks, making the
> Characters more plain and legible of what had bin practic'd and
> understood in the preceding Ages, and the observation whereof
> are of the same profit and convenience to King and People.

My sense of the matter is that if Clarendon were abruptly
required to vindicate (a verb he favoured) in under fifty words his
conception of the role of author in the second half of the seventeenth
century, he could hardly do better (always supposing he deigned to
answer) than to take these, his own words from *A Brief View and
Survey*, which appeared posthumously in 1676. And if he were further
obliged to defend, at equally short notice, his conception of the just
work of polity, he could—with propriety—direct his interrogator to
the same manuscript source.

That Clarendon could so—and so incidentally, as it must seem—focus a double vocation, an ethical twinning which he himself would not have stooped to comment on, is a necessary caveat against overconfidence in broad comparison and conjecture. Having said that, I would say also that Clarendon writes with a sense of authority and that he clearly requires a sufficient competence in his reader to distinguish between such authority and the stylistic 'exercise . . . [of] an absolute Dictatorship', 'imperious averment', a presumption of 'having the Soveraign power over all definitions', absolute confidence in the 'Sovereignty . . . of [one's] own capricious brain, and haughty understanding', all of which indicate vices of theory and practice characterizing the arch-seducer Hobbes. Clarendon takes for granted that there is a legitimate distinction to be drawn between Hobbes's imperiousness and his own forms of hauteur ('such inestimable Treasure . . . ventur'd against dirty people of no name'), though the dividing line is much less obvious to us now than it was to him.

It is equally the case that Clarendon points us in the general direction of a systematic alternative code of procedure. Contrary to Hobbes's 'imperious averment', there is 'a proper and devout custom of speaking', which the Hobbists deride but which still has power to 'vindicate . . . the Truth from the malice that would oppress it'. As I have suggested, Clarendon's style is intended to maintain and display that proper and devout custom of speaking; an exhibition of standards in direct opposition to the improper and impious and aggressive new way of Hobbes. It is meant to exemplify 'reflexion, without which there can be no thinking to [any good] purpose'. As I have also suggested, the 'devout custom' is evoked by an imitation of Hooker (an imitation that comes perilously close to travesty, none the less). Clarendon's propriety has a double root; it is partly the acknowledged excellence of Anglican custom and partly the lordly self-possession of one who is wholly untroubled by his contempt for dirty people of no name, the illiterate and dispossessed, and who at the heart of the matter writes as if he were deaf to the radical discrepancies among these allegiances and attitudes, between Anglican religious polity on the one hand and, on the other, the vision of the suffering servant prophesied by Isaiah and manifested in Christ.

Clarendon's style, therefore, however firmly it adheres to the principle of integrity and comeliness, in practice is bound to show signs of strain, of badly resolved perplexity, partly realized contradiction, and implicit self-contradiction. The strain is felt in some usages more than others; it appears particularly as the manner in which certain words are recurrently placed: for example 'custom', 'tradition', 'integrity', 'desperate', and—above all—'private'. Clarendon has 'ordain'd and constituted by custom and acceptation' (of the signification of words), and, again, 'that common practice of circumspection and providence, which custom and discretion hath introduced into human life'. But he notes also 'all the customes of the Nations' as proscribed by God to the Israelites, and classifies among the 'enormities of the Roman Church' its 'errors of Tradition'. Bramhall equates 'custome' with 'proclivity' and proclivity with 'vitious habits'; yet his 'old truth derived by inheritance or succession from mine ancestors' is surely also a form of custom. For Lucy, the 'natural' capacity shown by 'Beasts or Dogs' to 'love' what is 'profitable' for them and to detest that which is 'hurtful', can also be called *'natural appetite'*, which, in turn, can be viewed as *'custome'*. In his *Observations upon H. Grotius, 'De Jure Belli, & Pacis'* (1657), Robert Filmer argues that

> it is not the being of a custome that makes it lawfull, for then all customes, even evil customes, would be lawfull; but it is the approbation of the supreame power that gives a legality to the Custome: where there is no supream power over many nations, their Customes cannot be made legall.

As I understand the business, the authors of these early responses to *De Cive* and *Leviathan* are fully competent to negotiate, for the best terms each can get, among a compact body of ambiguities: ambiguities which are in part ethical, part civil, part etymological. Reading them, I again lose confidence in my ability to name the benefits and improvements which John Locke conferred on English philosophy, religion, polity and language when he set himself to nullify the capacity of words to excite 'Disputes' and to 'reduce' 'all . . . Terms of Ambiguity and Obscurity' to 'determined Collections of the simple *Ideas* they do or should stand for'. The rubric to the *OED*'s entry on the verb 'to reduce', that most characteristic term of seventeenth- and eighteenth-century ratiocination, is exemplary of the matter as it stood then and stands now:

> The original sense of the word, 'to bring back', has now almost entirely disappeared, the prominent modern sense being 'to bring down' or 'to diminish'. A clear arrangement of the various uses (many of them found only in the language of the 15–17th centuries) is rendered difficult by the extent to which the different shades of meaning tend to pass into or include each other.

It now strikes me that there is very little in Locke's programme of remedial analysis that has not been anticipated by Bramhall; and, further, that Bramhall is no less concerned than is Locke at the moral and emotional attrition which is the toll exacted by ambiguity, obscurity, and all forms of disputation. The difference between them is, in part, that Bramhall's moral theology is taken deeply into the body of his 'Etymologie' and that Locke's is not. To the blunt retort 'Then Locke has achieved with perfect finesse the task he set himself: and religion philosophy and the English language are the better for it', I would respond that the perplexed matter of tradition, or custom, as we have received it, gives evidence that to legislate as 'the end of Speech' 'that those Sounds, as Marks may make known [our] *Ideas* to the Hearer' is to presume to disconnect language from the consequences of our common imbecility. The Lockean prescription names a legitimate function of language; but its tacit proscriptions turn legitimacy into tyranny. As with other patrimonies, our language is both a blessing and a curse, but in the right hands it can mediate within itself, thereby transforming blessing into curse, curse into blessing. I note W. D. J. Cargill Thompson's insistence that Locke is not Hooker's heir, and that the supposed derivation is largely the issue of Whig myth-making. Hooker's theology is also involved with etymology; and Bramhall, who in theory anticipates Locke, is in practice closer to Hooker and, even, to Calvin.

I draw to this conclusion through my sense of the emphasis placed by Bramhall, as by Hooker before him, and by Calvin before that, on the nature of contingency, circumstance: 'For as much as actions are often altered and varied by the circumstances of Time, Place and Person'; 'Of such questions they cannot determine without rashnes, in as much as a great part of them consisteth in speciall circumstances'; 'And also the same could not be simply determined without rashness, forasmuch as a great parte of the order of this question consisteth in circumstances'.

Though Hooker appears to be copying Thomas Norton virtually word for word, it is probable that he is working directly from Calvin's Latin, to which his marginal annotation (*'Cal. instit.li.4.cap 20, Sect 8.'*) refers. This is a telling instance of the manner in which the hypothetical apprehension of contingency and circumstance can be—and, especially at this period, is—a most immediate realization, and a working through, of the contingent and circumstantial in which one is caught up or, all too often, merely caught. Hooker's 'Preface' is not, in the first instance, addressed to interested general

readers (as we construe 'interest' and 'reader') but to a compact, interested and inward body of English Presbyterian controversialists:
inward, I mean, with every word and phrase of Calvin's Latin
Institutes. Hooker so engages the cause, the men, the books, that it is
always with renewed surprise that one discovers, or is reminded, that
the foundation-works of that cause were twenty years old by the time
the first four books of *Ecclesiasticall Politie* were put into print.
Archbishop Whitgift, still at that time Dean of Lincoln and Master
of Trinity College, Cambridge, had hotly contested the Presbyterian
case on the spot in 1572–1573. More recently, the Anglican apologist
Richard Bancroft had taken on the Marprelates in terms as acridly
mocking as those of the pamphlets themselves.

It is generally accepted that Hooker was delegated, and in part
self-delegated, to the writing of his great apologia armed with a distinct working brief. As V. J. K. Brook observes:

> The *Ecclesiastical Polity* represents the crowning victory of
> Whitgift's campaign, raising the issues out of a mire of petty
> querulousness to a high level of reverence, toleration, humility.

Reverence, toleration and humility are not necessarily qualities of the
delegated stylist's personality. It should be understood, morever, that
Hooker was able to flex and direct a style of reverence, toleration and
humility because there were others—like Whitgift—able and prepared to turn the screws of suspension, deprivation, imprisonment
and, in a few cases (William Hackett, John Penry, John Greenwood
and Henry Barrow), execution. Hooker's delegated, arduous procedure is to make official doctrine and formal eloquence not seem but
be reciprocally 'proportionable': 'The Church of Christ is a bodie
mysticall. A bodie cannot stand, unless the partes thereof be proportionable'. Bramhall, in 1645 (published 1651), contends that

where *T.H.* demands how it is possible for the liberty of doing, or not doing this or that good or evil, to consist in God and Angels, without a liberty of doing or not doing good or evil. The answer is obvious and easy, *referendo singula singulis*, rendering every act to its right object respectively.

It may be worth repeating here that, on the evidence of this set of *Early Responses*, one engrained idea, of Hobbes's completing Francis Bacon's work for the eradication of Scholastic Philosophy from seventeenth-century intellectual life, must be strongly qualified. The 'Schole-men' are no more and no less agencies in Bramhall's argument than is the theory and practice of etymology. To the Bishop of St David's (William Lucy), in his *Observations* of 1663, the question of faith may be resolved by subsequent empirical consideration of initial dogmatic statements concerning, for example, duty ('afterward, upon experience, or examination, they find it congruent to the *will* of God; then they practice it accordingly with *confidence*').

All three instances could ultimately derive from a common Scholastic source. But I must here qualify my own claim. In terms of theory and general topos, it is possible to align Hooker's 'proportionable' with Lucy's '*Congruence*' and Bramhall's 'rendering every act to its right object respectively' and conclude that, over the span of seventy most turbulent years, they manifest a remarkable continuity and coherence. Such paraphrase, however, gives false readings by cancelling out individual pitch, and, in context, Bishop Lucy's pitch is markedly different from that of Hooker. In the light of my earlier comments on Hooker's style, it would be difficult to claim that we move from his *mystique* to Lucy's *politique*. The 'body mystical' of the *Lawes* itself is a feature of polity. Even so, one could say with some justice that it is of real concern to Hooker that the 'parts . . . proportionable' should be adducible both to Christian doctrine and to the eloquent structures of his defence of that doctrine. If we add that, in Lucy's 'find it congruent', the author is concerned to give as much emphasis to the activity of confirming as to the status of congruence, a change of pitch must be conceded to that. Bramhall in turn gives weight to his verb, 'rendering', from the Latin gerund *referendo*. Could one show that the Bishops of Derry and of St David's accommodate Hobbes in such details and that the post-Restoration cast of the Church of England will be a slow but progressive secularization intermitted by bouts of reactionary 'enthusiasm'? While the liturgical Service of Confirmation is retained throughout as the Anglican *rite de passage*, more is increasingly claimed by, and bitterly conceded to, the soteriological activity of confirming oneself in the faith, until the mystical pragmatism of the search itself becomes the validating activity of evangelical belief, both within the Church (for instance, John Newton of Olney) and among the several categories of separated brethren. The confrontation, in August 1739, between Bishop Butler and John Wesley provides an exemplary indication:

> B[ishop Butler]. And Mr. Whitefield says in his Journal: 'There are promises still to be fulfilled in me.' Sir, the pretending to extraordinary revelations and gifts of the Holy Ghost is a horrid thing—a very horrid thing!

There is, I believe, an unbroken continuity from the arguments feeding into, and arising out of, the Elizabethan 'Settlement' (less a settlement than a redistribution of weight and bias) to this disputation between two powerfully conservative Anglicans who were alike in their opposition to deism and the Deists. Wesley claimed to be empowered, by the terms of his Oxford Fellowship, to an 'indeterminate commission to preach the word of God in any part of the Church of England', or, failing that, by 'my business on earth . . . to do what good I can'. To Butler, Wesley was a trespasser on the property of the diocese of Bristol and on the propriety of behaviour deemed congruent with and within the limits of salvation. Wesley's 'business' was to endeavour to save the ignorant and depraved masses from the natural desperation of their lives and from the supernatural consequences of their despair. To Butler, I would conclude, Wesley's activities made him no better than a desperado.

Such observations may be dismissed as mere wordplay. My position here is that, with the 1559 Acts of Supremacy and of Uniformity, if not before, an element of wordplay was taken into the official language of state. Having restored—after the Marian abeyance—her father's title of 'Supreme Head' of the English Church, Elizabeth compounded with vociferous Puritan protest and gave royal assent to the substituted words 'Supreme Governor'. Gerald Bray calls it 'a change of form, but not of substance'. Christopher Morris has noted that, among other 'Elizabethan assumptions', '"reason of state" . . . was somehow different from normal reason'. The Acts of 1559 recapitulated and reinforced the fiction that a crisis of soteriology could be identified as latent and active sedition, as *lèse-majesté,* and as conduct threatening the common weal, the well-being of the state. Despairing men are desperate men; desperate men are instant and armed desperadoes. At times, as one reads, life-and-death decisions of state appear to be projections of the rhetorical figure *traductio.*

The Elizabethan Injunctions—also of 1559, but closely following those of Edward VI, of 1547—enjoined the parish clergy to stock up on 'comfortable places and sentences of Scripture' against the 'vice of damnable despair' if and when they were apprised of its presence among their parishioners—an anarchic flock very readily equated with 'ridiculous men and bewitched' (Bancroft), 'common persons and private men' (Whitgift), 'the common sort of men', 'the vulgar sort', 'the multitude' (all Hooker), 'the many headed multitude' (Bramhall, after

Horace, Sidney, et al.), 'dirty people of no name' (Clarendon), 'secret corner-meetings and assemblies in the night' (Hooker again, though it could easily be mistaken for Hobbes).

Just as some kind of mental *membrana* (as Ben Jonson might say) rendered these fine scholars and spiritual wrestlers incapable of recognizing, in such 'secret corner-meetings and assemblies in the night', the origins of the Christian Church in Jewish discipleship (Nicodemus visiting Jesus 'by night', John 3:2; the disciples at evening in the locked room, John 21:19), so something in the pitch of contingency and circumstance rendered them all too fluent in a kind of theatrical 'tragic' bombast and fustian: 'desperate cause', 'more desperately rebellious', 'innovators and seditious orators', 'Sophisters and seditious Oratours' (all Bramhall); 'acts of rage and despair', 'melancholy', 'desperate imaginations', 'seditious and erroneous Doctrines' (all Clarendon). It is like recovering phrases from a failed and discarded Tragedy of State. One can sense an affinity between such phrases and the language of Sidney's *Arcadia* (1590) or of Jonson's *Sejanus* (1603–1605) and *Catiline* (1611), but Sidney's and Jonson's critical intelligence is fully aware of cause and effect, and of the pathology of the humours for which a strident euphuism, interspersed with episodes of the laconically outrageous, offers an effective range of expression. Bramhall and Clarendon are at once magisterial and imbecile (to recall Hooker's word), but the proverbial 'Stone Dead hath no Fellow' none the less stands plumb with its uncanny power of register at the heart of Clarendon's account of the impeachment of Strafford.

Torquato Tasso, in his *Discourses on the Heroic Poem*, commented that 'Extremely beautiful and ornate ... are additions that imply opposition and contradiction'; he cites, from Petrarch's *Trionfo d'Amore* 4, 143–147: '*chiaro disnore e gloria oscura e nigra, / perfida lealtate e fido inganno*'. At some indeterminate date, possibly 1536–1537,

the Henrician scholar-diplomat Henry Parker, Lord Morley, translated the *Trionfi*, rendering the lines remarked by Tasso as:

> Cleare dishonoure, and glory obscure and darke;
> False lealtie left not there to warke.

If we consider what is held 'tacitly' (yet another word of their
conjuring) when Tasso remarks on the high ornamental value of certain rhetorical figures, figures which none the less turn upon moral
negations, annulments, cynical flauntings of the incongruent, it is
possible to perceive compromises and compromisings as forms of eloquence and forms of eloquence as compromised. Hobbes seems to
hold this commonplace as his patent. To put the issue in a slightly different form: *traductio* is the figure whereby you 'turne and translace a
word into many sundry shapes'; it is also traduction: 'the act of tra-
ducing or defaming, calumny, slander, traducement'. The *OED*
marks this sense as 'rare' and not before 1656, but as I have attempted
to show elsewhere, Sir Thomas Wyatt—to cite one striking example—was clearly on to the essential connection between speech-turns
and malpractice, 'safe' convention and malicious invention, in the
late 1530s. There are, of course, instances of 'traduction' which are
both eloquent and morally congruent. Hooker shows a particular
felicity in 'The prophet Abacuk remained faithfull in weaknes though
weake in faith', but Hooker would not have dissented from Sidney's
trope of worldly sweetness turned to

> poysonous sugar of flatterie: which some vsed, out of the innate
> basenesse of their hart, straight like dogges fawning vppon the
> greatest; . . . But his minde (being an apt matter to receiue what
> forme their amplifying speeches woulde lay vpon it) daunced so
> prettie a musicke to their false measure, that he thought himselfe

the wysest, the woorthyest, and best beloued, that euer gaue hon-
our to a royall tytle.

There is a sense in which, half a century to a century later, the
authors here reviewed—Clarendon in particular—have not notice-
ably extended the perimeter of Sidney's axiomatic ethical polity. Thus
Clarendon, from the Introduction to *A Brief View and Survey*:

> That saying of *Nosce teipsum*, in the sense of *Solon* who prescribed
> it, was a sober truth, but was never intended as an expedient to
> discover the similitude of the thoughts of other men by what he
> found in himself, but as the best means to suppress and destroy
> that pride and self-conceit, which might temt him to undervalue
> other men, and to plant that modesty and humility in himself, as
> would preserve him from such presumption.

Clarendon is, of course, contending that Hobbes has radically misconstrued the basic Humanist prescription for self-recovery; he is
much as 'Antiphilus his base-borne pride borne high by flatterie' is to
the author of the *Arcadia;* though Hobbes is chiefly the recipient of
self-flattery. He is both tyrant and false prophet.

The type of exemplary figure represented by Solon, particularly
as memorialized by Isocrates (and further memorialized by
Clarendon and Swift), stood in relation to issues of English polity in
a manner which is simply incomprehensible to the modern educator
and policy-maker. We return once more to the nature—or definition—of the 'necessary requisite'. For Clarendon, Bramhall and, I
will hazard, even for the Milton of *Areopagitica* and the *Tractate of
Education*, it is not a question of progress so much as of 'resuscitation'
(as C. A. Patrides discerned with characteristic acumen): 'The end
then of Learning is to *repair* the ruines of our first Parents by *regain-*

ing to know God aright' (my italics). It is even more, in the understanding of Clarendon's pregnant phrase, the necessary 'sober truth'.
Clarendon detested Bramhall; Thomas Tenison revered and defended
him. All three would have seen in Milton's republicanism and mor-
talism, if they were even aware of it, the groundwork for a godless
tyranny. The one common aspiration among these violently disunit-
ed spirits, otherwise united only in their opposition to Hobbes, was
a belief in, a working towards, the eloquence of 'sober truth': an eloquence which, in Bramhall, is something other than the cult of 'plain
dealing', and which for Clarendon is something other than the affectation of plain speaking. In the *Brief View and Survey,* Hobbes is seen
as 'pretending to so much plainness and perspicuity'.

If we are to understand from this that Hobbes is a false claimant
to such qualities, we are obliged to adjust our sense of the word, some
thirty pages on in Clarendon's book, when we read that Sidney
Godolphin's early death in the Civil War was 'an irreparable loss . . .
lamented by all men living who pretended to Virtue, how much divided soever in the prosecution of that quarrel'. Godolphin is mourned
by persons of integrity, whether Royalist or Parliamentarian, who can
recognize sober truth when they see it: persons whose claim to recognize true virtue can, for the most part, be taken on trust.

When Bramhall maintains that his controversy with Hobbes 'is
not about Words, but about Things', he makes the point somewhat
elliptically. The things do not anticipate Locke's 'Substances'; they
read like the metaphysical elements required by speculation, the
nature of things as conceived, or misconceived, by the understanding
or misunderstanding of fallible human minds: 'not what the words
Voluntary or Free do or may signifie, but whether all things be extrinsecally praedetermined to one'. The case that these ill-assorted, frequently incompatible, variously gifted antagonists bring against
Hobbes is one that is grounded in matters of claim and entitlement.

Such questions of entitlement are fundamentally political; Bramhall's Aristotelian observation that 'man . . . is a politicall creature' runs like a seventeenth-century thorough bass under the variety of opinions and counter-opinions presented in these six volumes. For each of them, the intersection of politics and language occurs in certain word-usages, as in property / propriety, private / public, but the crux, for them, is not etymology (present though that word is in their vocabulary) but *intention*. And with intention we find that they, and we, have re-engaged with the matter of English polity.

The question of polity is, at its most basic level as also in the most elevated language of response, that of entitlement to speak, one's right to claim authority, albeit as a private person contending in—and with—a public matter. The implications of 'They who to States and Governours of the Commonwealth direct their Speech, . . . or wanting such accesse in a private condition, write that which they foresee may advance the publick good', reach back through Hooker to such early Reform writings as Tyndale's *Obedience of a Christen Man* and anticipate the situation of both Bramhall when he wrote *A Defence of True Liberty* (deprived of his see and in exile with the remnant of the House of Stuart) and Clarendon.

Clarendon's situation as an exile, from 1646 until 1660 and again from 1667 until his death in 1674, was one of enforced privacy. He was private chiefly because deprived of office; there were none the less matters of state to which he was still privy. Reflections on the private as a condition of deprivation are less prominent in these arguments than are considerations of the private as an entitlement to property and a just claim to be treated with propriety. Clarendon's 'Epistle Dedicatory to the King's Most Excellent Majesty' is a strategic exception, but here the policy is counterpoised by a sense of the author's being sincerely (as they would say) cast down, dejected, wretched. There is a quality of politic chiaroscuro in the sincere interplay of public polemic and private sorrow in Clarendon's last work.

The Weight of the Word

The critical limitations of *Reason, Grace and Sentiment* are (as such limitations generally are) inseparable from a general limitation of insight and imagination.* Intellectually confident in its documentation of cant words when these are a part of the seventeenth- and eighteenth-century detritus, the book is oblivious to its own compliance with the prevailing jargon of modern communication. Attempts to discriminate and evaluate repeatedly collapse upon the words 'interesting', 'interestingly' or 'of more interest than': and this in a work that labours to define and distinguish the various senses which the word 'interest' carried during the period 1660–1780 ('the Interest of *Sects*', 'the interest of virtue', 'the true Interest of the Christian Religion', etc.). Such a tic ('very interesting', 'particularly interesting', 'extraordinarily interesting') is the kind of stylistic solecism which is reducible to a philosophy that some will find laudable. The author '[has] not taken the reader's knowledge of the period for granted' and

---

*Isabel Rivers, *Reason, Grace and Sentiment: A Study of the Language of Religion and Ethics in England 1660–1780. Volume I: Whichcote to Wesley.* 277 pages (Cambridge and New York: Cambridge University Press, 1991).

hopes that 'this method of presentation will make the book accessible to undergraduates as well as scholars'.

Questions of accessibility turn upon matters of context. In both sacred and secular writings we may receive, at any instant, a sense of things inaccessible suddenly made accessible, where grammar and desire are miraculously at one. The effect may appear to be studied (as in Milton or Hopkins) or spontaneous (as in the Wesleys or Wordsworth); what delights and silences us is the sustained moment of communion between the two kinds of eloquence and apprehension, whether in Cranmer's collects or Campion's 'Brag' or the great hymns of Watts and Charles Wesley.

I am not suggesting that consent to my paradigm would be widespread, either then or now: a variety of opinions on the matter characterized the period covered by *Reason, Grace and Sentiment*; the majority of them appear at first sight more consonant with Isabel Rivers's method of presentation than with my mode of dissent (for example, Gilbert Burnet's 'a *Preacher* is to fancy himself, as in the Room of the most unlearned Man in his whole Parish'; John Wesley's 'I design plain truth for plain people. . . . I labour to avoid all words which are not easy to be understood'). In fairly stating her own adherence to the principle of accessibility, Dr Rivers implicitly associates herself with one of the main strands in her thesis: that of the 'plain and natural Method' praised by Burnet in his *Pastoral Care*. Burnet acknowledged, with more fairness than some of his contemporaries, the just demands of more difficult forms of writing which 'require a good deal of previous Study' and ought not to be attempted before one is 'ready'. Dr Rivers fails to perceive that when all things are 'interesting' there is not 'readiness' but stasis; that authorial 'accessibility' is now no more than a commodity cry; and that her book, like its readership, is consequent upon the very forces and circumstances which it describes. Even if she is able to acknowledge this rationally, I do not think that she is moved by it affectively. If she were, the temper of her style would be other than it is:

> My subject is the language of religious and moral prose, and my methods are those of the literary historian of ideas. I have concentrated on language because I am interested in the history of religious and moral thought for its own sake, not in relation to another subject, such as science or politics, and because I believe that it is only through the careful study of language that meaning can be ascertained.

These sentences stand as an epitome of the book's larger failure to connect. The author's gratitude to her general editor and her publishers for 'agreeing' to a two-volume format is misplaced. You do not 'do justice to a very complex subject' by simply reduplicating an original misconstruction. Concentration, in Dr Rivers's 'I have concentrated on language', must be understood as heavy accumulation of data and not as intensity of perception. When 'concentration' means 'mass', it can also mean dissipation of perceptual and structural cogency, as I think is the case here.

I do not grasp, for instance, Dr Rivers's motive for proposing to discuss Locke's civil and religious thought as if she were considering two distinct philosophical entities ('For Locke's religious views see . . . Volume II') when, throughout the present volume, *Whichcote to Wesley*, she is at pains to show how his thought is implicated in arguments for and against a view of religion as 'fitted to man in his worldly state', with the same terms (drawn from the *Essay Concerning Human Understanding* as from *The Reasonableness of Christianity*) employed on either side of the contention by Anglican latitudinarians and dissenters alike. I cannot accept that those who pondered 'Degrees of Assent' (Book IV, Chapter xvi of the *Essay*) would have concluded that Locke had distinct 'religious views':

> This only may be said in general. That as the Arguments and Proofs, *pro* and *con,* upon due Examination, nicely weighing every particular Circumstance, shall to any one appear, upon the whole matter, in a greater or less degree, to preponderate on either side, so they are fitted to produce in the Mind such different Entertainment, as we call *Belief, Conjecture, Guess, Doubt, Wavering, Distrust, Disbelief,* etc.

I accept that Locke speaks elsewhere of 'Propositions (especially about Matters of Religion)', but he is there making a case that in 'unwary, as well as unbiass'd Understandings', such propositions may be 'riveted . . . by long Custom and Education beyond all possibility of being pull'd out again'. The rational and affective tempers of his thinking are mutually secured in that 'riveted'. Lumpish words like 'religious views' belong more to the mechanics of subediting than to the entertainments of Locke's prose.

Of the three moral and affective qualities named in the title of this study, 'sentiment' remains the most elusive; the inherent difficulties are compounded by the fact that Dr Rivers proposes to reserve its full discussion to Volume II, which will 'essentially explore the tension between the languages of reason and sentiment' as Volume I 'essentially explores the tension between the languages of reason and grace'. If her feeling for words and their implications were more consonant with the capacities of her chosen authors, she would have thought twice before reducing them to the level of that bit of etiolated jargon. The quality of 'sentiment' is itself a factor in the debate between 'grace' and 'reason'; it is, moreover, a quality which reveals itself mainly in grammar: vocabulary, syntactical order and affective device. As locution we hear it in Edward Stillingfleet's 'Without perplexing our minds about those more nice and subtile speculations', in Benjamin Whichcote's 'To stand upon nice and accurate Distinctions of [words], is needless; useless', in Burnet's 'I have ever thought, that the true Interest of the Christian Religion was best consulted, when nice disputing about Mysteries was laid aside and forgotten' and in William Law's 'It is not a Doctrine that requires learned or nice Speculations, in order to be rightly apprehended by us'.

The common factor in these emphases is the term 'nice', implying a finicky, over-subtle, 'scholastic' concern with minutiae and suggesting, in each of these authors, an assumption of a close agreement of common sense between writer and reader. 'Assumption' may here be understood as legitimate 'postulate' and as 'unwarrantable claim'; and I would argue that in the four citations given above, 'nice' is an assumption situated between those two senses of that term. In the seventeenth century, as the *OED* article states, 'it is difficult to say in what particular sense the writer intended ['nice'] to be taken'. A few years earlier than Stillingfleet, Jeremy Taylor argued that 'the way to destruction is broad and plausible, the way to heaven nice and austere'; some thirty years later than Stillingfleet, Dryden deployed the word with coarse refinement to dismiss the quaint, outmoded style of Donne: 'He . . . perplexes the Minds of the Fair Sex with nice Speculations of Philosophy, when he shou'd ingage their hearts, and entertain them with the softnesses of Love'. I do not think that Stillingfleet, Whichcote or Burnet would balk at the word 'broad', since latitude is what they desired, though they would be pained by Taylor's collocations. In attempting to describe their several styles of rational persuasion, one is touching on a symptomatic elision of the deliberated and the unwitting. To call the issue 'complacency' is not to insinuate a term that is unknown in seventeenth-century theological writings; it is not even to turn their own idiom against them. Richard Baxter writes of 'the love of Complacencie and Acceptation' as a Divine gesture; Isaac Barrow warns against the 'arbitrary opinion and fickle humour of the people; complacence in which is vain'. There is, even so, in the work of Whichcote, Barrow and even Law, an indifference to contextual 'otherness' which is too simple a corollary of their moral objection to the 'obstinate and contumacious'.

Whichcote wrote that 'by wickedness [a man] passes into a *Nature* contrary to his own'. I am willing to claim as an empirical fact that when you write at any serious pitch of obligation you enter into the nature of grammar and etymology, which is a nature contrary to your own. You cannot extricate yourself from this 'contrary nature' by some kind of philosophical fiat or gesture of spiritual withdrawal. Hobbes categorized 'Compleasance' as a 'Law of Nature': *'That every man strive to accommodate himselfe to the rest'*. In the palpable contrariness of *'strive / accommodate'* one recognizes the working of intelligence at a more than conceptual level; it is like Locke's 'riveted', where a word is struck into the body of a sentence in such a way that a 'particular sense' of the mind is at one with the particular sensuousness of an instinctual choice.

I anticipate two main objections to these ideas. The first is that the 'accommodation', the 'particular sense', which I derive from Hobbes and Locke appeals to the satirical *frisson* almost exclusively; it anticipates Pope ('familiar Toad') but not Watts or Charles Wesley. The second is that Whichcote and, especially, Law established clear theological reasons why the attraction of 'contrary' Nature is alien to a life of Christian discipline. There is arguably something obstinate and contumacious in an attempt to force their quality of spiritual desire ('the silent Longing of the Heart') into an unacceptable fashion of contextual sensuousness, a mere 'Accomplishment . . . of the lettered World' which Law would have dismissed as '*Form, and Fiction,* and empty beating of the Air'.

George Herbert is ruled out of Dr Rivers's discussion. Without his example we are inclined to assume spiritual initiatives in proposals which ought rather to be seen as derivations and attenuations. Burnet's remarks on the inappropriateness of learned sermons for rural congregations had been anticipated by Herbert's first Bemerton sermon of 1630 ('*since Almighty God does not intend to lead men to heaven by hard Questions*'). That this Laudian observant of the Canonical Hours could be so revered by the 'meer Nonconformist' Baxter, that his paraphrase of 'The 23d Psalme' should have been set, first by Henry Lawes as a courtly solo to the lute, then by John Playford in the plainest four-part harmony (perfectly matching the spirit of the Bemerton sermon and perfectly attuned to Nonconformist practice), is eloquent testimony to his reconciling of 'grace' and 'reason'. As Barnabas Oley observed when noting Herbert's '*singular Dexterity*' in administering reproof with gentleness, the quality of his reconciling art is embodied in the '*Garb and Phrase*' of his writing.

It is this sense of 'garb and phrase' which is missing from Dr Rivers's 'careful study of language', and I do not see how, without it, 'meaning' can be rightly 'ascertained'. The diligent listing of Barrow's use of the 'co-prefix' is an 'interesting' abstraction, not a 'concentration'. Meaning is not 'established', even in those writers who greatly desire to see it so; it is concatenation, ellipsis, lacuna: as much in those who speak 'pertinently, plainly, piercingly, and somewhat properly' as in those who strain after far-fetched conceits. Watts's 'meaning', as an apologist, is not determined, in 1707, by 'If any Expressions occur to the Reader that savour of an Opinion different from his own, yet he may observe these are generally such as are capable of an extensive Sense, and may be used with a charitable Latitude'. Nor is it determined, in 1747, by 'I hope I have kept the middle way between a libertinism of principles, and a narrow uncharitable spirit'. Watts's 'capable of an extensive Sense' in no way resembles Dr Rivers's 'I take "language" in a broad sense to include . . .'. She simply assumes the concurrence of language with one's expectations; his 'Sense' is a deliberated sentiment; an 'extensive Sense' is what, in fact, his sentence is. Such meaning is not to be 'ascertained'; it must be entertained, as we entertain, with our sense of the circumstantial shifts of forty years, the difference of implication between 'charitable Latitude' and 'libertinism of principles'. That passage from Locke's *Essay* ('This only may be said in general . . .'), to which I have previously referred, epitomizes the 'sensible pleasure', or the entertaining haziness, of philosophical latitude: the 'nice . . . weighing' of 'every particular Circumstance' turns into a syntactical comedy of manners, though one is not precisely sure what Locke's own manners are in this case. The grammar, nice yet licentious, is comparable to Barrow's description of the charitable man as 'virtuously voluptuous' and a 'laudable epicure'.

Coleridge's opinion was that Barrow wrote '*pertly* . . . at times, while his Thoughts are always grave, & fortunate'. There is nothing 'fortunate' in the citations which Dr Rivers gives from Barrow's sermon 'The Duty and Reward of Bounty to the Poor'; in these Barrow shows himself, as Taylor would say, 'broad and plausible'. But 'particular Circumstance' can no more be overlooked in matters of style than it can in 'due Examination' of the mind's entertainment or in questions of equity. We may take one sentence from Barrow's sermon 'Of Resignation to the Divine Will', speaking of Christ's submission to the details of his Passion: 'He was to stand (as it were) before the Mouth of Hell, belching Fire and Brimstone on his Face'. Set against Foxe, this appears as sentiment; there is no 'as it were' in his accounts of the protracted sufferings of such martyrs as John Lambert, John Hooper and Nicholas Ridley. Foxe has been termed a 'sensationalist', and even though, on the evidence of the *OED*, 'sensation' did not exist in any of its forms or senses during the period when *Actes and Monuments* was being compiled, one must concede that it is all here: the 'physical sensibility', the 'mental apprehension', the 'strong impression (e.g. of horror, admiration . . .) produced in a . . . body of spectators', the 'production of violent emotion as an aim in works of literature or art'.

Dr Rivers, who rightly emphasizes Foxe's significance for Bunyan ('to confirm the Truth by way of Suffering'), also observes that language 'was recognised at the outset as a dividing point between the latitude-men and the puritans' and that latitudinarians were eager to make 'corrections to the sixteenth-century theology that now seemed wrong-headed'. To glance again at the passages from Barrow and Locke is to acknowledge a small part of the cost of those corrections. On the other hand, one can set that sentence of Barrow against two from Burke's *Enquiry* of 1757:

> All *general* privations are great, because they are all terrible; *Vacuity, Darkness, Solitude* and *Silence*. With what a fire of imagination, yet with what severity of judgment, has Virgil amassed all these circumstances where he knows that all the images of a tremendous dignity ought to be united, at the mouth of hell!

In Barrow there is at least no 'tremendous dignity'; sentiment has not yet descended to aesthetic trifling. But of course there *is* descent (both in the sense of lineage and of deterioration) from Barrow's 'to stand (as it were) before the Mouth of Hell' to Burke's 'what a fire of imagination . . . !' This is what gravity (of sentiment) descends to when it lacks 'temper'.

It is an irony of sorts that this missing 'temper' is in fact a term prominently employed by writers of latitudinarian sympathy; by

Whichcote especially: 'When the Principles of our Religion become the *Temper* of our Spirits, then we are truly religious'; 'The *State* of Religion consists in a divine Frame and *Temper* of mind: and shews it self in a *Life* and Actions, conformable to the divine Will'; 'There is no Happiness, or Peace; but in the Compliance of the *Temper* of our Minds with the Reason of things: which is a Conformity with the Everlasting Law of Righteousness'. Of 'temper' in this sense there is ample evidence in Law: in the prescript for 'an exact and frequent method of devotion' which made him John Wesley's early spiritual mentor and in the pitch of a *'lively, zealous, watchful, self-denying spirit'*—the syntax itself a prescription for the soul's rebuttal of idle enthusiasm.

This is still within the bounds of ascetic theory: part of Law's 'relentless consistency in applying spiritual principles'. But as I have elsewhere suggested, one cannot simply assume consistency of insight and imagination from consistency of principle.

> To proceed; if you was to use yourself (as far as you can) to pray always in the *same* place . . . if any *little room*, (or if that cannot be) if any particular *part* of a room was thus used, this kind of consecration of it, as a place *holy* unto God, would have an effect upon your mind, and dispose you to such tempers, as would very much assist your devotion.

You could argue from this Law's high qualities as a spiritual director, tempering 'relentless consistency' with an acknowledgement of particular circumstance. Even so, the line between principle and sentiment is so fine here that the slippage of one word—'a kind of consecration' for Law's 'this kind of consecration'—would suffice to tip the fineness into boudoir mawkishness, would have 'an effect upon [the] mind' very different from that which Law intended. And yet any attempt to apply, reduce, or otherwise paraphrase Law's instruction inevitably (I believe) dissipates his particular grammar and leaves the 'kind' of consecration an open or indifferent question, susceptible to any ephemeral mood, disposition or 'temper'. I am not convinced that, at a time when 'nice' distinctions were considered tedious, Law's distinctions could be received with a concomitant finesse. Dr Johnson and John Wesley were spiritually strengthened by reading him, but the witness of those two exceptional spirits does not negate the force of the caveat: that the distance between grace and sentiment may be the breadth of a syllable, dissolved in an instant, rather than that slow-motion relay race of trend and tendency depicted by literary historians of ideas.

The question returns upon the nature of 'temper' and on Whichcote's, or his editors', latitude in reading the term. Its sense is firm enough when the target is mere temperament: 'To live after *Temper*, is below Reason, and short of Virtue'. My sense of Whichcote's characteristic usage (so far as one can accurately judge a reduced text like the *Aphorisms*) is that 'temper' is itself inclined towards 'inclination'—'mental condition', 'habitual disposition', 'frame of mind', 'humour'—and that statements which appear to offer an 'extant' medium (to adapt Baxter's phrase) in which inclination might be checked are in fact little more than gestures in that direction: 'Our Happiness depends upon Temper within, and Object without'. Even this falls short of the sense of 'temper' as 'due or proportionate mixture or combination of elements or qualities'. Whichcote's style, therefore, tends to follow inclination even where inclination is rebuked: 'A *wise* Man is more than Temper; a *good* Man much more'. It smacks of table-talk, though one is once more reminded that edited 'aphorisms' may have been picked out by a mind predisposed to relish the taste of 'opinion'.

The question was, even then, to some extent academic. George Herbert had already committed the matter to the 'garb and phrase' of his poetry and prose, verbal contextures which happily resolved the perplexities by which his successors were to be troubled a century later.

> In vain we tune our formal Songs,
>   In vain we strive to rise;
> *Hosannas* languish on our Tongues,
>   And our Devotion dies.

Watts's 'formal Songs' are, in his conviction of spiritual coldness, further off from him than Whichcote's 'Object without'. I have already suggested that it may be a limitation of Whichcote's theological idiom that makes him attribute an encounter with 'contrary' Nature to 'wickedness' rather than to experiential profession, as Donne does in the *Devotions*: 'But what have I done, either to *breed*, or to *breath* these *vapors?* They tell me it is . . . my *thoughtfulnesse;* was I not made to *thinke?* It is my study; doth not my *Calling* call for that?' Neither Whichcote nor Law (with his *Serious Call*) nor Watts seems to clinch original sin in relation to the formalities, the constraints and opportunities, of 'calling' in quite this way. Once you begin to thin the matter down to 'inward Sentiments' versus *'arbitrary signs'*, sentiment calls the tune to such effect that modern theologians are still in thrall to it. Owen Chadwick's life of Michael Ramsey records, or interprets, an early stage in Ramsey's spiritual way: 'He saw that the intellectual side of him could not be wrong, somehow he must baptize it'. One can understand the appeal of the metaphor (Chadwick is not the only contemporary theological writer to use it), but 'intellectual side' is an arbitrary distinction, and 'somehow' is itself, in this context, an 'arbitrary sign'. George Herbert had already, by the early 1630s, healed (presciently) the lesions of late-seventeenth- and eighteenth-century sentiment and its 'intellectual' side, the residues of which still trouble

Ramsey and his biographer. In 'Affliction (IV)', particularly, Herbert is not only more severe than the latitude-men and scientists in the detail of self-scrutiny; he recognizes the 'detail' for what it simultaneously is: a depressive sentiment, not an exclusive spiritual concept or a mystical hypothesis, however eloquent. If we recall Watts's 'In vain we tune our formal Songs' in the light of Herbert's poem, written some seventy years earlier, we recognize that Watts's anxiety has been rendered otiose by the words of the older poet:

> Then shall those powers, which work for grief,
>> Enter thy pay,
>> And day by day
> Labour thy praise, and my relief.

This is Whichcote's 'by wickedness [a man] passes into a *Nature* contrary to his own' put into reverse process. 'Contrary' Nature, which we do not doubt Herbert has experienced by direct suffering as much as by intuition, is set to redemptive 'labour' in a way that reduces Watts's line to a plaintive bleat and offers Chadwick (whose attention is elsewhere) a real logic of sacramental grammar in place of an etiolated 'somehow'. In Chadwick's book, not altogether surprisingly, it is Herbert's admiring imitator Walton who is given the penultimate valediction—'Of this blest man, let his just praise be given, / Heaven was in him, before he was in heaven'—an amiable style-book couplet with an attenuated Anglican 'metaphysical' cadence, but without the sense of theological discovery that Herbert's poem awakens line by line. It is not that one is confusing technical felicity with a theological category like 'sufficient grace': the theologians would be justified in coming down hard on that solecism. It is that no other English poet can convince us, as Herbert can, that the 'otherness' of figurative language is, even as we meet it, instantly turned upon itself 'in a sense most true'. Though poetry for Herbert does not enjoy a privileged place in the daily round, his poems have the dignity of any common task that is sufficient to offer up ordinariness to the life of grace.

Dr Rivers may object to my poetic excursus (as it must seem to her), since she clearly states at the commencement of her discussion that her 'subject is the language of religious and moral prose'. My answer must be that, in undertaking a study of the language of 'Reason, Grace and Sentiment' in England from 1660 to 1780, she had no choice but to consider the language of poetry together with that of prose. How, for instance, is one to follow the trace of eighteenth-century sentiment without the evidence of Addison's two *Spectator* papers of August 1712? If Addison's prose in these essays is what you would expect ('There is not a more pleasing exercise of the mind than gratitude'; 'In our retirements every thing disposes us to be serious'), the hymn concluding each paper is a modulation which relates to the question raised by Watts in his anxiety about 'formal songs'. The 'piece . . . of divine poetry' for Saturday, August 9 ('When all thy mercies, O my God'), is perhaps little more than a verse paraphrase of the latitudinarian psalm that is *The Spectator* no. 453 ('If gratitude is due from man to man, how much more from man to his Maker?' etc.). It proves the diffusive strength of the 'very pleasing sensation in the mind of a grateful man' in several ways: for instance, by 'doubling' the 'store' of platitude already present in the essay and by 'gently clear[ing]' the word 'transported' of any slight penal associations it has carried since 1666. The major qualification to all this mild success is one's sense that Addison is not equal to the terms of his own question 'O how shall words with equal warmth / The gratitude declare . . . ?' In Herbert as in Wesley we are convinced either that words do constitute a worthy correlative to the sensations of 'wonder, love, and praise' or that to the poet, in a particular circumstance, words are indeed cold and remote from the incommunicable longing of the heart. Addison's language weakly conciliates both possibilities with the result that a 'piece of divine poetry' is also (I think half-consciously so) a divine piece of poetry.

The second piece, the 'ode', as Addison calls it, from *Spectator* 465 ('The spacious firmament on high'), is a different matter. Its relation to Addison's other divine meditations in prose and verse is comparable with Burnet's distinction between 'a right notion of style' and 'a false pitch of a wrong sublime'. It is not exactly comparable because Burnet, in context, begs the question whether there is a true pitch of a right sublime. It is as if, in his ode, Addison intuitively perceives the 'rhetorick' of a right sublime which corrects the pitch of his own effusions but is not to be reduced to the level of Burnet's 'right notion of style'. This is the kind of resolution, it seems to me, which closely pertains to the 'very complex subject' that Dr Rivers seeks to address.

Her presentation of 'complexity' requires us to consider 'states of mind' and 'senses . . . natural and spiritual', with their commingled affects and effects ('disagreement . . . over . . . meaning', 'recurrent emphasis', 'disclaimer' and innumerable other modulations and modifications). At the same time, we are to note, as if in passing, any individual characteristics of eloquence, such as the 'peculiar edge' which Calamy praised in Richard Baxter's delivery of his 'thoughts'. The main weakness of Dr Rivers's thesis is her failure to recognize that a 'peculiar edge' can be something other than an attractive 'mettle' or even an exemplary cogency; that it can mark, stylistically, the ethical line between compliance and resistance, sentiment and reason, enthusiasm and meditative attention. Quoting as she does, both extensively and minutely, she none the less fails to 'read' the grammar that she has so painstakingly accumulated, like Baxter's 'consideration awakeneth our reason from its sleep, till it rouse up itself, as Sampson', or 'meditation produceth reason into act'. The grammar of 'consideration awakeneth our reason from its sleep' and 'meditation produceth reason into act' is like a template of the spiritual grammar of Herbert's poems or Law's prose or Charles Wesley's hymns. I do not think that language which moves with such a natural mimesis can be adequately translated into, or represented by, the parataxis 'Reason, Grace and Sentiment', which is uncommitted either to collocation or consequence.

What I have termed 'natural mimesis' is, in Charles Wesley, the 'spontaneous' movement of a creative spirit at once submissive to revealed authority and hard-pressed by brute fact. In his case, the 'peculiar edge' of the writing is the line which reason draws between enthusiasm and grace. The theme of Wesley's hymns is recurrently that of 'taste'; taste is also his 'temper', his instrument for endowing hard distinctions with a real effect of ease and freedom. Isaac Barrow had written, to encourage the practice of charity, that 'the communication of benefits to others [is] accompanied with a very delicious relish upon the mind of him that practises it'. Richard Baxter had declared that 'it is a sign of a distempered heart that loseth the relish of Scripture excellency'. Barrow makes 'relish' resemble the word of a sybarite; for Baxter it remains the seal of self-knowledge. The word is impacted with the self-contradictions and manifold abuse of 'the language of religion and ethics', a language which was Wesley's inescapable patrimony. That 'temper' which Dr Rivers cites, frequently yet inconsequentially, is concluded in Wesley as he concludes upon it. His greatest hymns are the key to the arch of 'Reason, Grace and Sentiment'.

If 'temper' in Wesley is also taste, and if taste is also the eucharistic 'taste', his rhetoric and 'inward Sentiments' would seem, in principle, so remarkably interfused that, as in Herbert, the one is transformed within the other. In practice, of Wesley's several thousand hymns, a few score at most have this effect of perfect balance, of 'peculiar edge', which separates the 'delicious relish' of spiritual self-regard from the experiential relish of the awakened heart discovering, or recovering, its true temper. If he is less consistent than Herbert, and less fine in his spirituality, he is not unworthy of the comparison. It might further be argued that the run-up against brute actuality, harsh though it was for Herbert, was harsher still for the Wesleys, and that this caused an excess of strain, an infusion of gall, which the hymns were bound to take and taste. Herbert had condescended, in the decent sense that then applied, to his unlettered flock; but seventeenth-century Bemerton was not eighteenth-century Wednesbury, or Olney, or the Kingswood collieries. The Anglican, high Tory Wesleys were in daily contact with circumstances which, among a vast number of greater and lesser effects, swept away the old style of condescension (it can still be heard in the isolated, reclusive William Law, who died in 1761) and with it much of the old language of grace as it had been known in Herbert's 'Redemption'.

'Condescension' is subject to the same circumstantial pressures as 'complacency'. The Wesleys had not foreseen the strength of antinomian complacency which their own eloquence largely excited and which took against them from the midst of their own following. Charles Wesley's language of 'grace' and 'taste' was, from an early stage, controversial in ways that Herbert's had less need to accommodate, though controversy, in the hymns, frequently appears as a preemptive note of accurate surprise ('Blest with this Antepast of Heaven!'). In moving, with the force of its exclamation, to embrace affirmations like John Owen's 'tasting how gracious the Lord is', in withdrawing upon the dry, bookish alertness of 'antepast', this line epitomizes Wesley's nervous vigilance towards his own style of faith. The Wesleys aroused enthusiasm and, at the same time, deprecated certain of its consequences.

Dr Rivers suggests that John Wesley's 'appeal to feeling is solipsistic' and that 'contemporaries were justified in their criticism'. I would rather say that both Wesleys grew increasingly aware of the

two-natured power of their evangelical oratory: how it awakened
many into a redemptive, spiritual, common life and drove some into
an anarchic emotional solitude. I question Whaling's statement that
'the philosophical or theological nature of the [eucharistic] sacrifice is
not [Charles Wesley's] concern; he is joyfully aware that Christ has
died sacrificially for all men . . .'. The emphasis on 'all men' *was*
'philosophical or theological'; that is to say, it was an Arminian reading of the nature of the Atonement, a reading deliberately pitched
against the Calvinist interpretation of Whitefield and his supporters.
There was, in addition, a persistent philosophical or theological difference between the Wesleys themselves, with John entering frequent
caveats against his brother's doctrinal language, as in this characteristic warning to a correspondent: 'Take care you are not hurt by any-
thing in the *Short Hymns* contrary to the doctrines you have long
received'.

I think it entirely possible for a hymn to be, at one and the same
time, joyful and 'unhappy'; that kind of oxymoron is inherent in the
creative matter, the ganglion of language and circumstance from
which the piece of divine poetry is created:

> Now, even now, we all plunge in.
> And drink the purple wave.

This is wretched because it is 'gushing' ('Gushing streams of life'. . .
are found in a preceding stanza). It is gushing because, at the crux of
his theological imagination, Wesley is finally unable to dispose and
reconcile the protean fluctuations of that extreme sentiment known
to admirers and detractors alike as religious 'enthusiasm'. Cowper, in
'The Castaway', working at the cold negative pole of the same emotion, is desperately laconic ('For then, by toil subdued, he drank /
The stifling wave, and then he sank'), but one is not offering such sty-

listic resolution as an answer to Wesley's problem. Cowper and Wesley, at this point, standing on opposite sides of the same central flaw or fault, are strikingly complementary in their felicity and wretchedness.

Such oxymoronic constructions find themselves awkwardly placed between the technical and the spiritual. The awkwardness, however, is entirely appropriate to the subject of Dr Rivers's thesis and to the spirit of my contention. 'Original sin, in Wesley's view, is the essential underpinning of Christianity'. This, the crucial statement in her book, affects throughout, implicitly if not explicitly, the temper of her argument, even when it is concerned with those latitude-men who appear, at first sight, to be paddling away from the unpleasant proximity of the thought. I could have wished Dr Rivers to have 'felt', in a variety of practical applications, the all-pervading relevance of Wesley's affirmation, as I could have wished her to recognize the close practical applicability of several other citations, like Baxter's argument for the 'natural "pondus", or necessitating principle' or his belief that 'good books are a very great mercy to the world'.

In order to keep the terms of this discussion 'open', I would allow that the commitment to an unqualified belief in original sin need not be the absolute prerequisite for taking seriously a 'natural "pondus", or necessitating principle' of English style. One could try to restrict the question to Hobbesian mechanics, his 'certain impulsion of nature' comparable to 'that whereby a stone moves downward', but a Calvinist like Jonathan Edwards adapted natural impulsion to sustain his conviction of a human nature 'as it were heavy as lead', and Hobbes himself asserted, in *De Corpore Politico*, that '*the Divine Moral Law, and the Law of Nature, is the Same*'. One could of course elect to read Hobbes's equation as metaphor, but I cannot myself see any way of escaping complete assent to the doctrine of original sin, which, in the contexture of this argument, may be understood as no more and no less than 'the imperfection which marks all human effort, especially where it aims to avoid it'. The 'human effort' in Dr Rivers's book cannot be gainsaid; her scholarship is arduous and scrupulous but is finally vitiated by the radical imperfections, the errors of premise and inference, which I have endeavoured to describe in detail. Painful though it is to say so, I believe that her desire to conciliate 'accessibility' is the equivalent of Baxter's 'idle heart in hearing'; it is an 'idleness' of the critical, historical and, indeed, the scholarly imagination that annuls so much of the formidable business of her research. Her introduction to *Reason, Grace and Sentiment* assumes the inescapable public contexture of our personal responsibility to the word while, at the same time, her inescapable personal idiom subordinates the public significance to a different priority which Jonathan Edwards called '*private* interest' ('interest' is her poor substitute for Ruskin's 'intrinsic value').

The contrast between a 'cold rational language of philosophical argument' and a 'warm affectionate language of evangelical preaching' which Dr Rivers associates with Watts (a distinction modified rather than confirmed by his lines about 'formal songs') has had, in the long term, deleterious effects. So has the widespread emphasis, among theologians as well as scientists, on words as 'arbitrary signs'. From the seventeenth century to the present day it has led to false conclusions, such as Rivers's own suggestion that Watts's 'tone and method of arguing are of more interest than his doctrinal solutions'. Literary historians of ideas justify their condescension by such 'signs' without registering how emphatically they are contradicted within the texture of, say, Baxter's own writings. Language, especially in the authors discussed here, *is* a doctrinal solution, in which 'solution' acts or suffers what it describes: *OED* sense 1.1*a* fusing with senses 11.5*a* & c (*transf.*), and 6*a*; with finesse or not, as the case may be; with or without direct authorial agency. This caveat is required in the case of Whichcote's *Aphorisms,* where, as has been suggested, the 'fusing' is less complete than the author's regard for 'temper' would lead one to expect. There is more gravity, in the sense that Hobbes and Jonathan Edwards would stress, more feeling for 'intrinsic Malignity', than the weight of an aphorism can sustain. One suggests here a distinction between aplomb (*à plomb,* 'according to the plummet') and Hobbes's 'certain impulsion of nature' or Edwards's 'internal mutual attraction . . . whereby the whole becomes one solid coherent body'. There is even a sense in which 'aplomb' works to defy, or deny, the Hobbesian gravity, persistently bobbing up in a Galsworthian sort of way: 'There is nothing so intrinsically Rational, as *Religion* is: nothing, that can so Justify itself: nothing, that hath so pure Reason to recommend itself; as Religion hath'. What is 'Rational' here is chiefly the concept: the grammar betrays a strong sentiment regarding the concept. However, as Dr Rivers observes, 'there are special, perhaps insoluble' textual problems with Whichcote's writings. She expertly notes these details (she is at her best on such points), though without drawing the most obvious conclusion from her own scrutiny.

The extent to which John Wesley interfered with the doctrinal solutions of his brother's hymns is well known and well documented. His editing was entirely 'reasonable', in that high-minded eighteenth-century way, which means that a good deal of 'sentiment' was also involved: sentiment, in the main, about the nature of 'grace'. But with Wesley we are spared, for decent high Tory, Anglican reasons, subjective impressions about the egalitarian rough house of words and ideas (an absurd reach-me-down version of seventeenth-century elitist 'taste'). Such impressions, on the impulse or inclination of scholars less diligent and less textually disciplined than Dr Rivers, bear us down into one solid coherent body of anarchy; a brute actu-

ality with which to confront the Wesleys, who so feared and resisted
the anarchic in all its religious and political manifestations.

   Charles Wesley: A Reader, edited by an American Methodist scholar of some standing, was published by the Oxford University Press in
1989. There was need for such a compilation, bringing together
'hymns, sermons, letters, and journal materials—many rare and hith-
erto unknown'—from the scattered work of this great devotional
poet. The reader who does not have the sources at his or her elbow
recognizes slowly (and with some natural reluctance) the extent of
what is amiss with the edition. The hymns are imprinted with gross
errors of transcription which anyone with even an elementary grasp
of metre and rhyme ought to have picked up, by educated intuition,
at proof-stage if not before. With certain exceptions, misreadings of
the manuscripts can be corrected by collation with *The Unpublished
Poetry of Charles Wesley*, Volume II (1990); among the exceptions are
pieces from 'MS John', for which recourse must be had to the
Methodist Church Archives in the John Rylands University Library
of Manchester. Among exemplary details we may record the following cluster: 'And Satan lays the lunacy and waste', page 387 ('And
Satan lays the vineyard waste', *Unpublished Poetry*, page 23); 'Purge all
our faith and blood away', page 386 ('Purge all our filth and blood
away', MS John); 'Which reaches for the when and now', page 387
('Which teaches God the when and how', *Unpublished Poetry*, page
28); 'That wicked one rival consume [our nature?]', page 385 ('That
wicked One reveal, consume', MS John). These errors strike me as
being qualitatively different from the general run of typographical
mishap ('*for* wordly *read* worldly', etc.) with which all who tempt
print are habitually afflicted. When 'filth' becomes 'faith' and 'vineyard' 'lunacy', we have fallen into an inverse theological dimension
where Wesley's doctrinal art is pitched back into anarchy and where
a good book is no longer a very great mercy to the world. The most

charitable view of the matter is a 'philosophical' one, leading to the conclusion that the editor of *Charles Wesley: A Reader* believes so absolutely in the primacy of 'concept' that words, to him, actually are 'arbitrary' and can be thus abandoned to their own natures. It is a type of literary antinomianism, extreme but not unique.

The 'obvious conclusion' which Dr Rivers has failed to draw from her own most useful remarks on the textual problems in Whichcote is the recognition of a misconceived *métier*. In the present undertaking, I believe, she has been ill-advised. A 'study' of the language of religion and ethics which cannot push itself beyond a repetitious 'interest' is merely adding weight to the 'stone' that 'moves downward'. There is, however, a present need for good critical editions of (among others) Baxter, Whichcote and Law, and Dr Rivers's manifest qualities would best be devoted to such an end. Against the odds and a good deal of evidence, I still regard the effort to bring secular scholarship (and poetics and the 'fine arts') into the field of theological judgment as something other than a search for the philosopher's stone. At the same time, one recognizes that the general drift of the tendency has been towards an effusive post-Symbolism (e.g., 'Images of Atonement in the Novels and Short Stories of William Faulkner') which coy and prurient exercises in the 'confessional' mode have further dissipated. The writings considered in *Reason, Grace and Sentiment,* at once more reserved and more of a revelation, form the nexus of a different order of theological understanding, inherent in etymology and the contextures of grammar and syntax, clamped to a paradox that the 'one solid coherent body' of the work may be its 'Intrinsic Goodness', its reconciling of style and faith, or an abandoned finality of mind and soul, an intrinsic malignity 'as it were heavy as lead'.

Dividing Legacies

T. S. Eliot's Clark Lectures, delivered at Trinity College, Cambridge, in 1926, were a distinguished contribution to a series which has not always received such good returns on its modest investment. Ronald Schuchard's meticulously annotated edition makes *The Varieties of Metaphysical Poetry* an indispensable work of reference, and not only for professional readers of Eliot.* The lecturer was evidently dissatisfied with what he had achieved in these papers and in the subsequent Turnbull Lectures of 1933, a second shot, no less inconclusive, at the same topic. He withheld the typescripts of both sets from publication, and one can see why, even though by the standards that now prevail his reluctance may seem excessively fastidious.

To adapt one of Eliot's own figures to the purpose of my argument, I would say that the proper weight of any formal topic is related to its centre of gravity and that this centre, not surprisingly, is the most difficult element to establish in the composition of any lecture

---

*T. S. Eliot, *The Varieties of Metaphysical Poetry: The Clark Lectures at Trinity College, Cambridge, 1926, and the Turnbull Lectures at the Johns Hopkins University, 1933*, edited and introduced by Ronald Schuchard (London: Faber & Faber, 1993; New York: Harcourt Brace Jovanovich, 1994).

or essay. The true centre of *The Varieties of Metaphysical Poetry* is not easy to ascertain, in part because Eliot has seen, but not fully addressed, the problem; his anxious shifts and reservations complicate rather than clarify the issue. He observes that 'we have . . . to consider the centre of gravity of metaphysical poetry to lie somewhere between Donne and Crashaw, but nearer the former than the latter'. Subsequently he backs away from 'what many of you will have expected, a neat and comprehensive definition', because in order to satisfy expectation 'I should have had to draw in the background much more completely, with the figures of James, and Charles, and Hooker, and Laud, and Hyde and Strafford'. It was a misjudgment not to bring these 'figures' under review, as it was to suggest that in any case they could be regarded as 'background'. It was a further miscalculation not to let go of the 'hypothetical' project, the comparison and contrast with 'Dante and his School' to which he had referred in his letter of thanks to Middleton Murry. (Murry, editor of *The Athenaeum,* had successfully nominated him for the Cambridge appointment after A. E. Housman had declined it.)

As is usually the case in such circumstances, the electors pressed Eliot hard for a theme and title; his nomination having been confirmed on March 6, 1925, his topic was 'approved' on April 14. It also appears probable that two studies, M. P. Ramsay's *Les Doctrines médiévales chez Donne* (1917) and Mario Praz's recently published *Secentismo e marinismo in Inghilterra,* which, at the time, appeared to point to the centre of gravity for his own discourse, in the event directed his thought away from its true centre. Schuchard observes that Eliot, soon after the conclusion of his Clark Lectures, moved to a consideration of the author of *The Lawes of Ecclesiasticall Politie* in the essay on Lancelot Andrewes, of September 1926, and that he returned to Hooker three years later in a contribution to *The Listener.* Though Schuchard does not say that Eliot's way of making up the arrears is equivalent to a properly developed discussion at the time, his footnote on this, a half-page of small, dense print, implies a weight and cogency which is not evident in any of Eliot's own references to the author of *The Lawes of Ecclesiasticall Politie*. Schuchard quotes from the *Listener* piece—'The style of Hooker, and the style of Bacon, have a stiffness due to their intellectual antecedents being Latin and not English prose'—and I must draw my own conclusions from what he cites. It has to be said that in proposing the three periods—'the *trecento* in Italy and the seventeenth century in England', together with the period 1870–1890 in France—as equivalently, if not interchangeably, 'metaphysical' for the purposes of his Cambridge lectures, Eliot irrecoverably misdirected his own argument away from its centre of gravity. It was a disciple of Eliot, the late Helen Gardner, who eventually made the necessary conjunction in her edition of Donne's *Divine Poems* (1951): 'To read the *Essays in Divinity* or the Sermons ... is to feel at once that Donne has absorbed Hooker's conception of the *via media* so deeply that it has become the basis of his own thinking'. This is of course a particularly happy discovery for a disciple of Eliot to have made since it was through his example, after 1927, that the *via media* once more came into acceptable critical parlance.

As we have seen, the metaphor 'centre of gravity' is Eliot's own, as is the equally suggestive 'points of triangulation'. These figures are useful, even essential, in helping to establish Eliot's necessary tone of tentative authority, perhaps the most attractive of his various *personae* and one which, as he thought, derived in part from the manner of F. H. Bradley, that 'curious blend of humility and irony, an attitude of extreme diffidence about his own work'.

It was Bradley who, in 1914, expressed gratification at 'the increasing devotion amongst us to metaphysical inquiry'. Twelve years later, at the commencement of the Clark Lectures, Eliot, though much indebted to Bradley, can less afford his relaxed amplitude of phrase. Where Bradley contrives to suggest a gratified disengagement from unnecessary particulars ('There has been, I think, a rise in the general level of English philosophical thought such as fifty years ago might well have seemed incredible'), Eliot contrives at the start to suggest a pursuit and scrutiny of the *'echt metaphysisch'* more close and stringent than any subsequent detail can match. While arguing to disengage the peculiar qualities of seventeenth-century metaphysical poetry in England from the broad connotations of philosophical metaphysics, he presents significant aspects of his case still from within the circuit of Bradley's comprehension, drawing his own terms of assessment, as Schuchard demonstrates, from such Bradleian passages as 'On our Knowledge of Immediate Experience' or 'Floating Ideas and the Imaginary'. In his preface (1964) to *Knowledge and Experience in the Philosophy of F. H. Bradley,* Eliot recalls how it was 'as a pupil of Harold Joachim, the disciple of Bradley who was closest to the master', that he came to 'an understanding of what I wanted to say and of how to say it'. He means—more certainly—the understanding of the philosopher than the saying of the poet, though it is not futile to consider 'Marina', at least, in the context of Bradley's critique of floating ideas ('ideas may be recognized as merely imaginary, and, taken in this character, they float suspended above the real world').

It is not, however, as a pupil of a disciple of Bradley that Eliot considers 'the style of Hooker, and the style of Bacon'. It is difficult to name the mask he has here chosen to assume: one is inclined to say 'protégé of George Saintsbury' except that Saintsbury was probably more solidly bottomed in his knowledge of that period. It is nonetheless apparent that when Eliot is wearied by 'the most arduous, the most concentrated critical labour of which detailed record exists' he slips, not into incoherence but into a mechanical alternative mode of discourse exemplified by, if not imitated from, Saintsbury, to whom

Homage to John Dryden (1924) is dedicated, or Charles Whibley, to whose memory *The Use of Poetry and the Use of Criticism* (1933) is inscribed. I mean by this that Eliot, who, in the correspondence pages of *The Athenaeum* (27 February 1920), attacked the 'apathy' of 'the so-called cultivated and civilised class', was to some extent a practitioner of its modes and to a further extent their beneficiary. Schuchard notes that Eliot's review of Housman's 1933 Leslie Stephen lecture, *The Name and Nature of Poetry*, was far from hostile; that an advance copy of 'The Journey of the Magi' was inscribed to Housman with the author's 'respectful homage'; and that Housman evidently appreciated and to some extent reciprocated the sympathy. It is germane to our sense of *A Shropshire Lad* and *Last Poems* to understand that Housman can invoke, as a rhetorical tribute to precedent, the classical *apatheia* and at the same moment appeal to a less elevated form of apathy, that indolence of 'cultivated' taste, which Eliot deplores in his letter to *The Athenaeum*. What is most, and what is least, admirable in Housman and in those who value him is contained within the tacit qualifications of that word. Eliot has more facets than this, but his singleness of purpose within his divided conditions and unhappy circumstances is more clearly, more ambitiously, stated than are Housman's own professions and demurrals. Again I refer to a particular source, Eliot's letter of April 1919 to one of his former teachers at Harvard, J.H. Woods:

> There are only two ways in which a writer can become important—to write a great deal, and have his writings appear everywhere, or to write very little. It is a question of temperament. I write very little and I should not become more powerful by increasing my output. My reputation in London is built upon one small volume of verse, and is kept up by printing two or three more poems in a year. The only thing that matters is that these should be perfect in their kind, so that each should be an event.

It is of course true that in writing to Woods at that time Eliot had a particularly difficult case to make on his own behalf. The professor thought very highly of Eliot's potential and prospects as an academic philosopher and had concerned himself about the practicalities of Eliot's return to Harvard to take up a teaching post in Philosophy. 'Please let us be reassured that your interest in Philosophy is as strong as before', Woods had written in June 1916, in the same letter which reported that Eliot's doctoral dissertation on F. H. Bradley had been accepted in partial fulfilment of the requirements for that degree. In the next few years Eliot's main task in writing not only to the Harvard philosophers but also to his parents would be to persuade them, and perhaps in a sense himself, that by remaining in London to write poetry and to pick up a living from various kinds of literary journey-man-work he had not irretrievably ruined his life and unforgivably blighted their expectations. Even with this concession to circumstance, however, I find that the letter places a remarkably heavy stress on the particulars of career-making. Eliot's self-evaluation is in terms of a calculating idealism; the effect is gratingly oxymoronic: 'important', 'powerful', 'reputation', 'event'; the commitment suggested by 'perfect in their kind' is abraded in the surrounding context.

Four years after the delivery of the Clark Lectures he had achieved an 'extraordinary power' (the words are G. Wilson Knight's) to influence literary opinion. In Peter Ackroyd's words, Eliot was always 'shrewd enough to make his peace with an age to which he did not truly belong'. Richard Wollheim's conjecture is that it was 'only after he had made some kind of initial submission to a force, felt in itself to be uncongenial or external, that he possessed the liberty to do something for himself or on his own account'. Eliot himself observed, having in mind Donne's Catholic patrimony and apostasy, 'Conflict is contact'; and immediately added, 'The air which Donne breathed was infused with Jesuitism'. But I should have supposed that 'contact', as argued here, is an entirely different state or process from infusion as he here conceives it. Eliot's scholarly intuition is acute: he anticipates the speculations of Martz, Gardner, Raspa and others who emphasize Donne's critical and creative involvement with Jesuit spirituality. His deductions are less effectively conveyed: 'For you can hardly fight anyone for very long without employing his weapons and using his methods; and to fight a man with ideas means adapting your ideas to his mind'. Not necessarily, though it may have been necessary for Eliot to convert a vulnerability into a truism. The tone of his delivery throughout both sets of lectures shows him acting, at least in part, on his own dubious maxim. He urges the significance of what he terms the 'psychologism' of Jesuit practice and believes that he has established its influence on Donne's style of thought. *The Oxford English Dictionary* (1989) gives two principal senses of 'psychologism'; neither of them strikes me as apposite to Eliot's purpose. 'Psychologism' is either a form of 'idealism as opposed to sensationalism' or 'the tendency to explain in psychological terms matters which are considered to be more properly explained in other ways'. The deficiency may be that of the compilers—it is possible that Eliot's usage significantly modifies the given senses, but on balance I doubt it. If it is in any way appropriate to employ a term not current before the nineteenth century, I would suggest that the Ignatian method seeks to move the exercitant by an edited sensationalism, e.g.: '*The fourth point* is to use in imagination the sense of touch, for example, by embracing and kissing the place where the persons walk or sit, always endeavouring to draw some spiritual fruit from this'. And if, alternatively, we attempt to apply *OED* sense 2 we arrive at conclusions directly opposed to Ignatian proprieties of explanation.

It is worth repeating that Eliot's instinct for spotting the significant detail in a line of thought or nexus of circumstance is that of a true scholar-critic. The conclusions which he derives from his scholarly and critical *aperçus* nevertheless strike me as being anachronistic, broadly impressionistic. I would accept that 'psychologism' in the *OED* sense 2, even if inadmissible as a description of Ignatian method, illuminates the poems of the period 1926–1930, in particular 'Marina', which has been called 'Eliot's most elusive poem'. In Denis Donoghue's judgment this poem 'makes sense' as being about 'waking up to find yourself a Christian, not knowing quite what to make of it all'. It is within this particular area of suggestion, at once contracted and expansive, that the second definition of 'psychologism' indeed makes sense. The voice of the poem is acutely conscious of attempting to explain, to itself and others, matters more properly explained in other ways. These other ways may reasonably be understood as those of Anglo-Catholic doctrine and practice; the way in which that understanding moves, and moves us, in the poem remains, at least as I understand it, essentially Bradleian. I note here the organization of *Essays on Truth and Reality* (1914), where the chapter on 'Faith' is immediately succeeded by the discussion of 'Floating Ideas and the Imaginary', a chapter to which Eliot made frequent reference in his doctoral dissertation. Bradley argues that 'the origin of faith, it seems to me clear, may be what we call emotional; and, even perhaps apart from emotion, faith can arise through what may be termed a non-active suggestion'. The rhythm and syntax of 'Marina' seem scarcely to rise out of the non-active (this is their achievement) while possessing sufficient resilience to pull away from the static horror of Hercules' cry of recognition (the Senecan epigraph).

I am far from suggesting that the final incoherence of the Clark Lectures is mysteriously vindicated in the coherences, the coherent elusiveness, of 'Marina'. The difficult economy of invention can do without that kind of condescension. That which misdirects itself in the academic context is not vicarious, not in payment for the subliminal self-discoveries of a Baudelairean Christian poet. The source of the error is in part, I believe, the scholarly oversight to which I have referred: Eliot's failure to take rightly the measure of Hooker. That Eliot himself apprehended the extent to which he had missed Hooker's significance is indicated by the proliferation of his successive returns upon the matter: in the essay on Andrewes later that year, in 'The Genesis of Philosophic Prose: Bacon and Hooker' (1929), in 'The Prose of the Preacher' (1929) and again in the Turnbull Lectures of January 1933. To say that 'the subject of Hooker's book is a very interesting one, and indeed very pertinent to some modern problems' is to be as far from the quick of the matter as when he says that Hooker's prose has a stiffness due to its intellectual antecedents being Latin and not English.

I had better explain what I mean in this instance by the quick of the matter. In April 1931 Eliot gave a BBC talk in the course of which he drew attention to the fineness of Shakespeare's dramatic sense; he focused on the words of the dying Charmian, in *Antony and Cleopatra,* spoken over the dead body of her mistress:

> It is well done, and fitting for a princess
> Descended of so many royal kings.
> Ah, soldier!

Eliot pointed out that Shakespeare added to the text of North's *Plutarch,* from which he was working, 'the two plain words, *ah, soldier*'. Eliot continued, 'I could not myself put into words the difference I feel between the passage if these two words *ah, soldier* were omitted and with them. But I know there is a difference, and that only Shakespeare could have made it'. In stating the issue as he does Eliot *has* of course put into words, very finely, the difference that he says he cannot explain. Christopher Ricks comments, 'If in some game I had to instance one paragraph from Eliot to show that he was a great critic, I should choose this, from a radio talk which he never himself reprinted. For it is an act of genius in the critic to see that the act of genius in the artist was the cry "Ah, Souldier'". From this, as from other sources, I draw my conclusion that within the semantic field, felicities and infelicities are herded indiscriminately together and that it requires a particular quality of aural sensitivity, a vigilance at once intuitive and disciplined, to make sense of one or the other or both. This we may call 'recognition', a term doubly applicable to Eliot's mind and art, for he is one who—psychologically and spiritually—commits himself to, and requires a very great deal from, evocations of rediscovery and redemption.

In the light of such affirmations it is at first bewildering to discover the frequency with which Schuchard is obliged to correct misquotations and 'minor mistranscriptions' in these lectures. One can go only so far in arguing that Eliot prepared the text under great pressure of various kinds; so does everyone, in one way or another; so did Péguy, famed for his impeccable proof-reading. It is of course true that, unlike the majority of Clark Lectures, Eliot's were not subsequently prepared by the author for the press. But his misquotations and minor mistranscriptions are also strongly instinctual; for example, his recollection that the butcher and the beaver marched shoulder to shoulder 'from necessity' and not 'merely from nervousness', as Lewis Carroll had imagined, or that Shakespeare's 'gnomic utterance' in *King Lear* (V. 2, 9–11) reads:

> Man must abide
> His going hence, even as his coming hither;
> Ripeness is all.

When I say 'instinctual' I mean instinctively metaphysical, and I suggest also that Eliot's metaphysics sometimes require the exquisite pointing of a word or two, as in 'Ah, soldier', and at other times do not. Bradley famously observed that metaphysics is 'the finding of bad reasons for what we believe upon instinct', and one might place 'Tradition and the Individual Talent', 'The Function of Criticism', 'Hamlet' and 'The Metaphysical Poets' in that category. But Bradley was also a 'rigorous metaphysician', permitted or self-permitted his relish of insouciance, and Eliot's doctoral dissertation upon him is not merely the 'painfully obscure work' that Wollheim declares it to be. Its argument resolves into clarity, particularly at points where a chord in Eliot's mind resonates to a note in Bradley or to something recalled (possibly) from Josiah Royce's seminar of 1913–1914. At one of these meetings Royce introduced to the discussion Charles Sanders Peirce's belief 'that there is a mysterious harmony between the mind of the scientist and the order of nature; for otherwise, supposing it were a mere matter of chance as to what hypotheses he should devise, he would rarely hit upon any true and adequate explanations'. Eliot needs words, in a metaphysical sense, as a manifestation of that 'mysterious harmony' by which the mind not only reconciles itself with the 'order of nature' but also prefigures that reconciliation. Eliot states, in his treatise on Bradley:

> In really great imaginative work the connections are felt to be bound by as logical necessity as any connections to be found anywhere; the apparent irrelevance is due to the fact that terms are used with more or other than their normal meaning, and to those who do not thoroughly penetrate their significance the relation between the aesthetic expansion and the objects expressed is not visible.

The key to our understanding here, as in much else concerning Eliot, is Bradley's 'My Station and Its Duties'. John Passmore, with what I take to be genial asperity, observes that 'My Station and Its Duties' also shows us what Bradley 'believed upon instinct'. The possibility of picking up the wrong key, for us as for Eliot, is present throughout a reading of Bradley. Take, for example, 'On Our Knowledge of Immediate Experience':

> We . . . have experience in which there is no distinction between my awareness and that of which it is aware. There is an immediate feeling, a knowing and being in one, with which knowledge begins; and, though this in a manner is transcended, it nevertheless remains throughout as the present foundation of my known world.

If we proceed no further we appear to be in that region of atonement ('there is an immediate feeling, a knowing and being in one') which is the focal point of desire in 'Marina' and 'Ash-Wednesday' and is intended to be heard as the proclaimed consummation of 'Little Gidding'. For Bradley, however, as I understand it, this is not the blessed finality but the necessary point of unavoidable departure. The attempt to stay or to recover will be regressive or retrograde. It is possible to understand how, given the Roycean-Bradleian inheritance, Eliot's discovery of Dante is inevitable, at one with 'the mysterious harmony between the mind of the scientist and the order of nature', and not only inevitable but foreordained, so that Bradley's primal 'knowing and being in one' is at the same time the final *sì come rota ch'igualmente è mossa* of the *Paradiso*. In accordance with this paradigm—Dante does not declare that he is paraphrasing Aquinas—one's words can take up another's; nor is it essential that the words so taken up should be exactly quoted. One is not, in fact, quoting but recognizing. I infer that the 'psychologism' runs somewhat in this manner. Indeed it could be said that the psychologism is unanswerably proved and justified by 'Ah, soldier', the two plain words which wholly transform with genius the dutiful words from North and which, three hundred years later, are formally recognized, by the reciprocating genius of Eliot, as great imaginative work.

It is equally the case, however, that if one accepts the metaphysical profile which I have drawn, it must be accepted—or conceded—that the obtrusion of Dante and exclusion of Hooker damage the structure of these lectures beyond immediate recovery. The necessary connection which Eliot failed to make was not that 'Hooker's philosophy was much more "mediaeval" than Donne's', true as that is, or that 'the intellectual achievement and the prose style of Hooker and Andrewes came to complete the structure of the English Church as the philosophy of the thirteenth century crowns the Catholic Church': these are fair points well within the competence of a decent man of letters such as Charles Whibley. Eliot's encounter with language, in the making of *Prufrock and Other Observations* and *Ara Vos Prec,* was already at a pitch above and beyond the range of such minor settlements. His sense of this is uncomfortably conveyed in small tonal irritants and irritations throughout the lectures: 'what many of you will have expected; a neat and comprehensive definition . . .', 'But I think that I warned you . . .', 'You will perhaps think it unjust of me'. . . The distinction to be emphasized here is between pitch and tone. The style of Eliot's address to his audience is a matter of tone; the burden of his analytical criticism is, or ought to be, the question of pitch. To meet with Hooker in significant engagement is to encounter questions of pitch: to take note that the word 'reason' as Hooker deploys it throughout *The Lawes of Ecclesiasticall Politie* has at least seven distinct senses. It signifies God's great original purpose and design and also mankind's highest capacity to recognize God's proposed design and to imitate it; it signifies a decent common sense as well as opin-

ion and prejudice; it is necessity and determinism and certain causes of certain effects; it is also used to suggest formal ratiocination.
Hooker's 'style' is to a large extent his semantic ingenuity, his ability to make these senses merge and part with equanimity, though
not always with equity. Of similar significance to our grasp of
Ecclesiasticall Politie is the skill with which Hooker can alter the
pitch of the word 'common': 'common received error', 'common
sense or fancy', 'a common opinion held by the Scribes', 'the common sort of men', 'common discretion and judgement', 'in every
action of common life', 'the common good', 'common misery', 'the
minds of the common sort', 'for common utility's sake'. Clearly,
'common discretion and judgement' is pitched differently from 'a
common opinion held by the Scribes', which is itself at a different
pitch than 'the minds of the common sort'. Hooker's *belief,* we may
say, is that each separate pitch is justified by an equivalent degree on
a scale determined by Chapter 13 of St Paul's Epistle to the Romans.
Hooker's *equivocation,* we may decide, is in the tacit invitation to
his readers to accept that hierarchical distinctions and brute natural
obduracies are alike resolved into equity by fiat of the commonweal
and the administrations of the 1559 *Book of Common Prayer.*

If, as Eliot claims, 'the centre of gravity of metaphysical poetry
[lies] somewhere between Donne and Crashaw, but nearer the former
than the latter', it is incumbent upon him to demonstrate that 'centre of gravity' is, critically speaking, a term of common utility. I am
not persuaded that he does so. The pitch of the argument can to an
extent be determined by the empirical judgment that one brings to
Eliot's use of the words 'thought', 'idea', 'figure', 'image', 'conceit'. In
terms of thought, notion, idea, Eliot appears anti-Cartesian in so far
as he dismisses the sixth *Meditation* as an 'extraordinarily crude and
stupid piece of reasoning' at the point where Descartes denies that
one can deduce the existence of the body from the 'distinct idea of

corporeal nature, which I have in my imagination'. It further appears, at an initial acquaintance, that Eliot values the pre-Cartesian elements in Donne's poetics that are at the same time Cartesianism turned upon itself: 'the sensuous interest of Donne in his own thoughts as objects'. 'I attempted to show', Eliot announced at the end of the fourth lecture, 'that this interest naturally led [Donne] to expression by conceits'. What is missing from Eliot's appraisal, however, is a convincing presentation of 'sensuous interest'; he gives us an idea, a notion, an indication, of sensuous interest. I am clear in my own mind that what I have called the pitch of Hooker's prose is also the sensuous interest of that prose; I am equally convinced that a discovery of the pitch of Donne's language in, say, 'A Nocturnall upon S. Lucies Day' or 'A Hymne to Christ, at the Authors last going into Germany' would also be a recognition of the sensuous interest of those poems. I do not detect that awareness in what Eliot finds to say in praise of Donne's figures felicitously 'teasing the idea', even 'creat[ing] the idea'; or in what he has to say, a shade less sympathetically, of our having (parenthetically) to 'swallow the idea of the indeterminability of time in the future state, and then pass on at once to the difficult idea, startlingly expressed, of the namelessness of the soul, of its distinction from the breathing composite of soul and body which we knew . . .'. I find in this sentence no sensuous interest, that is to say, no sense of pitch, no centre of gravity; one is again reminded how much critical description is in fact tautologous. Eliot concludes that 'the only thing that holds [Donne's] poems, or any one poem, together, is what we call unsatisfactorily the personality of Donne'. I believe that he is mistaken in this conclusion, and it is evident that he himself senses that something is wrong. He is forced to take up extrinsic 'personality', 'unsatisfactorily', as he admits, precisely because intrinsic pitch has not been attended to. 'Personality' has to stand as a substitute centre of gravity.

Professor Schuchard foresees a happy likelihood that 'the publication of Eliot's Clark Lectures on metaphysical poetry will have as much impact on our revaluation of his critical mind as did the facsimile edition of *The Waste Land* (1971) on our comprehension of his poetic mind'; I will end with a few observations on this speculation, though not with the enthusiasm of assent which its tone of *pietas* invites. Three years before he delivered the Clark Lectures Eliot had suggested, in 'The Function of Criticism' (1923), that 'probably . . . the larger part of the labour of an author in composing his work is critical labour', and he would rightly object to this belated editorial presumption that one can so neatly divide the 'critical' from the 'poetic' mind.

That, however, is not the most important issue arising from the publication of these lectures. I have attempted to show that throughout his argument Eliot aims at pitch but, for the most part, succeeds only in tone. I say 'succeeds' because tone is what people expect and suppose themselves familiar with. It was the pitch of *Prufrock and Other Observations* that disturbed and alienated readers; it was the tone of *Four Quartets* that assuaged and consoled them. That is to say, Eliot's poetry declines over thirty years from pitch into tone, and these late-published papers contribute significant evidence to the history of that decline.

In 'The Love Song of J. Alfred Prufrock' (1910–1911) the distinction between I, me, my, we, us, our, you, your, his, her, they, them, one, it, its is a proper distinction in pitch; in 'Little Gidding' (1942) communication is by tone:

> You are not here to verify,
> Instruct yourself, or inform curiosity
> Or carry report. You are here to kneel

Where prayer has been valid. And prayer is more
Than an order of words, the conscious occupation
Of the praying mind, or the sound of the voice praying.

How is the repeated 'you' to be understood? Is it the modern second
person singular or the second person plural, or is it the emphatic
demotic substitute for what the *OED* terms a 'quite toneless, proclitic
or enclitic, use of "one"'? Is Eliot instructing himself, self-confessor to
self-penitent, taking upon himself penitentially the burden of common trespass, or is he haranguing the uninitiated, some indeterminate other—or others—caught trespassing on his spiritual property?
Do these lines contain, even, a redundant echo from *The Waste Land,*
the exclamatory 'You' of line 76, the closest Eliot could get, in the
grammar of modern English, to the pitch of Baudelaire's 'Tu' in line
39 of 'Au Lecteur'? Whatever it is, it is no match for the quality of
pitch which Eliot caught in just two words, two just words, in *Antony
and Cleopatra.* Ricks, in his fine appraisal to which I have referred,
says that we cannot be sure of the 'posture proper to the cry' and that
the 'responsibility for settling upon the best response has been manifestly delegated' to us by Shakespeare. My argument does not require
that we should be relieved of the office proper to our intelligence. My
objection to the lines from 'Little Gidding' has nothing to do with
deliberated indeterminacy of pitch; I hear in them the semantic
equivalent of *tinnitus aurium,* and I say that one cannot rightly be
expected, as reader, to take responsibility for this condition.

Juxtapose the passage from 'Little Gidding' with the following
sentence from Wordsworth's 'Preface' (1800) to *Lyrical Ballads:*

It is supposed, that by the act of writing in verse an Author makes
a formal engagement that he will gratify certain known habits of

association, that he not only thus apprizes the Reader that certain classes of ideas and expressions will be found in his book, but that others will be carefully excluded.

Reading the lines from 'Little Gidding' in the light of Wordsworth's argument I find that Eliot stands in relation to Wordsworth's sense of pitch ('It is supposed, that') not as one similarly situated but as a commentator on the general tone or tonelessness of things. Certain classes of ideas and expressions will be found at Little Gidding—subsequently in 'Little Gidding'—rich in known habits of association, and others will be carefully excluded. If I add that of course I am not impugning the sincerity of Eliot's Anglo-Catholic devotion I fall into the same error which Eliot fell into when he was forced to address— 'unsatisfactorily'—'the personality of Donne'. And I have to disagree with Christopher Ricks when he finds that, in 'Little Gidding', 'antagonism to clichés—like the expression of antagonism through clichés—has been succeeded by confidence in their good sense, in their generous common humanity'. I do not claim that it is impossible for clichés in poetry to correspond to, or represent, a generous common humanity. Whitman, for instance, uses them in a vital and comradely way in *Drum-Taps*. I do say, however, that the 'apathy . . . more flagitious than abuse' to which Eliot acutely drew attention in 1920 is a determining factor in the tonality of his own later poetry and in its public reception, and that Ricks is uncharacteristically imperceptive in his response to this factor. I would ask him to place his 'generous common humanity' within the field of Hooker's common equivocation and to determine how much weight and pressure that generous humanity can sustain.

The residual beneficiaries of *Four Quartets* have been Larkin and Anglican literary 'spirituality', two seeming incompatibles fostered by a common species of torpor. If I were to ask Ricks how it is that, against all the evidence his own unrivalled critical intelligence could bring to the process, he is pleased to be numbered among Larkin's advocates, I anticipate that he might answer, 'Because he speaks to the human condition'.

Acknowledgments

The seven essays that make up this book have been previously published in periodicals, and I herewith make grateful acknowledgment to the editors who invited me to write them.

Five of the essays first appeared in *The Times Literary Supplement:* 'Common Weal, Common Woe' (April 21, 1989); 'Of Diligence and Jeopardy' (November 17, 1989); 'Keeping to the Middle Way' (December 23, 1994); 'The Eloquence of Sober Truth' (June 11, 1999); and 'The Weight of the Word' (under the title 'Style and Faith', December 27, 1991). 'A Pharisee to Pharisees' appeared in *English* (Summer 1989) and 'Dividing Legacies' in *Agenda* (vol. 34, no. 2, Summer 1996).

Some of my work on Hobbes, Bramhall, Clarendon has been anticipated chiefly by Samuel I. Mintz, *The Hunting of the Leviathan: Seventeenth-Century Reactions to the Materialism and Moral Philosophy of Thomas Hobbes* (Cambridge: Cambridge University Press, 1962), and by Mark Goldie, 'The Reception of Hobbes,' in J. H. Burns, ed., *The Cambridge History of Political Thought 1450–1700* (Cambridge: Cambridge University Press, 1991).

Rereading after many years Robert Penn Warren, *Selected Essays* (New York: Vintage Books, 1966), I am struck by the similarity of our emphases on 'the vollied glare' in Melville's poem 'The March into Virginia'. This is evidently an unconscious echoing on my part.

In the case of the *T.L.S.* pieces a number of reference notes subsequently dropped from my files, and a few have proved—to my limited competence—irretrievable. I beg to plead with J. I. Mombert (quoted elsewhere in this book) 'the imperfection which marks all human effort, especially where it aims to avoid it', though he had less cause than I to enter the plea.

During the writing of the individual essays my chief obligation was to the vigilance of my wife, Alice Goodman. During the time in which I have been collecting and preparing them for publication in book form, my friend and colleague Kenneth Haynes has saved me from many errors. For those errors that remain I bear sole responsibility.

Further debts are recorded among the Notes.

Notes

Epigraph

page
xi 'Knowledge cannot ... when we are come thither' / *The Sermons of John Donne*, ed. (with introductions and critical apparatus) George R. Potter and Evelyn M. Simpson, 10 volumes (Berkeley and Los Angeles: University of California Press, 1953–1962), III, p. 359.

xi 'If it were not for Sin. . .' / Benjamin Whichcote, *Moral and Religious Aphorisms*, 1753 (London: Elkin Matthews & Marrot, 1930), no. 731.

Preface

xiii 'The Hebrew word *bachan* . . . spectator' / John Calvin, *Commentary on the Book of Psalms,* transl. from the original Latin and collated with the author's French version by the Rev. James Anderson, reprint edition, 5 volumes (Grand Rapids, Mich.: Eerdmans, 1949), I, p. 165.

xiv 'The Holy Ghost . . . style too' / *The Sermons of John Donne*, ed. (with introductions and critical apparatus) George R. Potter and Evelyn M. Simpson, 10 volumes (Berkeley and Los Angeles: University of California Press, 1953–1962), V, p. 287.

Common Weal, Common Woe

1 Joseph Wright's *English Dialect Dictionary* / See James Milroy, *The Language of Gerard Manley Hopkins* (London: André Deutsch, 1977), p. 39. (*The English Dialect Dictionary, being the complete vocabulary of all dialect words still in use, or known to have been in use during the last two hundred years,* was published, in six volumes, by Henry Frowde [Oxford: Clarendon Press] from 1898 to 1905.)

1 'with the heyday of English philology' / Ibid., p. 49.

1 when the proposal ... February 1884 / See *The Oxford English Dictionary*, Second Edition, 20 volumes (Oxford: Clarendon Press, 1989), I, pp. xxxv–lvi ('The History of the Oxford English Dictionary'); see especially pp. xxxv, xxxvi, xlii.

1 'almost exactly ... date' / K. M. Elisabeth Murray, *Caught in the Web of Words: James A. H. Murray and the 'Oxford English Dictionary'*, with a preface by R. W. Burchfield (New Haven and London: Yale University Press, 1977), p. 312.

2 'the Oxford ... indicated' / *Dictionary of National Biography*, 1884–1901, ed. L. Stephen and S. Lee, Reprint Edition, 22 volumes (London: Smith, Elder & Co., 1909), XIX, p. 1120.

2 'still common in Ireland' / Richard Chenevix Trench, *English Past and Present*, 1855, Tenth Edition, revised (London: Macmillan, 1877), p. 202.

3 'accepted ... indifferent' / K. M. Elisabeth Murray, *Caught in the Web of Words*, p. 195.

3 'The Signification *(Sematology)*' / Thus in the 'Corrected Reissue' of the 1884–1928 *Oxford English Dictionary* (1933), 12 volumes, I, p. xxxi.

3 'The Signification, or *senses*' / *OED*, Second Edition (1989), I, p. xxviii.

4 Murray had conceded ... 'most difficult duties' / See *OED*, 'Corrected Reissue' (1933), I, p. xxxi.

4 'So also *pitch* ... than nothing and not-being' / *The Sermons and Devotional Writings of Gerard Manley Hopkins*, ed. C. Devlin, S.J. (London: Oxford University Press, 1959), p. 151.

4 'the peculiar meaning ... word' / Peter Milward, S.J., *A Commentary on G. M. Hopkins' 'The Wreck of the Deutschland'* (Tokyo: The Hokuseido Press, 1968), p. 86.

4 'though this scarcely ... definition which will' / Norman H. MacKenzie, *A Reader's Guide to Gerard Manley Hopkins* (London: Thames & Hudson, 1981), p. 34.

4 'a Dictionary ... language' / *OED*, Second Edition (1989), I, p. xxxvi, column 1.

4 'short dictionaries ... actually need help' / William Empson, *The Structure of Complex Words*, 1951, Third Edition (London: Chatto and Windus, 1977), p. 396.

4 'the interactions ... included' / Ibid., p. 391.

5 'straddle' / Ibid., p. 394.

5 'going together' / Ibid., p. 392.

5   'long . . . significations' / *OED*, 'Corrected Reissue' (1933), I, p. xxxi.

5   'that was not . . . universally practised in those parts' / *The History of the Rebellion and Civil Wars in England, by Edward Earl of Clarendon: Also, his Life, Written by Himself,* 2 volumes (Oxford: Oxford University Press, 1843), I, p. 533.

6   'he had a memory . . . dexterity and addresse' / *Characters from the Histories and Memoirs of the Seventeenth Century,* ed. D. Nichol Smith (Oxford: Clarendon Press, 1918), p. 94.

6   'Ther neede no more be sayd . . . dexterity . . .' / Ibid., p. 153.

6   'temper and spirit' / *Clarendon: Selections,* ed. G. Huehns (London: Oxford University Press, 1955), p. 374.

6   'posture of affairs' / Ibid., p. 375.

7   In the original text . . . five sentences / See Sir Thomas Elyot, *The Boke named the Gouernour,* 1531 (London: Dent/Everyman's Library, n.d. [1907]), p. 2.

7   Murray . . . photographs / K. M. Elisabeth Murray, *Caught in the Web of Words,* frontispiece and passim.

8   'for if words . . . POWERS' / Samuel Taylor Coleridge, Preface to *Aids to Reflection,* 1825, in *The Collected Works of Samuel Taylor Coleridge, Volume 9: Aids to Reflection,* ed. J. Beer (Bollingen Series LXXV; Princeton: Princeton University Press, 1993), p. 10.

8   'Parts of speech . . . human mind' / Ralph Waldo Emerson, *Nature,* 1836, in *Emerson: Essays and Lectures,* ed. J. Porte (New York: The Library of America, 1983), p. 24.

8   'iron determination . . . work' / K. M. Elisabeth Murray, *Caught in the Web of Words,* p. 289.

8   'the creative . . . embrace' / Samuel Taylor Coleridge, *Biographia Literaria,* 1817, in *The Collected Works of Samuel Taylor Coleridge, Volume 7: Biographia Literaria,* ed. J. Engell and W. J. Bate, 2 volumes (Bollingen Series LXXV; Princeton: Princeton University Press, 1983), II, p. 26.

8   'diverging . . . faculties' / Ibid.

8   'famous quotations' / K. M. Elisabeth Murray, *Caught in the Web of Words,* p. 223.

8   'crack-jaw . . . surgical words' / Ibid, pp. 221–222.

8   'acknowledge . . . times'/ Ibid., p. 223.

9   'to every man . . . *all* English' / *OED*, 'Corrected Reissue' (1933), I, p. xxvii.

9   'in the interest of English Literature' / K. M. Elisabeth Murray, *Caught in the Web of Words*, p. 158.

9   'He held . . . time'/ Ibid., p. 24.

9   'superfluous quotations' / Ibid., p. 274.

9   'the need . . . authors' / *OED*, 'Corrected Reissue' (1933), I, p. xxxii.

10 'of an unusually . . . nature' / *The Periodical*, Oxford University Press, XIII:143 (15 February 1928), p. 12.

10 'Bradley knew Shelley . . . rich poetry' / *The Collected Papers of Henry Bradley, With a Memoir by Robert Bridges,* 1928 (College Park, Maryland: McGrath Publishing Company, 1970), p. 24.

10 'the author . . . few Germans can' / Ibid., p. 34.

10 'tact' . . . William Sotheby / *Collected Letters of Samuel Taylor Coleridge,* ed. E. L. Griggs, 5 volumes (Oxford: Clarendon Press, 1966), II, p. 444.

10 When *The Times* . . . 'literary masterpiece' / K. M. Elisabeth Murray, *Caught in the Web of Words*, p. 224.

11 T. H. Green's phrase / *Works of Thomas Hill Green,* ed. R. L. Nettleship, 3 vols., 5th impression (London: Longmans, Green, 1906), III, p. 400.

11 'willed contrivance . . . readers' / Eric Griffiths, *The Printed Voice of Victorian Poetry* (Oxford: Clarendon Press, 1989), pp. 275–276.

11 'the Brute Actuality of things and facts' / Charles Sanders Peirce, 'A Neglected Argument for the Reality of God', 1908, *Selected Writings (Values in a Universe of Chance)*, ed. P. P. Wiener, 1958 (New York: Dover Publications, 1966), p. 359.

11 'a simultaneous . . . contrivance' / Griffiths, *Printed Voice of Victorian Poetry*, p. 275.

11 'this double character . . . words' / Ibid., p. 276.

11 'man of science . . . human speech' / K. M. Elisabeth Murray, *Caught in the Web of Words*, pp. 292–293.

11 'I am not . . . newspaper' / Ibid., p. 292.

12 'men who speak . . . not understand' / William Wordsworth, Preface to *Lyrical Ballads*, 1802, in *The Poems*, ed. J. O. Hayden, 2 volumes (Harmondworth: Penguin Books, 1977), I, p. 879.

12 'unfortunately slain . . . hand' / Thomas Hobbes, *Leviathan*, 1651, ed. C. B. Macpherson (Harmondsworth: Penguin Books, 1968), p. 718.

12 'give us . . . permit' / 'Direction to Readers for the Dictionary' in K. M. Elisabeth Murray, *Caught in the Web of Words*, p. 348 (Appendix II).

13   'the volunteer sub-editors . . . slips' / *OED*, 'Corrected Reissue' (1933), I, p. xvi.

13   'practical utility . . . direction' / Ibid., I, p. xxvii.

13   'hee unobserv'd . . . privat returnd' / This is the final line of *Paradise Regain'd*.

14   'who every one . . . before the Judge'/ John Bunyan, *The Pilgrim's Progress*, 1678, ed. N. H. Keeble (London: Oxford University Press, 1984), p. 79.

15   'the knavery . . . haunt' / Hobbes, *Leviathan*, p. 92.

15   'timorous, and supperstitious' / Ibid.

15   'exact . . . ambiguity' / Ibid., p. 116.

15   'Perspicuous Words' / Ibid.

15   'juggling . . . knavery' / Ibid., p. 176.

15   'the run of thought . . . different things' / *The Journals and Papers of Gerard Manley Hopkins*, ed. H. House and G. Storey (London: Oxford University Press, 1959), p. 119.

16   'that the scripture . . . english tonge' / William Tyndale, *The Obedience of a Christen Man and How Christen Rulers Ought to Governe*, Antwerp, 1528; facsimile edition (Amsterdam: Theatrum Orbis Terrarum / Norwood, N.J: Walter J. Johnson, 1977), f.p. xii[recto].

16   'The love . . . direction' / Trench, *English Past and Present*, p. 3.

16   'devoted . . . tradition' / *The Collected Papers of Henry Bradley*, p. 51.

16   'it is the privilege . . . possessed by it' / Coleridge, *On the Constitution of the Church and State*, p. 13.

17   'an interesting . . . institutions' / Ibid., p. lxi.

17   'die experienced . . . vollied glare' / Herman Melville, 'The March into Virginia, Ending in the First Manassas (July, 1861)', in *Battle-Pieces and Aspects of the War*, 1866 (New York: Da Capo, 1995), pp. 22–23.

18   'Every fact . . . never cease to be true' / K. M. Elisabeth Murray, *Caught in the Web of Words*, pp. 187, 366 n57.

18   'Cannon . . . thunder'd' / Alfred, Lord Tennyson, 'The Charge of the Light Brigade', *Tennyson: A Selected Edition*, ed. C. Ricks (Berkeley and Los Angeles: University of California Press, 1989), p. 509.

18   'the elixir . . . thousand years' / *A Dictionary of the English Language . . . by Samuel Johnson* (London, 1755) (London: Times Books, 1979), 'Preface', p. [9].

18   'the recognition . . . Queen Victoria' / K. M. Elisabeth Murray, *Caught in the Web of Words*, p. 289.

18   'national benefits' / Coleridge, *On the Constitution of the Church and State*, pp. 71–72.

19   as Peter Milward says / Milward, *A Commentary on 'The Wreck of the Deutschland'*, p. 106.

20   'that terrible . . . calamity' / John Henry Cardinal Newman, *Apologia Pro Vita Sua*, 1864, ed. M. J. Svaglic (Oxford: Clarendon Press, 1967), pp. 217–218.

Of Diligence and Jeopardy

21   the Wallis edition / *The New Testament, Translated by William Tyndale 1534: A Reprint of the Edition of 1534 with the Translator's Prefaces and Notes and the Variants of the Edition of 1525*, edited for the Royal Society of Literature by N. Hardy Wallis, with an introduction by the Right Honourable Francis Foot (Cambridge: Cambridge University Press, 1938).

22   Tyndale's Erasmian reply . . . 'than hee did' / See S. L. Greenslade, *The Work of William Tindale*, with an Essay on Tindale and the English Language by G. D. Bone (London and Glasgow: Blackie and Son, n.d [1938]), p. 61.

22   as A. W. Pollard argues / See *The Holy Bible: An exact reprint in Roman type, page for page, of the Authorized Version published in the year 1611*, with an introduction by Alfred W. Pollard (Oxford: Oxford University Press, 1985), p. 10.

22   Fry's 1862 reprint of Tyndale's New Testament / *The first New Testament printed in the English language (1525 or 1526), translated from the Greek by William Tyndale*, reproduced in facsimile from the Copy in the Baptist College, Bristol, with an Introduction by Francis Fry (Bristol: Printed for the Editor, 1862).

22   'The Prophete Jonas' / *'The Prophete Jonas', with an introduction before teachinge to understonde him and the right use also of all the Scripture, etc. etc., by William Tyndale*, reproduced in facsimile, 'to which is added Coverdale's version of Jonah', with an introduction by Francis Fry (London: Willis and Sotheran, 1863).

22   Mombert's . . . Pentateuch / *William Tyndale's Five Books of Moses, called The Pentateuch*, 1530, ed. J. I. Mombert, 1884 (Carbondale: Southern Illinois University Press, 1967).

22   'does not give the *letter* in facsimile' / Ibid, p. cii.

22   'the ready use . . . ends to be served' / Ibid, p. lxvii.

22   'in order to clarify the text' / *New Testament* (1534), ed. Wallis, p. xv.

22   'large body . . . students' / Ibid, p. xiii.

22   'dedicated . . . 450 years' / *Tyndale's New Testament, translated from the Greek by William Tyndale in 1534*. A modern-spelling edition, with an introduction by David Daniell (New Haven and London: Yale University Press, 1989), p. xxx.

23   'the processe, . . . the texte' / *The Pentateuch*, ed. Mombert, p. 3.

23   'the imperfection . . . accuracy' / Ibid, p. vii.

23   'It is uncomfortable . . . glossing' / *Tyndale's New Testament*, ed. Daniell, p. xxxi.

23   'There is . . . across the world' / Ibid, p. vii.

23   'Count it . . . fynnesshed' / *The New Testament: The Text of the Worms edition of 1526, in original spelling, as translated by William Tyndale*, edited for the Tyndale Society by W. R. Cooper, with a preface by David Daniell (London: The British Library, 2000), p. 554.

23   'Lyke as a sicke man . . . an whole man' / *New Testament* (1534), ed. Wallis, p. 310 (translating Luther, 'Vorrede auff die Epistel S. Pauli an die Römer', at VII, 2).

24   'the doctrine . . . unbelievable' / Paul Rigby, *Original Sin in Augustine's Confessions* (Ottawa: University of Ottawa Press, 1987), p. 1.

24   'there is . . . unreality' / St Augustine, *Enchiridion, or Manual to Laurentius concerning Faith, Hope and Charity*, trans., with an introduction and notes, by E. Evans (London: The Society for Promoting Christian Knowledge, 1953), p. xxiii.

24   'gredie to do euell' / *New Testament* (1534), ed. Wallis, p. 326.

24   'without faith' . . . 'with oute . . . God' / *The Pentateuch*, ed. Mombert, p. 385; *New Testament* (1534), ed. Wallis, p. 302.

24   'when a man . . . cannot' / St Augustine, *The Problem of Free Choice [De Libero Arbitrio]*, trans. D. M. Pontifex (Westminster, Md.: Newman Press, 1955), p. 192.

24   'le mal . . . le serf-arbitre' / Paul Ricoeur, *Le Conflit des interprétations: essais d'herméneutique* (Paris: Éditions du Seuil, 1969), p. 281.

24   'grace and apostleshyppe' / *New Testament* (1534), ed. Wallis, p. 319.

24   'terrible curving in on itself' / *Luther's Works, Volume 25: Lectures on Romans*, 1515–1516, ed. J. Pelikan, H. C. Oswald and H. T. Lehmann (St Louis: Concordia Publishing House, 1972), p. 346.

24   'We never . . . salvation' / Paul Ricoeur, '"Original Sin": A Study in Meaning,' trans. P. McCormick, in *The Conflict of Interpretations:*

Essays in Hermeneutics, ed. D. Ihde (Evanston, Ill.: Northwestern University Press, 1974), p. 286.

25   'the involuntariness . . . voluntary' / Ibid.

25   'all the synne . . . frailte' / Tyndale, '*The Prophete Jonas*', A iiii[recto] ('W. T. Vnto the Christian Reader').

25   'ouermoch . . . vnchristenlye' / *The Pentateuch,* ed. Mombert, p. 396.

25   'the dampnacion . . . ceremonies' / *New Testament* (1534), ed. Wallis, p. 399.

25   'the Idolatrie . . . imaginacion' / *The Pentateuch,* ed. Mombert, p. 165.

25   'dyed in the faith' / Ibid, p. 293.

25   (though the anonymous . . . not be his) / See Erasmus, *Enchiridion militis Christiani: An English Version,* ed. A. M. O'Donnell (Oxford: Oxford University Press for the Early English Text Society, 1981), pp. xlix–liii.

25   'some affections . . . doutfull' / Ibid., p. 68.

25   'These affections . . . resemble' / Ibid.

25   'after so lo[n]ge . . . teachi[n]ge' / William Tyndale, *The Obedience of a Christen Man and How Christen Rulers Ought to Governe*, Antwerp, 1528; facsimile edition (Amsterdam: Theatrum Orbis Terrarum / Norwood, N.J: Walter J. Johnson, 1977), p. xxiii.

26   yf christes . . . yf we be not all perfecte y[e] fyrst daye' / Ibid., p. xxiii[verso]. I would wish to indicate a few details, in the introduction to the present volume, which strike me as being 'not all perfecte'. These objections become, in my usage, matters of mere 'worldly busynesse' and perhaps do an injustice to the editor whose argument, if I read aright its 'True Christianity always releases' (*Tyndale's New Testament,* ed. Daniell, p. xxviii) (that is, as a statement, not a paraphrase), is able to give to Tyndale's doctrine a degree of assent which my own argument lacks. It is equally the case, however, that Tyndale, in his 1526 colophon 'To the Reder', invited correction of 'ought . . . oversene thorowe negligence' (*New Testament* [1526], ed. W. R. Cooper, p. 554), and these suggestions could perhaps be offered and received in that spirit. There appears to be no authority for *Enchiridion militis Christi* (pp. viii, xvii) as the title of Erasmus's book; the final word should be *Christiani.* The 'Translators to the Reader' preface of the 1611 Bible is not really 'difficult to find' (x); it is included in the Oxford University Press 'Exact Reprint in Roman Type' of 1833 which was reproduced and reissued in 1985. It is not strictly true to say that 'Black letter was the standard, indeed the only, printing type from Gutenberg and

Caxton until the later sixteenth century' (xiv). In Tyndale's
Pentateuch (1530) only Genesis and Numbers are printed in black-
letter; the three remaining books are in roman. In the revised edition
(1534) Genesis itself is reset in roman.

26 'the ring of Establishment authority,' *Tyndale's New Testament,* ed.
Daniell, p. xxiv.

26 'In their new . . . English' / Ibid., p. viii.

27 'Tyndale was not a committee' / Ibid., p. xxviii.

27 'Tyndale's . . . history', etc. / Ibid., p. vii.

27 'has a short . . . works' / Ibid., p. xxxii.

27 'the significance . . . craftsman' / Ibid., p. xxiii.

27 'the excellence . . . praised' / Norman Davis, *William Tyndale's English
of Controversy,* The Chambers Memorial Lecture delivered at The
University College, London, March 4, 1971 (London: H. K. Lewis for
The University College, 1971), p. 3.

28 'the Apostle . . . Bible' / *The Pentateuch,* ed. Mombert, p. vii.

28 'Tyndale . . . all humanity' / *Tyndale's New Testament,* ed. Daniell,
p. xxviii.

28 'bloudy . . . heritike' / Tyndale, *Obedience,* pp. xxiiii, xxiii^verso.

28 'when all . . . person . . .' / *The Pentateuch,* ed. Mombert, p. 161.

28 'goodly lawes of loue' / Ibid, p. 164.

28 'the edyfyi[n]ge . . . beleve)' / *New Testament* (1526), ed. W. R. Cooper,
p. 555.

28 'Latin-inspired . . . classes' / *Tyndale's New Testament,* ed. Daniell,
p. xxviii.

29 'If literature . . . importance' / John Davy Hayward, *Prose Literature
Since 1939,* Arts in Britain, Pamphlet No. 5 (London: Longmans,
Green & Co. for The British Council, 1947), p. 47.

29 'The Authorised Version . . . "trouble"' / Ibid., p. xxviii.

29 'incomparable . . . gentlemen' / *Donne's Sermons: Selected Passages,*
with an Essay by Logan Pearsall Smith (Oxford: Clarendon Press,
1919), p. xxxvi (editor's introduction).

29 'The opinions . . . British Council' / Hayward, *Prose Literature*: standard official disclaimer.

29 'Cleaue vnto . . . storye' / *The Pentateuch,* ed. Mombert, p. 162.

29 'The litterall . . . spirituall' / Tyndale, *Obedience,* p. cxxxiiii^verso.

29 'Sublime . . . perfection' / *Tyndale's New Testament,* ed. Daniell, pp.
xiv, ix, x.

30 'committees . . . ears' / Ibid., p. viii.

30 'the vivid . . . Hebrews show' / Ibid., pp. xviii, viii, xvii, x, xvii, xxvii, xx, xxvii.

30 'wonderful . . . reasoning' / Ibid., pp. xxi, xxiii.

30 'accessible Tyndale' / Ibid., p. xxvii.

30 'the laye people' / *The Pentateuch,* ed. Mombert, p. 3.

31 'impossible . . . tonge' / Ibid., p. 3.

31 'a boke . . . handes' / Ibid, p. 517.

31 'I thynke . . . brede of the soule' / *New Testament* (1534), ed. Wallis, p. 293.

31 'the old punctuation . . . clause' / G. D. Bone in Greenslade, *The Work of William Tindale,* p. 61.

31 'the moare . . . it is' / *New Testament* (1534), ed. Wallis, p. 293.

31 'Tyndale understood . . . along' / *Tyndale's New Testament,* ed. Daniell, p. xxi.

31 'dragged through . . . sorrows . . .' / St Augustine, *Enchiridion,* p. 24.

31 'led, through . . . sufferings . . .' / *St. Augustine: Confessions and Enchiridion,* trans. and ed. A. C. Outler (London: SCM Press, 1955), p. 354.

32 'uncovered' / *Tyndale's New Testament,* ed. Daniell, p. vii.

32 Leviticus 18 . . . every instance / See *The Pentateuch,* ed. Mombert, pp. 350–352.

32 'With modernised . . . it once was' / *Tyndale's New Testament,* ed. Daniell, p. vii.

32 The ne- / we . . . Nouember. ' / *Historical Catalogue of Printed Editions of the English Bible 1525–1961,* revised and expanded from the edition of T. H. Darlow and H. F. Moule, 1903, ed. A. S. Herbert (London: British and Foreign Bible Society, 1968), p. 6.

32 'There is no . . . Pater' / G. D. Bone in Greenslade, *The Work of William Tindale,* pp. 67–68.

32 'writing . . . wanted' / Davis, *William Tyndale's English of Controversy.*

33 'though we read . . . nothinge at all' / *The Pentateuch,* ed. Mombert, p. 7 ('A prologe shewinge the vse of the scripture').

33 'It is not . . . oure eyes . . .' / Ibid.

33 'ydle . . . wordes' / Ibid.

33 'in manye . . . playne ynough etc' / *New Testament* (1534), ed. Wallis, p. 3.

33 'equitie . . . dealing' / A. C. Southern, ed., *Elizabethan Recusant Prose 1559–1582* (London: Sands and Co., n.d. [1950], p. 154; Robert

Southwell, *An Humble Supplication to Her Maiesty,* 1591, ed. R. C. Bald (Cambridge: Cambridge University Press, 1953), p. 3.

34 'to put . . . another' / *OED,* Second Edition (1989), I, p. 576, citations: 'apply'.

34 'that we maye . . . sores' / *The Pentateuch,* ed. Mombert, p. 7.

34 'brethren . . . fayth' / *New Testament* (1534), ed. Wallis, p. 3.

34 'the weake stomackes' / Ibid.

34 'that since . . . we live in' / 'A "New Look" for the Good Book', press release issued by the REB Office, Oxford University Press, June 8, 1989, pp. 1–2.

34 'bloudy' / Tyndale, *Obedience,* f. xxiv.

34 'think tank' / REB press release, June 8, 1989.

34 'even . . . tirantes' / Tyndale, *'The Prophete Jonas',* A iii^{verso}.

35 'process . . . text' / See *The Pentateuch,* ed. Mombert, p. 3.

35 'terreble . . . tre[m]bled at' / Ibid., p. 521.

35 'for then wee . . . damnacion' / *The First and Second Prayer Books of Edward VI,* with an introduction by the Right Reverend E. C. S. Gibson, Bishop of Gloucester (London: Dent / Everyman's Library, 1910), p. 215.

35 'When my wife . . . worthily' / REB Press Release, June 8, 1989.

35 'leatherex . . . blocking' / 'The Design of the Revised English Bible', press release issued by the REB Office, Oxford University Press, June 29, 1989, p. 2.

35 'yf wee receyue . . . unworthely' / *First and Second Prayer Books of Edward VI,* p. 215.

35 'yf they . . . ordinaunces' / *The Pentateuch,* ed. Mombert, p. 517.

35 'The Kingdom . . . country' / Karl Barth, *The Epistle to the Romans,* 1918, trans. E. C. Hoskyns, Sixth Edition (London: Oxford University Press, 1933), p. 263.

35 'The Gospel . . . plead' / Ibid., p. 38.

36 'If the Bible's . . . their congregations' / REB press release, June 8, 1989, p. 1.

36 'The revision . . . possible' / *The Revised English Bible with Apocrypha* (Oxford and Cambridge: at the University Presses, 1989), Introduction to the New Testament, p. iv.

36 'The translators . . . all the time' / Ibid., p. iii.

36 'Fields . . . Benjamin . . .' / Ibid., p. 687 (Jeremiah, 32:44).

37 'each sentence . . . uppermost' / G. D. Bone in Greenslade, *The Work of William Tindale,* p. 61.

37   'kepe myne ordinaunces' / *The Pentateuch,* ed. Mombert, p. 354.

37   'guiding principle ... English' / *REB,* Introduction to the Old Testament, p. xvii.

37   'He was a prisoner ... territory' / Gordon Rupp, 'Sermon preached at the Commemoration of Benefactors', *Emmanuel College* [Cambridge] *Magazine, Quatercentenary Issue 1584: 1984* (Cambridge: Printed for the College, 1984), p. 24.

37   'was a great ... melt away ...' / Ibid.

37   'Me[n] shal bye ... Beniamin ...' / *The Geneva Bible,* a facsimile of the 1560 edition (Madison: University of Wisconsin Press, 1969).

37   'archaisms ... terms' / *REB,* Introduction to the New Testament, p. iv.

37   'field at Anathoth' / Jeremiah, 32:8–9.

38   'processe ... texte' / *The Pentateuch,* ed. Mombert, p. 4.

38   'it is read ... out loud' / REB press release, June 8, 1989, p. 3.

38   'a living tool' / Ibid.

38   'the circumstances before and after' / *New Testament* (1534), ed. Wallis, p. 3 ('W. T. Vnto the Reader').

38   'Conscientious ... Bible' / REB press release, June 8, 1989.

38   'For to every man ... business ...' / *The Oxford English Dictionary,* 12 volumes (Oxford: Clarendon Press, 1933), I, p. xxvii.

38   'For the domain ... business ...' / *The Oxford English Dictionary,* Second Edition, 20 volumes (Oxford: Clarendon Press, 1989), I, p. xxiv.

38   'historical principles' / The original title was *A New English Dictionary on Historical Principles.*

39   'The office ... another' / Charles Dickens, *Great Expectations* (Oxford: Oxford University Press, 1993), p. 222.

39   'The Joint Committee ... Mary Stewart' / REB press release, June 8, 1989, p. 3.

39   'due humility' / D. Coggan, 'Preface to the Revised English Bible', *The Revised English Bible with Apocrypha* (Oxford and Cambridge: at the University Presses, 1989), p. ix.

39   'intelligibility' / Ibid., p. viii.

39   'wide range ... backgrounds' / Ibid.

40   'bycause ... besyed' / Erasmus, *Enchiridion militis Christiani,* pp. 14–15.

40   'temporall ... princes' / Ibid.

40   'the besynesse of the world' / Ibid.

41   'fluent ... appearance' / REB press release, June 8, 1989.

42   'it is better ... ma[n]' / Tyndale, *Obedience,* p. xxxiii[verso].

43	'bondage . . . inuencions' / *New Testament* (1534), ed. Wallis, p. 457.
43	'The Gospel . . . own sake' / Barth, *The Epistle to the Romans,* pp. 38–39.
43	'captiuite of ceremonies' / *New Testament* (1534), ed. Wallis, p. 399.
43	'affirmation of resurrection' / Barth, *The Epistle to the Romans,* p. 39.

Keeping to the Middle Way

45	Robert Burton / Burton's *Anatomy of Melancholy* was first published in Oxford in 1621. Cited here is the Clarendon Edition, based on a complete collation of the six seventeenth-century editions and published in six volumes by the Clarendon Press, Oxford, 1989–2001. Volumes 1–3 (Text) were edited by Thomas C. Faulkner, Nicholas K. Kiessling and Rhonda L. Blair, with an introduction by J. B. Bamborough; Volumes 4–6 (Commentary, together with biobibliographical and topical indexes) were edited by J. B. Bamborough and Martin Dodsworth.
45	'Divine' and 'schollar' / Burton, *Anatomy,* I, pp. 20, 11.
45	'It is most true . . . workes' / Ibid., p. 13.
46	'tug between two interests' / William Empson, *The Structure of Complex Words,* 1951, Third Edition (London: Chatto and Windus, 1977), p. 2.
46	'unrighteous subtleties' / Burton, *Anatomy,* III, p. 351.
46	'mad pranks' / Ibid., p. 343.
46	Ramist 'fad' / Walter J. Ong, S.J., *Ramus, Method, and the Decay of Dialogue: From the Art of Discourse to the Art of Reason* (Cambridge, Mass.: Harvard University Press, 1958), p. 315.
46	Though Burton . . . the work itself / See Burton, *Anatomy,* I, p. 11.
47	although Ramus . . . once / Ibid., VI, p. 409: *Biobibliography,* RAMUS.
47	'Divines use . . . commonly best' / Burton, *Anatomy,* I, p. 11.
47	'the composition . . . Schollar' / Ibid.
47	a priest of the Ecclesia Anglicana / Ibid., I, p. 20.
47	no taste for 'controversie' / Ibid., I, p. 21 *et seq.*
47	Whitgift's . . . *Admonition* / *Studies in Richard Hooker: Essays Preliminary to an Edition of His Works,* ed. W. Speed Hill (Cleveland and London: Case Western Reserve University, 1972), p. 16.
47	Jewel's *Apologie* . . . Hooker's *Ecclesiastical Politie* / John Jewel, Bishop of Salisbury, *An Apologie, or aunswer in defence of the Church of*

England . . . Newly set forth in Latine, and nowe translated into Englishe, London, 1562 (Amsterdam: Theatrum Orbis Terrarum, 1972); John Whitgift, *Answer to the Admonition* (1572); Richard Hooker, *Of the Lawes of Ecclesiasticall Politie* (1593).

47 'The *medium* is best' / Burton, *Anatomy,* III, p. 394.

47 'sobriety . . . God' / Ibid., p. 361.

47 'keepe . . . diligence' (Proverbs 4:23 / Ibid, p. 434.

48 Tertullian's *regula . . . irreformabilis* / Tertullian, *De virginibus velandis,* cited (in English) by Hooker in *Lawes,* III, 10.7: 'The rule of faith, saith Tertullian, is but one and that a lone immoveable, and impossible to be framed or cast anew'. *The Folger Library Edition of the Works of Richard Hooker,* ed. W. Speed Hill, 7 volumes (Cambridge, Mass.: Harvard University Press, 1977–1998), I, p. 244; II, p. 586.

48 Though Hooker . . . 'like circumstances' / Hooker, *Works,* I, pp. 244–245.

48 'oftentimes . . . Mercy' / John Donne, *Essays in Divinity,* ed. H. Gardner (Oxford, at the Clarendon Press, 1952), p. 91.

49 'an horrour . . . paynfull deth' / *The Yale Edition of the Works of St. Thomas More,* 14 volumes (New Haven and London: Yale University Press, 1963–1985), XII, pp. 277, 281 *(A Dialogue of Comfort Against Tribulation).*

49 J. R. Knott . . . detail / John R. Knott, *Discourses of Martyrdom in English Literature, 1563–1694* (Cambridge: Cambridge University Press, 1993), pp. 80 n105, 46 n45.

49 Warren Wooden / Warren W. Wooden, *John Foxe* (Boston: Twayne Publishers, 1983).

49 'persecucion for the fayth' / More, *Works,* XII, p. 292.

49 'No greater . . . religion' / Burton, *Anatomy,* III, p. 366.

49 'It is incredible . . . these many yeares' / Ibid.

49 'even all those . . . true regenerate man' / Ibid., p. 29.

50 'loose . . . in all kingdomes' / Ibid., p. 396.

50 'absorbed . . . thinking' / John Donne, *The Divine Poems,* ed. H. Gardner (Oxford: Clarendon Press, 1952; reprinted from corrected sheets, 1959), p. xxi n1.

50 Hooker . . . 'distempered affections' / Hooker, *Works,* I, p. 302.

50 'inordinate melancholies . . . dejections of spirit' / *The Sermons of John Donne,* ed. (with introductions and critical apparatus) George

R. Potter and Evelyn M. Simpson, 10 volumes (Berkeley and Los Angeles: University of California Press, 1953–1962), V, pp. 283–284.

50   Burton . . . to divert it / Burton, *Anatomy*, III, pp. 351, 427.

50   'We are naturally . . . impedime[n]t or let' / Hooker, *Works,* I, pp. 96–97.

50   'our manifolde sinnes and wickednes' / *The Prayer-Book of Queen Elizabeth,* 1559 (London: Griffin Farran & Co., 1890), p. 42.

51   'the loue . . . dulie ordered' / Hooker, *Works,* II, p. 113.

51   'to thintent . . . co[m]mon profit' / Jewel, *Apologie,* p. 17^{recto}.

51   'ye multitude of idle cerimones' / Ibid., p. 16^{verso}.

51   'common advise . . . publiquely done' / Hooker, *Works,* II, p. 116.

51   'any blinde . . . common prayer' / Ibid.

51   'all the good . . . the new' / Jewel, *Apologie,* p. 17^{recto}.

51   'the vulgar sort amongst you' / Hooker, *Works,* I, p. 14.

51   'the gullish commonalty' / Burton, *Anatomy,* III, p. 351.

51   'may appere . . . *Res plebeia'* / Sir Thomas Elyot, *The Boke named the Gouernour,* 1531 (London: Dent / Everyman's Library, n.d. [1907]), p. 2.

52   'to appease . . . appeasyng of the same' / *The First and Second Prayer Books of Edward VI* (London: Dent / Everyman's Library, 1910), p. 5.

52   I [the melancholic] am . . . restored in good time / Burton, *Anatomy,* III, p. 441.

53   Calvin's magnanimity / *The Institution of Christian Religion,* Written in Latine by M. John Calvine and translated into English according to the authors last edition by Thomas Norton (London: Vautrollier, for Toy, 1578), pp. 100–100^{verso} [II: 2, 15].

53   'Of marueilous . . . threescore yeares with them' / Hooker, *Works,* I, p. 76.

53   'diligent observuer . . . vulgar folly' / Ibid., II, p. 18.

53   'It is a wonder . . . [further into the dark]' / Burton, *Anatomy,* III, pp. 355–356.

54   'Apparitions . . . Darknesse' / See Hobbes, *Leviathan,* ed. C. B. Macpherson (Harmondsworth: Penguin Books, 1968), pp. 91–93.

54   'mu[n]grel *Democratia* / *The Works of Thomas Nashe,* ed. R. B. McKerrow, 5 volumes (London: Sidgwick and Jackson, 1910), III, p. 168.

54   'For that which is common . . . no mans' / Burton, *Anatomy,* I, p. 88.

54   'That which is . . . despised' / Nashe, *Works,* II, p. 166.

54   'Sheepe demolish . . . &c' / Burton, *Anatomy,* I, p. 55.

54 More's protest in *Utopia* / *The Utopia of Sir Thomas More*, ed. J. H. Lupton (Oxford: Clarendon Press, 1895), pp. 51–56.

54 'vnder-hand cloaking . . . pretences' / Nashe, *Works*, I, p. 220.

54 'pretences . . . poore' / Donne, *Sermons*, III, p. 363.

54 'censorys' . . . commyn wele' / Thomas Starkey, *A Dialogue Between Pole and Lupset*, ed. T. F. Mayer (London: Royal Historical Society, 1989), pp. 103, 136.

54 'to translate . . . action' / Alistair Fox and John Guy, *Reassessing the Henrician Age: Humanism, Politics, and Reform, 1500–1550* (Oxford: Blackwell, 1986), p. 51.

55 'to insist . . . motes in the Sun' / Burton, *Anatomy*, I, p. 55.

55 'that as *Salust* . . . fingers end' / Ibid., p. 79. The ascription to Sallust is—on scholarly authority—incorrect. See Burton, *Anatomy*, IV, p. 122 (Commentary).

55 'not only . . . salvation' / William Randolf Mueller, *The Anatomy of Robert Burton's England* (Berkeley: University of California Press, 1952).

55 *Commune Bonum*/Nashe, *Works*, III, p. 168.

55 *Bonum simplex* of Augustine / Donne, *Sermons*, V, p. 287.

55 When I behold . . . of the one or of the other / Hooker, *Works*, II, p. 342.

56 'our narrow . . . looks farther' / Donne, *Sermons*, VIII, p. 274.

56 '*spiritus vertiginis* . . . not that I do so' / Ibid., X, p. 56.

56 'spirituall wantonnesse' / Ibid., III, p. 353.

56 'a spirituall drunkenesse . . . themselves' / Burton, *Anatomy*, I, p. 65.

57 'increase' . . . even the 'sumptuous' / Nashe, *Works*, III, pp. 145; II, pp. 28–32; III, pp. 148–149, 171.

57 'profligated . . . bankerupt' / Ibid., III, pp. 168, 149.

57 He contrives to show . . . 'neuer mentions it' / Ibid., p. 6.

57 'it is the function . . . the truest' / Cited in *The Yale Edition of the Works of St. Thomas More*, XIII, pp. lxxix–lxxx.

57 'exuberant fertility and abundance' / Ibid.

57 as Burton said of Lucian / See Burton, *Anatomy*, III, p. 374.

57 'ferall vices' / Ibid., I, p. 84.

58 'whole catalogue . . . any thing' / Hooker, *Works*, III, pp. 178, 212.

58 'gallantry . . . preferred' / Burton, *Anatomy*, I, pp. 5, 54.

58 'boiles of the common-wealth' / Ibid., p. 76.

58 'expert . . . poore' / Donne, *Sermons*, VI, p. 304.

58 'rubbish menialty' / Nashe, *Works*, III, p. 183.

58 'the more ignorant . . . people' / Hobbes, *Leviathan*, p. 175.

58   'dirty people of no name' / Edward Hyde (Edward, Earl of Clarendon), *A Brief View and Survey of . . . Mr. Hobbes His Leviathan* (London, 1674), in *Early Responses to Hobbes*, edited by G. A. J. Rogers, 6 volumes (New York and London: Routledge / Thoemmes Press, 1996), p. 320.

58   'I am one of the common people' / Cited by K. Thomas, 'Social Origins of Hobbes's Political Thought,' in *Hobbes Studies*, ed. K. C. Brown (Oxford: Blackwell, 1965), p. 200.

58   'my fathers house . . . in the Land' / John Bunyan, *Grace Abounding to the Chief of Sinners*, 1666, ed. R. Sharrock (Oxford: Clarendon Press, 1962), p. 5.

58   'Grace . . . to the flesh' / Ibid.

59   'the brilliant . . . energy' / Wyndham Lewis, *Time and Western Man* (London: Chatto and Windus, 1927), p. 123.

59   *'Mundus furiosus'* / Burton, *Anatomy*, I, p. 45.

59   *ataxia* / Ibid., p. 68.

59   'so many . . . whirlegigs' / Nashe, *Works*, III, p. 178.

59   'king of fishes' / Ibid., p. 149.

59   'light friskin of . . . witte' / Ibid., p. 151.

59   'extemporean stile' / Burton, *Anatomy*, I, p. 17.

59   'intelligence . . . at bay' / Ezra Pound, 'Rémy de Gourmont', in Ezra Pound, *Selected Prose, 1909–1965*, ed. W. Cookson (London: Faber, 1973), p. 386.

59   'may wee not . . . *hipocritis*' / Nashe, *Works*, I, p. 22.

59   'I cannot forbid . . . idle text' / Ibid., pp. 154–155.

60   'melancholy men . . . *excutiat*' / Burton, *Anatomy*, I, p. 24.

60   'CAVETE FAELICES' / Ibid., III, p. 446.

60   'expertus . . . satis' / Ibid., I, p. 14; II, p. 8; III, p. 395.

60   'fleshly minded . . . vpon him' / Nashe, *Works*, I, pp. 201–202.

60   'We [devils] . . . burne them' / Ibid., p. 218.

60   'Their [pagan philosophers] . . . Hell fire' / Burton, *Anatomy*, I, p. 30.

60   'naked to the worlds mercy' / Ibid., p. 34.

60   'wandering . . . absurdities' / Hobbes, *Leviathan*, p. 117.

61   'Patience . . . of the minde' / Sir William Cornwallis, *Discourses upon Seneca the Tragedian*, London, 1601; a facsimile reproduction, ed. R. H. Bowers (Gainesville, Fla.: Scholars' Facsimiles & Reprints, 1952), p. H4^{recto}.

61   'In summe . . . past cause' / Hobbes, *Leviathan*, p. 96.

61   *'effudi . . . meus'* / Burton, *Anatomy*, I, p. 17.

61   'For if . . . let them runne' / Hobbes, *Leviathan,* p. 194.

61   'God speaks . . . *soluta*' / Donne, *Sermons,* II, p. 50.

61   'For he . . . mans life' / Burton, *Anatomy,* III, pp. 409, 422.

62   *stultus* and its cognates / Ibid., I, e.g., pp. 12, 25, 26, 28, 29, 31, 31, 32, 34,
        41, 48, 54, 56, 57, 58, 60, 62, 63, 65, 99, 100, 101, 102, 103, 104, 105, 111.

62   'close & couert dealing' / More, *Works,* II, pp. xcvi, 82.

62   'What they call . . . like a foole' / *The Oxford English Dictionary,*
        Second Edition, 20 volumes (Oxford: Clarendon Press, 1989), XVI,
        p. 989.

62   'We must make . . . in this kinde' / Burton, *Anatomy,* III, pp. 424,
        443, 416.

62   'Extemporean . . . affected' / Ibid., I, p. 12.

63   *Be not solitary, be not idle* / Ibid., III, p. 445.

63   This likewise . . . to enjoy it / Ibid., III, p. 334.

63   'endlesse . . . abruptlie' / Nashe, *Works,* I, p. 245.

63   'praecipitate, ambitious age' / Burton, *Anatomy,* I, p. 9.

63   'Be styll . . . I am God' / Psalm 46:10 (*Geneva Bible,* 1560).

64   If any man . . . *'rise and walke'* / Burton, *Anatomy,* III, p. 444.

64   'confused company . . . speake' / Ibid., p. 471.

64   'smatterer' / Ibid.

64   'accurate musicke . . . phantasie' / Ibid., p. 443.

64   'equall musick . . . equall possession' / Donne, *Sermons,* VIII, p. 191.

64-65   'by . . . steppes . . . knowledge' / Hooker, *Works,* I, p. 74.

65   'the name . . . ambition' / Donne, *Sermons,* VIII, pp. 184–185.

65   'whether it be . . . in you' / Hooker, *Works,* I, p. 51.

65   'We must make . . . *ex vi morbi*' / Burton, *Anatomy,* III, p. 424.

65   'things doubtfull' / Hooker, *Works,* I, p. 50.

65   'a rule . . . our faith' / Donne, *Sermons,* VII, p. 262.

65   'inordinate melancholies . . . sinfull melancholy' / Donne, *Sermons,*
        V, pp. 283–284; p. 295; IV, p. 328; p. 329; VII, p. 269; III, p. 270.

66   He confesses . . . bring to it / See *John Donne: Biathanatos,* ed. E. W.
        Sullivan II (Newark: University of Delaware Press, 1984), p. 29.

66   Seale then . . . Everlasting night / Donne, *The Divine Poems,* pp. 48–49.

66   a commonplace found in More's *Utopia* / *The Utopia of Sir Thomas
        More,* p. 290.

66   It is, however, necessary . . . English translations / Though the 1611
        Old Testament has 'everlasting desolations', 'everlasting burnings' and
        'everlasting reproach', the epithet is largely an attribute of the power
        and majesty of God or of the rewards of the righteous. In the 1611

New Testament, the phrase 'everlasting life' occurs thirteen times, twelve of which are unchanged from Tyndale's translation of 1526. The most powerful common application may have been that of John 6:40, used in the Order for the Burial of the Dead in the first Edwardian Prayer Book of 1549 (but dropped from the revised forms), closely followed by the 'euerlasting lyfe', 'lyfe euerlasting' from the Ministration of Baptism and the Solemnization of Matrimony in the 1549, 1552, and 1559 Prayer Books.

67 'first, last, everlasting day' / 'The Anniversarie,' in John Donne, *The Elegies* and *The Songs and Sonnets,* ed. H. Gardner (Oxford: Clarendon Press, 1966), p. 71.

67 'most fearefull . . . Malediction' / John Donne, *Devotions upon Emergent Occasions*, ed. A. Raspa (Montreal and London: McGill–Queen's University Press, 1975), pp. 79–80.

67 The Gentils . . . very Essence / Donne, *Sermons,* VII, p. 272.

67 *Nox est . . . dormienda* / Catullus, 5.6.

67 *Nox tibi . . . dies* / Propertius, 2.15.24.

67 'turns from . . . associative magic' / Donne, *Sermons on the Psalms and Gospels,* ed. E. M. Simpson (Berkeley and Los Angeles: University of California Press, 1967), p. 26 (editor's introduction).

67 'A Nocturnall upon S. Lucies Day' / Donne, *Elegies* and *Songs and Sonnets,* pp. 84–85.

68 'Others commend . . . harpe' / Burton, *Anatomy,* III, p. 443.

68 *ad sanam mentem* / Ibid., p. 424.

68 'fierce with darke keeping' / Francis Bacon, *The Twoo Bookes of the Proficience and Advancement of Learning,* London, 1605; facsimile edition (Amsterdam: Theatrum Orbis Terrarum, 1970), *The first booke,* p. 21[recto].

68 'The power . . . glorie' / Hooker, *Works,* II, p. 425.

68 'rescu[ed] from degradation' / Edgar Wind, *Pagan Mysteries in the Renaissance* (London: Faber, 1958), p. 174.

68 Man receaued . . . able' / Calvin, *Institution,* p. 68[verso] (I: 15, 8).

69 Ever since *Euah* . . . tempted and tempting / Nashe, *Works,* II, p. 136.

69 'I am . . . contagious' / Donne, *Sermons,* IX, p. 311.

69 'our selves . . . destruction' / Donne, *Devotions upon Emergent Occasions,* p. 63.

69 'melancholy . . . 'tis all one' / Burton, *Anatomy,* I, p. 25.

69 'the whole . . . induction' / Ibid., p. 65.

69 Thy soule . . . expect and tarry / Ibid., III, p. 442.

70 'depart[ing] . . . treasured up' / Donne, *Sermons*, V, p. 289.
70 the 'harmonie . . . the other' / Bacon, *Twoo Bookes*, p. 20.

A Pharisee to Pharisees

The text of 'The Night' used in this study is that of *The Works of Henry Vaughan*, ed. L. C. Martin, 2 volumes (Oxford: Clarendon Press, 1914), pp. 522–523. The poem is as follows:

John 2.3 [3.2]

Through that pure *Virgin-shrine*,
That sacred vail drawn o'r thy glorious noon
That men might look and live as Glo-worms shine.
    And face the Moon:
    Wise *Nicodemus* saw such light   5
    As made him know his God by night.

    Most blest believer he!
Who in that land of darkness and blinde eyes
Thy long expected healing wings could see,
    When thou didst rise,   10
    And what can never more be done,
    Did at mid-night speak with the Sun!

    O who will tell me, where
He found thee at that dead and silent hour!
What hallow'd solitary ground did bear   15
    So rare a flower,
    Within whose sacred leafs did lie
    The fulness of the Deity.

    No mercy-seat of gold,
No dead and dusty *Cherub*, nor carv'd stone,   20
But his own living works did my Lord hold
    And lodge alone;
    Where *trees* and *herbs* did watch and peep
    And wonder, while the *Jews* did sleep.

Dear night! this worlds defeat;   25
The stop to busie fools; cares check and curb;
The day of Spirits; my souls calm retreat
    Which none disturb!
    Christs progress, and his prayer time;
    The hours to which high Heaven doth chime.   30

Gods silent, searching flight:
When my Lords head is fill'd with dew, and all
His locks are wet with the clear drops of night;
    His still, soft call;
    His knocking time; The souls dumb watch,   35
    When Spirits their fair kinred catch.

Were all my loud, evil days
Calm and unhaunted as is thy dark Tent,
Whose peace but by some *Angels* wing or voice
    Is seldom rent;   40
    Then I in Heaven all the long year
    Would keep, and never wander here.

But living where the Sun
Doth all things wake, and where all mix and tyre
Themselves and others, I consent and run   45
    To ev'ry myre,
    And by this worlds ill-guiding light,
    Erre more then I can do by night.

There is in God (some say)
A deep, but dazling darkness; As men here   50
Say it is late and dusky, because they
    See not all clear;
    O for that night! where I in him
    Might live invisible and dim.

72   Therefore he came under cover of darkness / See Edwyn Clement
    Hoskyns, *The Fourth Gospel*, ed. F. N. Davey, 2 volumes (London:

Faber, 1940), I, p. 226: 'darkness and night are in the Fourth Gospel sinister words . . . Nicodemus occupies a dangerous position betwixt and between; and this is suggested from the very beginning of the narrative'. See also Richard Ollard, *Clarendon and His Friends* (London: Oxford University Press, 1987), p. 69: in the spring of 1642 Edward Hyde deemed it prudent to visit Charles I 'only in the dark . . . upon emergent occasions'.

73   Like representatives . . . chop-logic upon it / See J. F. S. Post, *Henry Vaughan: The Unfolding Vision* (Princeton: Princeton University Press, 1982), pp. 202–203: 'Vaughan unfolds and develops a complex parallel between the Pharisee Nicodemus and himself that both establishes their "kinred" (I.36) connections and underscores their basic differences'. My suggestion is that we, as glossers and glozers, approach Vaughan's poem like well-meaning Pharisees. We may or may not see the light.

73   'to words and rhythms' / Frank Kermode, 'The Private Imagery of Henry Vaughan', in *The Review of English Studies*, New Series, Volume 1, Oxford, 1950, p. 206.

73   'his own . . . limited wisdom' / Post, *Henry Vaughan*, p. 203.

74   a 'bookish poet' / Kermode, 'Private Imagery', p. 206.

74   'the academic . . . a man to pray' / H. A. Williams, 'Theology and Self-Awareness', in *Soundings*, ed. A. R. Vidler (Cambridge: Cambridge University Press, 1963), p. 71.

74   'refuses . . . corrupt times' / Post, *Henry Vaughan*, p. 208.

74   Vaughan's embroilment . . . apocalyptic signs / Ibid., pp. 188–189.

74   'quickens to a palpable ecstasy' / E. C. Pettet, *Of Paradise and Light: A Study of Vaughan's 'Silex Scintillans'* (Cambridge: Cambridge University Press, 1960), p. 149.

75   'blest mosaic thorn' / *Hymns and Spiritual Songs for the Fasts and Festivals of the Church of England*, 1765, XXXII, in *The Collected Poems of Christopher Smart*, ed. N. Callan, 2 volumes (London: Routledge, 1949), II, p. 847.

75   'Others might expound . . . the text' / M. M. Mahood, *Poetry and Humanism*, Second Edition, 1950 (New York: W. W. Norton, 1970), p. 255.

76   In *Abr'hams* Tent . . . shady *Even* / Vaughan, *Works*, I, p. 404.

77   'One of the largest . . . magnetism' / Mahood, *Poetry and Humanism*, pp. 271–272.

77   'active commerce . . . existence' / Ibid.

77 'By 1650 . . . vanished' / L. L. Martz, *The Paradise Within: Studies in Vaughan, Traherne and Milton* (New Haven and London: Yale University Press, 1964), p. 13 n8.

78 'The logical . . . *Olives*' / Kermode, 'Private Imagery', p. 223.

78 'in these times . . . triall' / Vaughan, *Works*, p. 149.

78 'The *Sonne* . . . *Olives*' / Ibid., p. 138.

78 '*I write . . . presence of darknes*' / Ibid., p. 217.

79 're-creates . . . reality' / S. L. Bethell, *The Cultural Revolution of the Seventeenth Century,* second impression, 1951 (London: Dennis Dobson, 1963), p. 134.

79 Auden . . . angst / W. H. Auden, *New Year Letter* (London: Faber, 1941), pp. 35, 108.

80 'making our last . . . Nativity' / Sir Thomas Browne, *The Major Works,* ed. C. A. Patrides (Harmondsworth: Penguin Books, 1977), p. 284.

80 'rhyming' in a sense . . . sounds / Alice Goodman drew my attention to this.

80 'the creation . . . coincidence' / Sigurd Burckhardt, 'The Poet as Fool and Priest', in *English Literary History*, Volume 23, 1956, p. 281.

80 'union . . . extremes' / Mahood, *Poetry and Humanism*, p. 279.

80 'committed . . . hermeticism' / Kermode, 'Private Imagery', p. 208; see also Browne, *Major Works,* pp. 30, 103 n28.

80 'the troublesom . . . Rimeing' / in the prefatory note added in 1668 to *Paradise Lost.*

80 '*tagge his Verses*' / *Aubrey's Brief Lives*, ed. O. L. Dick (Harmondsworth: Penguin Books, 1972), p. 364.

80 'the childish . . . riming' / *Campion's Works*, ed. P. Vivian (Oxford: Clarendon Press, 1909), p. 37.

80 His own lyrics . . . contention / E.g., ibid., pp. 11, 13, 16, 17, 20, 22, 132, 140, 165, 172, 185 ['loue : moue']; 12, 14, 15, 22, 132, 161, 165, 168, 186 ['loue : proue']. And there are further instances.

80 'Rose-cheekt *Lawra*' / Ibid., pp. 50–51.

81 Changing shapes . . . loue / Ibid., p. 234.

81 'the light-darkness . . . Vaughan' / Bethell, *Cultural Revolution,* p. 157.

81-83 But in Vaughan . . . ('The Water-fall') / Vaughan, *Works,* pp. 7, 39, 398, 419, 423, 425–426, 434, 438–439, 449, 451–452, 466, 481, 488, 502, 511, 517, 519, 521, 524, 528, 529, 537.

83   to 'compose' . . . by authority' / Senses given in *The Oxford English Dictionary*, Second Edition, 20 volumes (Oxford: Clarendon Press, 1989).

83   'manufactured . . . has gone' / Pettet, *Of Paradise and Light*, p. 153.

84   'despite . . . into rapture' / Post, *Henry Vaughan*, p. 207.

84   'Lux est umbra Dei' / Browne, *Major Works*, pp. 71, 314 n50.

84   'adumbration' / Ibid.

84   'a thorough-going intellectual' / A. Rudrum, 'Some Remarks on Henry Vaughan's Secular Poems', in *Poetry Wales*, Volume 11, no. 2: *A Special Issue on Henry Vaughan*, p. 49.

85   '*Servus inutilis: peccator maximus*' / Vaughan's epitaph (1695), on his tombstone in Llansantffraed, Brecon. See F. E. Hutchinson, *Henry Vaughan: A Life and Interpretation* (Oxford: Clarendon Press, 1947), p. 240.

85   'contingency' / senses and dates of occurrence given in *OED*, Second Edition (1989).

85   'Dionysian' / *Henry Vaughan: The Complete Poems*, ed. A. Rudrum (New Haven and London: Yale University Press, 1981), p. 629 (editorial commentary).

85   'detached . . . with either' / Post, *Henry Vaughan*, p. 209.

86   'conversion . . . experience' / Kermode, 'Private Imagery', p. 206; see also Pettet, *Of Paradise and Light*, pp. 16–17.

86   'No one read . . . imagination' / Post, *Henry Vaughan*, p. 111.

86   'shining ring . . . intimated' / Pettet, *Of Paradise and Light*, p. 5.

86   light-darkness eschatology / In *Olor Iscanus* (1651), in his translation of 'Casimirus, Lib. 4. Ode 15', Vaughan employs 'light : *night*' at 11.13–14 where Sarbiewski's Latin does not require it. G. Hils, in his translation of the same ode, is both closer to the text and rather more surprising in his English word-finding, though one cannot make large claims for his skill. See Vaughan, *Works*, I, p. 88; Mathias Casimire Sarbiewski, *The Odes of Casimire*, trans. G. Hils (London, 1646); reprint edition, ed. M. S. Roestvig (Los Angeles: The Augustan Reprint Society [Publication no. 44], 1953), pp. 76–77. The point I wish to make is that Vaughan's 'light : *night*' is here mechanical, not metaphysical, and that 'The Night' regenerates the mere tag of 'Lib. 4, Ode 15' as well as the pretty conceit of 'To Amoret'.

86   'Christian theology . . . theology sweeps above it' / Walter J. Ong, S.J., *The Barbarian Within and Other Fugitive Essays and Studies* (New York: Macmillan, 1962), p. 104. See also Thomas Vaughan, *Lumen de*

Lumine ('When I seriously consider the system or fabric of this world
I find it to be a certain series, a link or chain which is extended . . .
from that which is beneath all apprehension to that which is above all
apprehension'), in *The Works of Thomas Vaughan,* ed. A. E. Waite
(London: Theosophical Publishing House, 1919), p. 269. This passage
is quoted in M. M. Mahood's admirable essay in her *Poetry and
Humanism,* pp. 279–280.

The Eloquence of Sober Truth

89 *Early Responses to Hobbes* / The six volumes boxed as *Early Responses
    to Hobbes* are reproduced in facsimile from their original editions,
    and each work is paged individually. They are here given their com-
    plete titles and listed by date of publication: John Bramhall, Bishop
    of Derry, *A Defence of True Liberty from Antecedent and Extrinsicall
    Necessity* (1655); George Lawson, *The Political Part of Mr Hobbs his
    Leviathan* (1657); William Lucy, Bishop of St David's, *Observations,
    Censures, and Confutations of Notorious Errours in Mr. Hobbs his
    Leviathan and other books* (1663); John Eachard, *Mr Hobb's State of
    Nature considered* (1672); Edward Hyde (Edward, Earl of Clarendon),
    *A Brief View and Survey of the Dangerous and Pernicious errors to
    Church and state in Mr. Hobbes's Leviathan* (1674); and Thomas
    Tenison, *The Creed of Mr Hobbes Examined* (1670), bound with pam-
    phlets by Robert Filmer, Seth Ward, Pierre Bayle et al. (1652–1738).

90 'a mighty . . . words' / George Watson, 'The Reader in Clarendon's
    History of the Rebellion', in *Review of English Studies* (New Series,
    Volume 25, no. 100, 1974), p. 398.

91 'this our imbecillitie' / *The Folger Library Edition of the Works of
    Richard Hooker,* ed. W. Speed Hill, 7 volumes (Cambridge, Mass.:
    Harvard University Press, 1977–1998), IV, p. 103.

91 'peaceful and lofty sentences' / A. P. D'Entrèves, *The Medieval
    Contribution to Political Thought* (London: Oxford University Press,
    1939), p. 89.

91 'diligent and distinct consideration' / Hooker, *Works,* IV, p. 101.

91 'subtiltie of Satan' / Ibid., V, p. 78 ('A Learned and Comfortable
    Sermon of the Certaintie and Perpetuitie of Faith in the Elect', 1585).

92 'works of nature . . . performed' / Ibid., I, p. 67.

92 'admirable dexteritie of wit' / Ibid., p. 3.

92   cannot be taken . . . respect / See W. P. J. Cargill Thompson, 'The Philosopher of the "Politic Society"', in *Studies in Richard Hooker: Essays Preliminary to an Edition of His Works*, ed. W. Speed Hill (Cleveland: Case Western Reserve University, 1972), pp. 14–15.

92   when Hooker . . . mince words / Hooker, *Works*, I, p. 76. See also *Studies in Richard Hooker*, ed. W. Speed Hill, p. 175.

92   '[his] attitude . . . censure' / Egil Grislis, 'The Hermeneutical Problem in Hooker', in *Studies in Richard Hooker*, ed. W. Speed Hill, p. 203.

92   Conscious as Hyde . . . if not his confusion / See Richard Ollard, *Clarendon and His Friends* (Oxford: Oxford University Press, 1988), pp. 111–112.

92   'may [not] loose . . . virtue' / See Watson, 'The Reader in Clarendon's *History of the Rebellion*', p. 403.

92   'seasonably and appositely' / *Characters from the Histories and Memoirs of the Seventeenth Century*, ed. D. Nichol Smith (Oxford: Clarendon Press, 1918), p. 94.

93   'cozen and deceave' / Ibid., p. 153.

93   The Earl of Strafford . . . 'pride' / See *Clarendon: Selections from 'The History of the Rebellion and Civil Wars' and 'The Life by Himself'*, ed. G. Huehns (London: Oxford University Press, 1955), p. 147.

93   'the late . . . Rebellion' / Clarendon, *Brief View*, pp. 56, 54.

93   'made his Defence . . . eloquence' / *Clarendon: Selections*, p. 137 (capitals as in First Edition, 1702, I, p. 173).

93   'deceitfull men . . . particulars' / Bramhall, *Defence*, p. 19.

93   [A] precedent . . . deliberation / Ibid., p. 47.

94   When he writ . . . all this night / Lucy, *Observations*, p. 6.

94   In Bramhall's . . . between them / See Bramhall, *Defence*, p. 14.

94   'changeth shapes in . . . particular' / Ibid., p. 104.

94   the common errors . . . desperation / See ibid., pp. 3, 7, 71, 74.

94   'descend . . . question' / Ibid., pp. 19, 139.

94   'take every word . . . Objections' / Lucy, *Observations*, p. 308.

94   'genuine sense' / Bramhall, *Defense*, p. 40.

94   'rip up . . . business' / Ibid., p. 158.

94   'voluntary' . . . genuine sense / Ibid., pp. 37–48.

95   'explicitly . . . loci' / Walter J. Ong, S.J., *Ramus, Method, and the Decay of Dialogue: From the Art of Discourse to the Art of Reason* (Cambridge, Mass.: Harvard University Press, 1958), p. 315.

95   Burton's . . . the indeterminate / See Robert Burton, *The Anatomy of Melancholy*, ed. T. C. Faulkner et al., 6 volumes (Oxford: Clarendon Press, 1989–2001), III, p. 458; *The Countesse of Pembrokes Arcadia, written by Sir Philippe Sidnei*, facsimile reproduction of the 1891 photographic facsimile of the original 1590 edition (Kent, Ohio: Kent State University Press, 1970), Book I, ch. 5.

95   'affections . . . in the other' / Bramhall, *Defence*, p. 4.

95   'inhaerent' 'vertue' / Thomas Hobbes, *Leviathan*, 1651, ed. C. B. Macpherson (Harmondsworth: Penguin Books, 1968), p. 75.

95   'this controversy . . . praedetermined to one' / Bramhall, *Defence*, p. 41.

96   'meer Logomachy' / Ibid., p. 130.

96   'true morall liberty . . . between us' / Ibid., p. 212.

96   'unfortunately . . . hand' / Hobbes, *Leviathan*, p. 718.

96   Hobbes's . . . Clarendon / E.g., Sidney, *Arcadia*, p. 269; Walter Ralegh, *The History of the World*, ed. C. A. Patrides (London: Macmillan, 1971), pp. 56–57 (on the character of Henry VIII); *Clarendon: Selections*, pp. 54–55 (on the character of Lord Falkland), pp. 200, 229 (on European reactions to the execution of Charles I).

96   'tautology' and 'wresting' / E.g., Lucy, *Observations*, pp. 354–355, 357, 365; Clarendon, *Brief View*, pp. 73, 75, 107.

97   'meer animosity', 'antipathy' / Bramhall, *Defence*, pp. 229, 200.

97   'melancholy', 'desperate imaginations' / Clarendon, *Brief View*, p. 179.

97   'very far from . . . *thoughts*' / Ibid., p. 12.

97   'terms of Art . . . the key' / Ibid., pp. 21–22.

97   to make 'Animadversions upon' / Lucy, *Observations*, facsimile title page (1663); Clarendon, *Brief View*, pp. 2, 5, 16, 59, 204, 231.

97   'Conster . . . no otherwise' / Hooker, *Works*, V, p. 165 ('A Learned Discourse of Justification . . .', 1586).

97   Father Ong . . . argument / See Walter J. Ong, S.J., *The Presence of the Word* (New Haven and London: Yale University Press, 1967), p. 87.

97   One would add . . . period / See Jean Mohl, *John Milton and His Commonplace Book* (New York: Ungar, 1969).

98   'this present . . . braine' / Hooker, *Works*, I, p. 83.

98   'Sophisters . . . multitude' / Bramhall, *Defence*, p. 249; see also pp. 157–158 ('Innovators and seditious Oratours, who are the true causes of the present troubles of Europe').

98	'Shakespeare' / See *Coriolanus*, Act II, Scene 3 ('many-headed multitude').
98	But how far . . . 1640s? / See John Ripley, *'Coriolanus' on Stage in England and America, 1609–1994* (Madison, Wis.: Farleigh Dickinson University Press, 1998), p. 343. Ripley finds no record of performance between 1609 and 1681 (an adaption by Nahum Tate).
98	'many headed multitude' / Sidney, *Arcadia*, p. 220.
98	from Horace's first *Epistle* / *The Oxford English Dictionary*, Second Edition (Oxford: Clarendon Press, 1989), citations: many-headed.
98	'natural ability or capacity' / Ibid., citations: genius.
98	'form . . . and model' / *Clarendon: Selections*, pp. 65–66.
98	'Sudden Glory . . . a signe of Pusillanimity' / Hobbes, *Leviathan*, p. 125.
98	his own negative . . . timidity / See *OED*, citations: pusillanimity.
98	'The Light . . . ambiguity' / Hobbes, *Leviathan*, p. 116.
98-99	even . . . bad odour / See *OED*, citations: snuff, vb.
99	'crafty ambitious persons' . . . purposes / Hobbes, *Leviathan*, pp. 91–93.
99	'our Senses' . . . true Religion / Ibid., p. 409. I have received enlightenment on this passage from an unpublished essay by Dr. Steve Bishop.
100	'for if . . . let them runne' / Hobbes, *Leviathan*, p. 194.
100	'the Holy Ghost . . . of language' / *The Sermons of John Donne*, ed. (with introductions and critical apparatus) George R. Potter and Evelyn M. Simpson, 10 volumes (Berkeley and Los Angeles: University of California Press, 1953–1962), VI, p. 55.
100	'to please . . . innocently' / Hobbes, *Leviathan*, pp. 101–102.
100	But living . . . myre / *The Works of Henry Vaughan*, ed. L. C. Martin, 2 volumes (Oxford: Clarendon Press, 1914), II, pp. 522–523.
101	Wilt thou . . . their doore? / John Donne, *The Divine Poems*, ed. H. Gardner (Oxford: Clarendon Press, 1952; reprinted from corrected sheets, 1959), p. 51.
101	'even as thou . . . mercy of thee' / *The Two Liturgies AD 1549 and AD 1552; with Other Documents Set Forth by Authority in the Reign of King Edward VI*, ed. J. Ketley (Cambridge, at the University Press, 1844), p. 471 (spelling regularized to the standard of 1844).
101	'the result . . . typography' / Ong, op. cit., p. 86.
101	the first recorded . . . *The Alchemist* / See *OED*, citations: register.
102	'subdue . . . transported with' / *Clarendon: Selections*, p. 19.

102	'uncharitableness' and 'ignorance' / Ibid., p. 51; Clarendon, *Brief View,* p. 91, taking up a phrase in Hobbes, *Leviathan,* p. 272.
102	'heat and animosity' . . . 'heat and passion' / Clarendon, *Selections,* p. 106.
102	'where that . . . dust and heat' / John Milton, *Selected Prose,* ed. C. A. Patrides (Harmondsworth: Penguin, 1974), p. 213.
102	'the incomparable Grotius' / Clarendon, *Brief View,* p. 141.
102	'the general . . . can be determined' / John Edward Sadler, *J. A. Comenius and the Concept of Universal Education* (London: Allen and Unwin, 1966), p. 188.
102	'exquisite reasons . . . demonstrative' / Milton, *Selected Prose,* p. 211.
102	'Rules of Arithmetic . . . experiment' / Clarendon, *Brief View,* p. 79.
102	'Etymologie' / Clarendon, *Brief View,* pp. 182, 204; Lucy, *Observations,* pp. 64, 280.
102	'the ambiguous . . . free' / Bramhall, *Defence,* p. 16.
102	'mist of words . . . his Structure' / Clarendon, *Brief View,* p. 26.
103	'the Liberty . . . monstrous Soveraign' / Ibid., pp. 55, 56.
103	'Property . . . precious term' / Ibid., p. 56.
103	'Occupancy' is 'a sacred title' / Lucy, *Observations,* p. 440.
103	'Lands and Goods' / Clarendon, *Brief View,* p. 107.
103	the Copies . . . King and People / Ibid., p. 110.
103	vindicate (a verb he favoured) / Ibid., pp. 37, 45, 223. See also p. 108, 'vindications', p. 244, 'vindicator'. See also *Selections,* ed. Huehns, pp. 1, 6, 8.
104	'exercise . . . understanding' / Clarendon, *Brief View,* pp. 16, 46, 185–186, 230.
104	'such inestimable . . . no name' / Ibid., pp. 319–320.
104	'a proper . . . speaking' / Ibid., p. 37.
104	'vindicate . . . oppress it' / Ibid.
104	'reflexion . . . purpose' / Ibid., p. 11.
105	the vision of the suffering servant / See Isaiah 53:2–5; Philippians 2:7–8.
105	'private' / Clarendon, *Brief View,* e.g., pp. 77, 79, 100, 105.
105	'ordain'd . . . acceptation' / Ibid., p. 22.
105	'that common . . . human life' / Ibid., p. 29.
105	'all the customes of the Nations' / Ibid., pp. 76–77.
105	'enormities . . . Tradition' / Ibid., p. 302.
105	Bramhall equates 'custome' . . . 'habits' / See Bramhall, *Defence,* p. 177.
105	'old truth . . . ancestors' / Ibid., p. 195.

105   For Lucy . . . *'custome'* / See Lucy, *Observations,* p. 75.

105   it is not . . . made legall / Robert Filmer, *Observations Concerning the Originall of Government* (in *Early Responses to Hobbes: Pamphlets*), p. 31 [actually 33].

106   'Disputes . . . stand for' / John Locke, *An Essay Concerning Human Understanding,* ed. P. H. Nidditch (Oxford: Clarendon Press, 1975), pp. 511–512.

106   The original sense . . . include each other / *OED,* citations: reduce.

107   'the end . . . the Hearer' / Locke, *Essay,* p. 405.

107   W. D. J. Carghill Thompson's . . . myth-making / See Thompson, 'The Philosopher of the "Politic Society"', p. 40.

107   'For as much . . . Person' / Bramhall, *Defence,* p. 47.

107   'Of such questions . . . circumstances' / Hooker, *Works,* I, p. 14.

107   'And also the same . . . circumstances' / *The Institution of Christian Religion, Written in Latine by M. John Calvine, and Translated into English according to the authors last edition, by Thomas Norton* (London: Thomas Vautrollier for Humfrey Toy, 1578), p. 623^{verso} [IV, 20.8].

108   Archbishop Whitgift . . . 1572–1573 / See V. J. K. Brook, *Whitgift and the English Church* (London: English Universities Press, 1957), pp. 33, 42–44.

108   More recently . . . pamphlets themselves / Ibid., p. 127.

108   *The Ecclesiastical Polity* . . . humility / Ibid., p. 152.

108   'The Church . . . proportionable' / Hooker, *Works,* I, p. 23.

109   where *T.H.* demands . . . respectively / Bramhall, *Defence,* p. 22.

109   The 'Schole-men' . . . etymology / Ibid., pp. 29, 152, 156, 158, 172–173, 198, 200, 226, 236.

109   'afterward . . . *confidence*' / Lucy, *Observations,* p. 130.

109   Hooker's 'proportionable' . . . 'respectively' / Hooker, *Works,* I, p. 23; Lucy, *Observations,* p. 130; Bramhall, *Defence,* p. 22.

110   John Newton of Olney / See *An Authentic Narrative of some Remarkable and Interesting Particulars in the Life of John Newton* [1764] (New York: Evert Duyckinck, 1806), e.g., pp. 59–60, 92.

110   B[ishop Butler] . . . a very horrid thing! / *The Rise of Methodism: A Source Book,* ed. R. M. Cameron (New York: Philosophical Library, 1954), pp. 287–288.

110   'indeterminate . . . what good I can' / Ibid., pp. 288–289.

111   'a change of form . . . substance' / Gerald Bray, *Documents of the English Reformation* (Minneapolis: Fortress Press, 1994), p. 113.

111 'Elizabethan assumptions . . . normal reason' / Christopher Morris, *Political Thought in England: Tyndale to Hooker* (London: Oxford University Press, 1953), p. 106.

111 At times . . . *traductio* / Followed particularly by Clarendon, *Brief View,* e.g., pp. 108, 166, 174, 231, 253. See also Bramhall, *Defence,* pp. 7, 71.

111 'comfortable places . . . despair' / Bray, *Documents,* p. 339.

111 'ridiculous men' . . . (Bancroft) / Brook, *Whitgift,* p. 146.

111 'common persons' . . . (Whitgift) / Ibid., p. 90.

111 'the common' . . . (Hooker) / Hooker, *Works,* I, pp. 14–15.

111 'the many headed multitude' . . . (Bramhall . . . et al.) / Bramhall, *Defence,* p. 249.

112 'dirty people . . .' (Clarendon) / Clarendon, *Brief View,* p. 320.

112 'secret corner-meetings . . .' (Hooker . . . Hobbes), / Hooker, *Works,* I, p. 47.

112 'desperate cause . . . Oratours' / Bramhall, *Defence,* pp. 7, 71, 158, 249.

112 'acts of rage . . . Doctrines' / Clarendon, *Brief View,* pp. 108, 179, 272.

112 'Stone Dead hath no Fellow' / *Clarendon: Selections,* p. 141; J. Simpson and J. Speake, eds., *The Concise Oxford Dictionary of Proverbs* (Oxford: Oxford University Press, 1992), p. 242.

112 'Extremely beautiful . . . *fido inganno*' / Torquato Tasso, *Discourses on the Heroic Poem,* trans. M. Cavalchini and I. Samuel (Oxford: Clarendon Press, 1973), p. 178.

113 Cleare dishonoure . . . to warke / Henry Parker, Lord Morley, *Tryumphes of Fraunces Petrarcke,* ed. D. P. Carnicelli (Cambridge, Mass.: Harvard University Press, 1973), p. 178.

113 'tacitly' . . . conjuring / See Clarendon, *Brief View,* pp. 122, 140; Bramhall, *Defence,* p. 133 ('a politick deafness').

113 'turne and translace . . . sundry shapes' / George Puttenham, *The Arte of English Poesie,* ed. G. D. Willcock and A. Walker (Cambridge: Cambridge University Press, 1936), p. 203.

113 Sir Thomas Wyatt . . . 1530s / See Kenneth Muir, *Life and Letters of Sir Thomas Wyatt* (Liverpool: Liverpool University Press, 1963), pp. 189, 197, 203; Geoffrey Hill, *The Enemy's Country* (Oxford: Clarendon Press, 1991), pp. 27–32.

113 'The prophet . . . faith' / Hooker, *Works,* V, p. 76.

113 poysonous sugar . . . royall tytle / Sidney, *Arcadia,* pp. 228, 228[verso].

114 That saying . . . such presumption / Clarendon, *Brief View,* p. 15.

114 'Antiphilus . . . flatterie' / Sidney, *Arcadia,* p. 227[verso].

114   The type of exemplary . . . Clarendon and Swift / See Clarendon, *Brief View*, p. 15; Jonathan Swift, *A Discourse of the Contests and Dissentions Between the Nobles and the Commons in Athens and Rome*, ed. F. H. Ellis (Oxford: Clarendon Press, 1967), pp. 90, 92, 93, 97–98.

114   as C. A. Patrides discerned / See Milton, *Selected Prose*, p. 196 (editorial note).

114   'The end then . . . God aright' / Ibid., p. 182.

115   'sober truth' / Clarendon, *Brief View*, p. 15.

115   'plain dealing' / Ibid., p. 289, and compare p. 282.

115   'pretending . . . perspicuity' / Clarendon, *Brief View*, p. 289; see also p. 282.

115   'an irreparable loss . . . quarrel' / Ibid., p. 320.

115   Locke's 'Substances' / See Locke, *Essay*, pp. 520–521.

115   'not what the words . . . praedetermined to one' / Bramhall, *Defence*, p. 41.

116   'man . . . creature' / Ibid., p. 107.

116   *intention* / *OED*, various senses. For analyses of motive and intention, see, e.g., Bramhall, *Defence*, pp. 19, 37, 74; Lucy, *Observations*, p. 205; Robert Filmer, *Observations on Milton* (in *Early Responses to Hobbes: Pamphlets*), p. 18; Robert Filmer, *Observations on Grotius* (in *Early Responses to Hobbes*), p. 27; Clarendon, *Brief View*, pp. 235–236, 272 [actually 262].

116   'They who . . . publick good' / Milton, *Selected Prose*, p. 196.

116   Tyndale's *Obedience of a Christen Man* / *The Work of William Tyndale*, ed. G. E. Duffield (Appleford: Sutton Courtenay Press, 1964), p. xxxiii; quotes part of a letter from Thomas Cromwell's agent Stephen Vaughan, who reported Tyndale's willingness to 'suffer what pain or torture, yea, what death his grace will' provided that the king would 'grant only a bare text of the scripture to be put forth among his people'.

116   Clarendon's 'Epistle . . . Majesty' / Clarendon, *Brief View*, six unnumbered prefatory pages.

The Weight of the Word

117   'interesting . . . of more interest than' / Isabel Rivers, *Reason, Grace and Sentiment: A Study of the Language of Religion and Ethics in England 1660–1780. Volume I: Whichcote to Wesley.* (Cambridge and

New York: Cambridge University Press, 1991), e.g., pp. 13, 17, 49, 50, 56, 57, 61, 71, 80, 99, 148, 168, 179, 210, 213, 226, 239.

117   'the Interest of *Sects* . . . Religion' / Ibid., pp. 70–71, 82, 102, 170–171, 190.

117   'very interesting . . . extraordinarily interesting' / Ibid., pp. 115, 117, 161, 162, 168, 195.

117   '[has] not taken . . . scholars' / Ibid., p. 4.

118   Campion's 'Brag' / See A. C. Southern, ed., *Elizabethan Recusant Prose 1559–1582* (London: Sands and Co., n.d. [1950], pp. 153–155.

118   'a *Preacher* . . . Parish' / Rivers, *Reason,* p. 50.

118   'I design . . . understood' / Ibid., p. 215.

118   'plain and natural Method' / Ibid., p. 34.

118   'require . . . Study' / Ibid., p. 19.

119   My subject is . . . ascertained / Ibid., pp. 2–3.

119   'do justice . . . subject' / Ibid., p. xii.

119   'For Locke's . . . Volume II' / Ibid., p. 48 n98.

119   'fitted . . . worldly state' / Ibid., p. 58.

120   This only . . . *Disbelief,* etc. / John Locke, *An Essay Concerning Human Understanding,* 1690, ed. P. H. Nidditch (Oxford: Clarendon Press, 1975), p. 663.

120   'Propositions . . . Religion)' / Ibid., p. 712.

120   'unwary . . . Understandings' / Ibid.

120   'riveted . . . pull'd out again' / Ibid.

120   'essentially . . . grace' / Rivers, *Reason,* p. 1.

121   'Without perplexing . . . speculations' / Edward Stillingfleet (1662), *The Oxford English Dictionary,* Second Edition (Oxford: Clarendon Press, 1989), citations: nice.

121   'To stand upon nice . . . useless' / Benjamin Whichcote, *Moral and Religious Aphorisms,* 1753 (London: Elkin Matthews & Marrot, 1930), no. 1008.

121   'I have ever thought . . . forgotten' / Rivers, *Reason,* pp. 70–71.

121   'It is not . . . by us' / William Law, *The Collected Works of the Reverend William Law,* 9 volumes, London: for J. Richardson, 1762; reprint edition (Setley: G. Moreton, 1892–1893), VI, p. 73.

121   'the way . . . austere' / Jeremy Taylor, *The Great Exemplar* (London: 1649), cited in *OED,* Second Edition, X, p. 387.

121   'He . . . perplexes . . . Love' / *The Poems of John Dryden,* ed. J. Kinsley, 4 volumes (Oxford: Clarendon Press, 1958), II, p. 604.

122   'the love of Complacencie and Acceptation' / Richard Baxter, *Of Saving Faith* (London, 1658), cited in *OED*, Second Edition, III, p. 606.

122   'arbitrary . . . vain' / Isaac Barrow, *Works* (London, 1689), cited in *OED*, Second Edition, III, p. 606.

122   'by wickedness . . . his own' / Whichcote, *Aphorisms*, no. 642.

122   'Compleasance . . . *to the rest*' / Thomas Hobbes, *Leviathan*, ed. C. B. Macpherson (Harmondsworth: Penguin Books, 1968), p. 209.

122   'familiar Toad' / Alexander Pope, 'An Epistle from Mr. Pope to Dr. Arbuthnot', line 319. See *The Poems of Alexander Pope*, ed. J. Butt (New Haven: Yale University Press, 1963), p. 608.

122   'the silent . . . Heart') / Law, *Works*, VII, p. 133.

122   'Accomplishment . . . World' / Ibid., p. 142.

123   '*Form* . . . the Air' / Ibid., p. 119.

123   '*since Almighty . . . Questions*' / Izaac Walton, *The Lives of John Donne, Sir Henry Wolton*, etc. (London: Oxford University Press / The World's Classics, 1927), p. 295.

123   'meer Nonconformist' / See N. H. Keeble, *Richard Baxter: Puritan Man of Letters* (Oxford: Clarendon Press, 1982), pp. 18–19.

123   Barrow's . . . 'co-prefix' / Rivers, *Reason*, pp. 77–78.

123   'pertinently . . . properly' / Ibid., p. 125.

123   'If any expressions . . . Latitude' / Isaac Watts, *Hymns and Spiritual Songs 1704–48: A Critical Edition*, ed. S. L. Bishop (London: Faith Press, 1962), p. liii.

124   'I hope . . . uncharitable spirit' / cited in Rivers, *Reason*, p. 179.

124   'I take "language" . . . include' / Ibid., p. 3.

124   'virtuously . . . epicure' / Isaac Barrow, cited in ibid., p. 78.

124   '*pertly* . . . fortunate' / *The Notebooks of Samuel Taylor Coleridge 1794–1804*, ed. K. Coburn, Bollingen Series L, 2 volumes (New York: Pantheon Books, 1957), I (Text), No. 1655.

124   'He was to stand . . . Face' / Isaac Barrow, *Of Civil Contentment, Patience and Resignation to the Will of God, In Several Sermons* (London: for Round, Tonson and Taylor, 1714), p. 232.

124   Set against Foxe . . . Ridley / *Foxe's Book of Martyrs*, ed. and abridged by G. A. Williamson (London: Secker and Warburg, 1965), pp. 132–137, 219–228, 290–312.

125   'physical sensibility' . . . 'literature or art' / *OED*, citations: sensation.

125   'to confirm . . . Suffering' / Rivers, *Reason*, p. 105.

125   'was recognised . . . puritans' / Ibid., p. 53.

125   'corrections . . . wrong-headed / Ibid., p. 76.

125   'All *general* privations . . . hell!' / Edmund Burke, *A Philosophical Enquiry into the Origin of our Ideas of the Sublime and Beautiful*, ed. J. T. Boulton (London: Routledge, 1958), p. 71.

126   'When the Principles . . . religious' / Whichcote, *Aphorisms*, no. 28.

126   'The *State* . . . Will' / Ibid., no. 853.

126   'There is no . . . Righteousness' / Ibid., no. 902.

126   'an exact . . . devotion' / Law, *Works*, IV, p. 162.

126   '*lively* . . . *spirit*' / Ibid., p. 133.

126   'relentless . . . principles' / *A Burning and a Shining Light: English Spirituality in the Age of Wesley*, ed. D. L. Jeffrey (Grand Rapids, Mich.: Eerdmans, 1987), p. 120.

126   To proceed . . . devotion / Law, *Works*, IV, p. 136.

127   'To live . . . Virtue' / Whichcote, *Aphorisms*, no. 250.

127   'Our Happiness . . . without' / Ibid., no. 857.

127   'due or proportionate . . . qualities' / *OED*, citations: temper.

127   'A *wise* . . . more' / Whichcote, *Aphorisms*, no. 250.

128   In vain . . . Devotion dies / Watts, *Hymns and Spiritual Songs*, p. 194 (Book II: 34).

128   'But what . . . call for that?' / John Donne, *Devotions upon Emergent Occasions*, ed. A. Raspa (Montreal and London: McGill–Queen's University Press, 1975), p. 63 (Twelfth Meditation).

128   *Serious Call* / William Law, *A Serious Call to a Devout and Holy Life*, 1728, The Second Edition, Corrected (London: for William Innys, 1732), p. 244.

128   'He saw . . . baptize it' / Owen Chadwick, *Michael Ramsey: A Life* (Oxford: Clarendon Press, 1990), p. 42.

129   Then shall . . . my relief / *The Works of George Herbert*, ed. F. E. Hutchinson (Oxford: Clarendon Press, 1941), p. 90.

129   'Of this blest . . . in heaven' / Chadwick, *Michael Ramsey*, p. 398.

129   'in a sense most true' / Herbert, *Works*, pp. 167–168.

130   'subject . . . moral prose' / Rivers, *Reason*, p. 2.

130   Addison's two *Spectator* papers / Nos. 453 (August 9, 1712) and 465 (August 23, 1712) of *The Spectator*, 7 volumes (London: for Tonson and Draper, n.d.), VI, pp. 222–225, 269–273.

130   'There is not . . . gratitude' / Ibid., p. 222.

130   'In our retirements . . . serious' / Ibid., p. 272.

130   'If gratitude . . . Maker?' / Ibid., p. 222.

130   'O how . . . declare . . . ?' / Ibid., p. 224 (hymn, verse 2).

131   'piece of divine poetry' / Ibid., p. 223.

131   Burnet's distinction . . . 'sublime' / See *Characters from the Histories
       and Memoirs of the Seventeenth Century*, ed. D. Nichol Smith
       (Oxford: Clarendon Press, 1918), p. 252.

131   'states of mind' . . . 'disclaimer' / Rivers, *Reason*, pp. 84, 236, 152, 176.

131   'peculiar edge' . . . 'thoughts' / Ibid., p. 115.

131   'consideration . . . Sampson' / Ibid., p. 146.

131   'meditation . . . act' / Ibid.

132   'the communication . . . practises it' / Barrow, cited in Rivers, *Reason*,
       p. 78.

132   'it is a sign . . . excellency' / Rivers, *Reason*, p. 114.

133   'Blest . . . Heaven!' / *Representative Verse of Charles Wesley*, ed. F. Baker
       (London: Epworth Press, 1962), p. 3 ('Christ the Friend of Sinners').

133   'tasting how gracious the Lord is' / Rivers, *Reason*, p. 128.

133   'appeal . . . criticism' / Ibid., p. 241.

134   'the philosophical . . . all men' / John and Charles Wesley, *Selected
       Prayers, Hymns, Journal Notes, Sermons, Letters and Treatises*, ed. F.
       Whaling (New York: Paulist Press, 1981), p. 31.

134   'Take care . . . long received' / Letter to Dorothy Furly, September 15,
       1762. See *The Letters of the Rev. John Wesley, A.M.*, ed. J. Telford, 8 vol-
       umes (London: The Epworth Press, 1931), IV, p. 189.

134   Now, even now, . . . purple wave / *The Eucharistic Hymns of John and
       Charles Wesley*, ed. J. E. Rattenbury (London: The Epworth Press,
       1948), p. 204.

134   'For then . . . he sank' / *The Poems of William Cowper*, ed. J. D. Baird
       and C. Ryskamp (Oxford: Clarendon Press, 1980–1995), I, p. 215.

135   'original sin . . . Christianity' / Rivers, *Reason*, p. 227.

135   'natural "pondus" . . . principle' / Ibid., p. 162.

135   'good books . . . world' / Ibid., p. 116.

135   'certain impulsion . . . downward' / Hobbes, cited in *Jonathan
       Edwards: Representative Selections*, ed. C. H. Faust and T. H. Johnson
       (New York: Hill & Wang, 1962), p. lxxii.

135   'as it were heavy as lead' / Ibid., p. 162.

135   *'the Divine . . . the Same'* / *Hobbes's Tripos in Three Discourses* (London:
       for Matt Gilliflower, Henry Rogers, 1684), p. 254.

136   'the imperfection . . . avoid it' / *William Tyndale's Five Books of Moses,
       called The Pentateuch*, 1530, ed. J. I. Mombert, 1884 (Carbondale:
       Southern Illinois University Press, 1967), p. vii.

136   'idle heart in hearing' / Rivers, *Reason*, p. 115.

136 '*private* interest' / *Jonathan Edwards*, p. 360.

136 Ruskin's 'intrinsic value' / E.g., John Ruskin, *Unto this Last and Other Essays on Art and Political Economy* (London: Dent/Everyman Library, 1907), pp. 203–209.

136 'cold . . . preaching' / Rivers, *Reason*, p. 175.

136 'arbitrary signs' / Ibid, p. 125.

136 'tone . . . solutions' / Ibid., p. 179.

137 'intrinsic Malignity' / Whichcote, *Aphorisms*, nos. 486, 918.

137 'internal . . . body' / *Jonathan Edwards*, p. 362.

137 'There is nothing . . . hath' / Whichcote, *Aphorisms*, no. 457.

137 'there are . . . insoluble' / Rivers, *Reason*, p. 38; see also p. 43.

138 *Charles Wesley: A Reader* / Ed. J. R. Tyson (Oxford and New York: Oxford University Press, 1989).

138 *The Unpublished Poetry of Charles Wesley* / Ed. S. T. Kimbrough, Jr., and O. A. Beckerlegge, 3 volumes (Nashville: Abingdon Press, 1988–1993).

139 'Intrinsic Goodness' / Whichcote, *Aphorisms*, no. 540.

Dividing Legacies

142 'we have . . . than the latter' / T. S. Eliot, *The Varieties of Metaphysical Poetry: The Clark Lectures at Trinity College, Cambridge, 1926, and the Turnbull Lectures at the Johns Hopkins University, 1933*, ed. Ronald Schuchard (London: Faber & Faber, 1993; New York: Harcourt Brace Jovanovich, 1994), p. 199.

142 'I should have had . . . Strafford' / Ibid., p. 224.

142 'Dante and his School . . . Middleton Murry / Ibid., pp. 6–7, 10–11 (Editor's Introduction).

142 As is usually the case . . . on April 14 / Ibid., p. 7.

142 It also appears . . . from its true centre / Ibid., p. 10 (Editor's Introduction).

143 'The style . . . not English prose' / Ibid., p. 224n.

143 It has to be said that . . . gravity / Ibid., pp. 58–59.

143 'To read . . . his own thinking' / John Donne, *The Divine Poems*, ed. H. Gardner (Oxford: Clarendon Press, 1952; reprinted from corrected sheets, 1959), p. xxi n1.

143 the *via media* . . . parlance / See particularly 'John Bramhall' (1927), in T. S. Eliot, *Selected Essays,* Second Edition (London: Faber, 1934), pp. 344–352.

143 'points of triangulation' / Eliot, *Varieties of Metaphysical Poetry,* p. 61.

143 'curious blend . . . his own work' / 'Francis Herbert Bradley' (1927), in Eliot, *Selected Essays,* p. 406.

143 'the increasing . . . metaphysical inquiry' / F. H. Bradley, *Essays on Truth and Reality,* 1914 (Oxford: Clarendon Press, 1950), p. vi (Preface).

144 'There has been . . . incredible' / Ibid.

144 '*echt metaphysisch*' . . . detail can match / Eliot, *Varieties of Metaphysical Poetry,* p. 48.

144 'On Our Knowledge . . . Imaginary' / Ibid., pp. 55n, 88n.

144 'as a pupil . . . how to say it' / T. S. Eliot, *Knowledge and Experience in the Philosophy of F. H. Bradley* (London: Faber, 1964), p. 9.

144 ('ideas may be . . . the real world') / Bradley, *Essays,* p. 29.

144 'the most arduous . . . record exists' / Hugh Kenner, *The Invisible Poet: T. S. Eliot* (London: Faber, 1960), p. 81.

145 attacked . . . 'civilised class' / *The Letters of T. S. Eliot, Volume I: 1898–1922,* ed. V. Eliot (London: Faber, 1988), pp. 369–370.

145 Schuchard notes . . . reciprocated the sympathy / Eliot, *Varieties of Metaphysical Poetry,* pp. 29–30.

145 rhetorical tribute . . . classical *apatheia* / I say 'rhetorical tribute to precedent' because *apatheia* is a Stoic virtue or quality. Housman claimed that he was neither Stoic nor Epicurean but Cyrenaic. See *Letters of A. E. Housman,* ed. H. Maas (Cambridge, Mass.: Harvard University Press, 1971), p. 329.

145 There are only two ways . . . an event / *Letters of T. S. Eliot,* I, p. 285.

146 'Please let us be . . . before' / Ibid., p. 285.

146 Woods had written . . . for that degree / Ibid., p. 143.

146 'extraordinary power' . . . literary opinion / G. Wilson Knight, 'T. S. Eliot, Some Literary Impressions', in *T. S. Eliot: The Man and His Work,* ed. A. Tate, 1966 (Harmondsworth: Penguin Books, 1971), p. 246.

146 'shrewd enough . . . truly belong' / Peter Ackroyd, *T. S. Eliot* (London: Hamish Hamilton, 1984), p. 330.

146 'only after . . . on his own account' / Richard Wollheim, 'Eliot and F. H. Bradley: An Account', in *Eliot in Perspective: A Symposium,* ed. G. Martin (London: Macmillan, 1970), p. 190.

146 'Conflict . . . Jesuitism' / Eliot, *Varieties of Metaphysical Poetry,* p. 89.

147 'For you can hardly . . . to his mind' / Ibid.

147 'psychologism' . . . Donne's style of thought / Ibid.

147 'The *fourth point* . . . fruit from this' / *The Spiritual Exercises of St. Ignatius,* trans. A. Mottola (New York: Image Books, 1964), p. 72.

148 'Eliot's most elusive poem' / Kenner, *The Invisible Poet,* p. 234.

148 'waking up . . . make of it all' / Denis Donoghue, *The Old Moderns: Essays on Literature and Theory* (New York: Knopf, 1994), p. 119.

148 'the origin . . . non-active suggestion' / Bradley, *Essays,* p. 22; see also Eliot, *Varieties of Metaphysical Poetry,* p. 88n.

149 That Eliot himself . . . January 1933 / Eliot, *Varieties of Metaphysical Poetry,* pp. 64, 65 (editor's notes); pp. 257, 259.

149 'the subject . . . modern problems' / Ibid., p. 224n.

149 'If in some game . . . "Ah, Souldier"' / Christopher Ricks, *T. S. Eliot and Prejudice* (London: Faber, 1988), pp. 159–160. The bibliographical information and the Shakespeare quotation are also given by Ricks.

150 misquotations and 'minor mistranscriptions' / Eliot, *Varieties of Metaphysical Poetry,* pp. 33–36 (editor's note on text and editorial principles). A clutch of misquotations is corrected on pp. 52n, 56n; see also 89n. For Schuchard's term 'minor mistranscriptions', see, e.g., pp. 103n, 108n, 116n, 124n, 134n.

150 Shakespeare's 'gnomic utterance' . . . Ripeness is all / Ibid., pp. 52n, 53n. See also pp. 35–36 for editorial references to F. Kermode (1975) and C. Ricks (1977) on creative misquotation.

151 'the finding . . . upon instinct' / Quoted in John Passmore, *A Hundred Years of Philosophy,* Second Edition, 1957 (Harmondsworth: Penguin Books, 1966), p. 61n. I acknowledge a general indebtedness over many years to Passmore's invaluable book.

151 'Tradition' . . . 'The Metaphysical Poets' / These essays, first published separately in 1919, 1921 and 1923, appear together in Eliot, *Selected Essays,* and elsewhere, as also in *Selected Prose of T. S. Eliot,* ed. F. Kermode (New York: Harcourt Brace Jovanovich, 1975), pp. 37–76.

151 'rigorous metaphysician' / Passmore, *A Hundred Years of Philosophy,* p. 60.

151 'painfully obscure work' / Wollheim, 'Eliot and F. H. Bradley', p. 170. This should not be read as Wollheim's final opinion of the quality of Eliot's dissertation.

151   'that there is . . . adequate explanations' / *Josiah Royce's Seminar,*
      1913–1914, as recorded in the Notebooks of Harry T. Costello, ed. G.
      Smith (New Brunswick, N.J.: Rutgers University Press, 1963), p. 42.
      Eliot was a member of the seminar, to which he presented a paper on
      December 9, 1913. Royce quoted, or paraphrased, Peirce's observation
      at the seminar held on October 28, 1913. Costello's notes do not reveal
      whether or not Eliot was present at that meeting.

151   In really great . . . not visible / Eliot, *Knowledge and Experience,* p. 75.

151   'My Station and Its Duties' / F. H. Bradley, *Ethical Studies,* Second
      Edition, revised, 1876 (Oxford: Clarendon Press, 1927), pp. 160–213.

152   'believed upon instinct' / Passmore, *A Hundred Years of Philosophy,*
      p. 61n.

152   We . . . have experience . . . my known world / Bradley, *Essays,* pp.
      159–160.

152   Eliot's discovery . . . Aquinas / Text as in Dante Alighieri, *La Divina*
      Comedia, ed. and ann. C. H. Grandgent, rev. C. S. Singleton, 1933
      (Cambridge, Mass.: Harvard University Press, 1972), p. 930. For my
      reference to Aquinas, see ibid., n144.

153   'Hooker's philosophy . . . than Donne's / Eliot, *Varieties of Metaphysical*
      Poetry, p. 68n.

153   'the intellectual . . . Catholic Church' / Ibid., p. 224n.

153   'what many of you . . . unjust of me' / Ibid., pp. 224, 190.

153   To meet with Hooker . . . formal ratiocination / Richard Hooker,
      Ecclesiastical Polity: Selections, ed. A. Pollard (Manchester: Carcanet
      Press, 1990), e.g., pp. 39 (sense 1), 53 (sense 2), 55 (sense 3), 19 (sense
      4), 50 (sense 5), 128 (sense 6), 84 (sense 7).

154   Of similar significance . . . 'the minds of the common sort' / Ibid.,
      pp. 52, 53, 103, 105, 110, 64, 129, 134, 135–136.

154   'extraordinary . . . imagination' / Eliot, *Varieties of Metaphysical*
      Poetry, p. 138.

155   'I attempted . . . conceits' / Ibid.

155   'teasing the idea . . . soul and body which we knew' / Ibid., pp. 85,
      132, 155.

155   'the only . . . personality of Donne' / Ibid., p. 155.

156   'the publication . . . poetic mind' / Ibid., pp. 1–2.

156   'probably . . . labour' / Eliot, *Selected Essays,* p. 30.

156   In 'The Love Song . . .' . . . voice praying / *The Complete Poems and*
      Plays of T. S. Eliot (London: Faber, 1969), pp. 13–17 ('Prufrock'), p. 192
      ('Little Gidding').

157   'posture . . . delegated' to us by Shakespeare / Ricks, *T. S. Eliot and Prejudice*, pp. 161–162.

158   'It is supposed' . . . carefully excluded / *Wordsworth's Preface to 'Lyrical Ballads'*, ed. W. J. B. Owen (Copenhagen: Rosenkilde & Bagger, 1957), p. 114.

158   'antagonism . . . common humanity' / Ricks, *T. S. Eliot and Prejudice*, p. 255.

158   Whitman . . . *Drum-Taps* / E.g., in 'A March in the Ranks Hard-Prest, and the Road Unknown', lines 7, 12–14, in *Whitman: Poetry and Prose*, ed. J. Kaplan (New York: The Library of America, 1982), p. 440.

158   'apathy . . . abuse' / *Letters of T. S. Eliot*, I, p. 369.

158   The residual beneficiaries . . . in 1920 / Ibid., p. 370. By 'Anglican literary "spirituality"' I have especially in mind the prevailing sentiment which takes *Four Quartets* to be not only in the contemplative tradition but also in the canon and which bases its own *bienpensant* soliloquies on that misapprehension. I take, as an exemplary instance of a prevalent type, John Booty's *Meditating on Four Quartets* (Cambridge, Mass.: Cowley Press, 1983). My criticism is not directed at the work of prayer of the contemplative orders.

159   I anticipate . . . 'human condition' / See Christopher Ricks, 'Philip Larkin', in *The Force of Poetry* (Oxford: Oxford University Press, 1984), pp. 274–284; e.g.: 'Larkin's classical temper shows its mettle when he deplores modernism, whether in jazz, poetry, or painting: "I dislike such things not because they are new, but because they are irresponsible exploitations of technique in contradiction of human life as we know it. This is my essential criticism of modernism, whether perpetrated by Parker, Pound or Picasso; it helps us neither to enjoy nor endure"' (p. 278). The 'temper' here is not 'classical' but postprandial. It is no more 'classical' to 'deplore' modernism than it is to invoke the wit and wisdom of Dr Johnson. Johnson was knowledgeable and skilled in the tragi-comedy of spleen: in this he recollects a classical line of wit and anticipates important facets of modernism's comedy—as in Beckett, Wyndham Lewis and early Eliot. The locution 'shows its mettle' ('quality of disposition or temperament') could be read as a punning escape-clause, as meaning 'shows itself for what it is', but I do not associate this kind of covert mechanism with the broad integrity of Ricks's critical practice. It is clear, I think, that we are to read 'spirit' as 'courage', and that he believes

Larkin to possess an inherent virtue of reactionary personality which turns even 'his greatest soft sell' (p. 279) into an awareness of 'destination', which in turn 'itself arrives at one of Larkin's greatest destinations, the end of "The Whitsun Weddings"' (p. 280). If I cannot accept 'great destinations' it is because I am conscious of being urged to an acceptance of a patrimony that is nowhere proven. In rejecting the Larkin package I am made to reject Wilfred Owen too, and Blunden, and Gray, in addition to which I am beneficiary of Dr Johnson's tacit approval. I must conclude that there is a tone that Larkin represents which is stronger even than Ricks's acute sense of pitch; what Larkin represents is an assumption, a narrow English possessiveness, with regard to 'good sense' and 'generous common humanity'. 'Good sense', so propertied, so keen to admit others, at a price, to its properties, strikes me as a deplorable kind of *bienséance*. During his lifetime Larkin was granted endless credit by the bank of Opinion, and the rage which in some quarters greeted his posthumously published *Letters* was that of people who consider themselves betrayed by one of their own kind. In fact Larkin betrayed no one, least of all himself. What he is seen to be in the letters he was and is in the poems. The notion of accessibility of his work acknowledged the ease with which readers could overlay it with transparencies of their own preference. Mill, who condescended to Wordsworth's poetry, allowed it the major significance of reflecting Mill's own love of mountains, thereby rescuing Mill from depression. Mill's intellectual heirs ('a person's taste is as much his own particular concern as his opinion or his purse') found it convenient to suppose that Larkin's peculiar concern as a poet was exactly conformable to their pursed opinions ('human life as we know it'). *The Waste Land*, at its first appearance, could only be understood exegetically; that is its remaining strength. *Four Quartets*, from its existence as an entity, was granted the major significance of reflecting Anglican *einfühlung*, a tendency that finds exemplary utterance in Booty's 'Whether fully conscious of the fact or not, Eliot seems to have here the right order for our time' (*Meditating on Four Quartets*, p. 60).

NAME INDEX

Subject Index

INDEX OF BIBLICAL PASSAGES

About the Author

Geoffrey Hill was born in Bromsgrove, Worcestershire, in 1932. A graduate of Keble College, Oxford, he taught for many years at the University of Leeds, then lectured at Cambridge as a Fellow of Emmanuel College. He is the author of nine books of poetry and of *New and Collected Poems, 1952–1982.* His stage version of *Brand,* a dramatic poem by Ibsen, was commissioned by the National Theatre, London, and performed there in 1978. His earlier critical writings have been collected in two volumes, *The Lords of Limit* and *The Enemy's Country,* the latter based on his Clark Lectures delivered at Cambridge in 1986. Since 1988 he has lived in Massachusetts and taught at Boston University, where he is currently Professor of Literature and Religion and co-director of the Editorial Institute.